Croydon Libraries

You are welcome to borrow this book for up to 28 days. (L)
If you do not return or renew it by the latest date stamped
below you will be asked to pay overdue charges. You may
renew books in person, by phone or via the Council's website
www.croydon.gov.uk

SELSDON LIBRARY
020 8657 7210

G-F.

MOBILE LIBRARY 020 8657 7210	3 NOV 2009	Ref Con.
- OCT 2007	19 JUN 2010	26/1/16.
1 5 NOV 2007	TRANS COU 2/7/10	
1 7 DEC 2007	COULSDON LIBRARY 0207 8845180	
4/08	2 0 SEP 2010	
1 1 AUG 2008	2 8 JUN 2011	
Unt to ASH	2 0 AUG 2011	
10/08	2 7 SEP 2011	
ASHBURTON LIBRARY 020 8656 4148		
	1 7 AUG 2012	
P3	2 7 OCT 2012	
19.2.10		

Moths

MOTHS

Karl Manders

Chatto & Windus
LONDON

Published by Chatto & Windus 2007

2 4 6 8 10 9 7 5 3 1

Isl   e,

Random House Publishers India Private Limited
301 World Trade Tower, Hotel Intercontinental Grand Complex,
Barakhamba Lane, New Delhi 110 001, India

The Random House Group Limited Reg. No. 954009
www.randomhouse.co.uk

A CIP catalogue record for this book
is available from the British Library

ISBN 9780701181062

Papers used by Random House are natural,
recyclable products made from wood grown in sustainable forests.
The manufacturing processes conform to the environmental
regulations of the country of origin

Typeset by Palimpsest Book Production Limited, Grangemouth, Stirlingshire

Printed and bound in Great Britain by
Mackays of Chatham plc, Chatham, Kent

Author's note

I am aware that certain events described here are not represented with strict accuracy. While the landmarks of Eddie Rozner's career (including his performance in a private audience with Stalin) are faithfully represented, their chronology has not been strictly observed. In defence of this distortion (and others too minor and too numerous to mention) I plead poetic licence, and apologise to readers who are offended by the corruption of historical truth. What is beyond dispute, and which I have not elaborated, is that millions of people suffered unimaginable privations in the punishment colonies of GULAG when they were innocent of any crime. This is a story. It did not happen. But a lot of it did.

Karl Manders, Zelhem, Gelderland, 2007

Acknowledgments

For the correct titles and functions of Soviet agencies, and for many other details of that era, I have taken as my authority *Stalin's Secret War*, by Nikolai Tolstoy.

The quotation which appears on p 103 is from Gene Stratton-Porter's classic entomological memoir, *Moths of the Limberlost*.

Prologue

DOLBOY LOOKED in the mirror and saw a room lit with tasselled lamps in pastel shades. He saw striped walls of leaf-green and pink, blotted with cherubim prints: cherubs with tears on their cheeks, cherubs licking jam off wooden spoons, cherubs with fists of flowers, innocently torn. He inhabited a realm of winsome creatures assembled to remind him of his purpose, which was the enactment of a dream life, the life of a toy. He looked in the mirror and saw an immaculate infant, his fine hair drifting in sculpted waves, his cheeks full and perfect, his lips like grapes above his dimpled chin. He looked in the mirrors of his mirrored eyes and enjoyed the ignorant bliss of wanting nothing. And then it was gone.

A man in khaki fabric hoisted him to a height from which he had never before seen the world. He felt like a fly, a heavy fly. Upturned faces all around coaxed and urged him to respond, but it was no good: he could not love his war-returned uncle. Soon a vertiginous fear delivered him to a bout of sobbing and wriggling he could not control, as the thrusting faces grew more horrid and insistent, and the giant hands compressed his ribs. Dolboy wished for his lamplit room, with its hill of woollen dolls, and its cherubs, but his wish was not granted. So he closed his eyes and made time run backwards.

When he was unborn, when he was no thing, his mother's mother and his mother's father separately crossed and recrossed the River Oder and the River Vltava, and even once the River Donau, without ever knowing that they searched for each other, until one day in Karlovy Vary she glanced up from her glass of tea and knew in an instant that she did, and he too, and their search was over. She saw in an eyeblink that she would die if she spent another day apart from him, and that one day when a cold wind skittered across the Pripet marshes she would die for him anyway. He had no such premonition, but felt an uproarious excitement flood his body as they recognised each other. In spite of oaths and protestations from both their families, they married in haste, and fulfilled every suspicion about their first meeting by presenting only eight months later Dolboy's mother.

While great leaders shook their fists and contemplated dominance of Roman proportions for one nation or another, Dolboy's maternal grandparents continued their river crossings. Soon they crossed and recrossed with all of their belongings in a cart drawn by a dun horse, then with a handcart, and finally, with their rags and kettles on their backs. On a day when one of the great nations decided that Dolboy's grandfather must put on a uniform, he hid from soldiers in the puddled potato fields which stretched from horizon to horizon with scarcely a tree or a barn for punctuation, and when he emerged it was too late: his adamant wife lay destroyed on the clay, and his wild-eyed daughter curled against her, gnawing her fist.

In all of eternity and all of space there is but one perfect mate girl rocked to and fro over her lace cushion, unable to take another step in the world. Every mid-morning, while drinkers struggled to regain consciousness, or blundered about the fields, their womenfolk went to the vodka house to see what the lace maker had dreamed into being, and windows all around were trimmed with her valances, and women's throats with her collars.

When Dolboy's father saw the lace maker, he felt the excitement of a connoisseur who has spent a long time rummaging hopefully through trash. He was the son of a merchant family which had ventured westward over several centuries, and indulged its indecision by settling first in one plump city of the Hanseatic League and then in another: now in Szczecin and now in Bremen, until out of weariness they became rooted in Zutphen, with its great towers and its milling barges. As a reward for attending his studies, he was travelling to meetings with suppliers of wine, leather, jewellery, nuts, icons, musical instruments and whatever commodity his family's inventories supplied to complete a diverting itinerary. He had drifted further eastward than he needed, not knowing that his listless meandering, like all our blindness, concealed a fateful purpose. He glimpsed her one morning in the dim vault he had never meant to visit, and offered to buy everything she had. She denied him, for fear of leaving her regulars unsatisfied. The next day she was unbending, and on the third day stubborn, so that Dolboy's father was maddened. But on the fourth day she allowed him to follow her upstairs, and let his hands rove where they would, across and over and in her unaccustomed body, because although she had never known a man beside her father, she felt the promptings of womanhood that her mother had known when she looked up from a glass of tea to see her destined husband.

She unhooked her clothing, and when Dolboy's father stood off and did likewise, she glanced without surprise at the lengthening limb he unloosed. Had she not seen animals in the field? And following their example, she fell on hands and knees, arching her back and thrusting her buttocks high. He clapped his hands first on her horselike haunches, then held her hair like reins, tugging her head back, and further back as his stroke grew stronger, and she found a new vocabulary of pain and pleasure combined.

There is a persisting belief, but not among old wives, that a newly fractured hymen is an impediment to conception. This belief is unfounded. Like his grandmother before her, Dolboy's mother greeted her gift with an ovum. His father returned every day, and at the end of a week, the job having been thoroughly done, he disappeared with his boxes and long coat into the steam and smoke of the Dresden train. Dolboy's mother got on with her lace making, and had no doubt that she would receive her foreign visitor again.

Long before he had completed his ensuing tour of Jutland, and taken ship in sight of the wind-scoured Friesland coast to the IJsselmeer, Dolboy's father feared that he had been precipitate. Why had he left so soon such a compliant partner? He tried to conjure with his own hand the sensation of plumbing Dolboy's mother, closing his eyes to recapture her image. But if Nature allowed such memories their full power, humankind would have perished daydreaming. If we could accurately recall the pleasure of copulation, there would be no need to repeat it. And so the long-awaited joy of returning under sail with baggy-trousered countrymen to his home on the Oude IJssel river was dulled by a deep and insistent longing to remind himself more fully of the sharpest pleasure he had ever known.

When after many months he had persuaded his father to authorise another excursion, he travelled eastward by land, changing trains at gaslit halts in forests of dripping spruce, and perching among newly-dug mangolds on horsedrawn carts where trains were too slow. He arrived a worn man at the vodka house, to find the lace maker in round health, her navel standing out like the boss of a barbarian's shield, her nipples magnified. For a week he mounted her three times daily, and for another week twice. Almost as much as their afternoon couplings he enjoyed the hour before, when he watched across the room her quiet dispensing of lace, while imagining the strange, involuntary responses to which she would soon give throat.

And then he felt compelled to depart with no prior warning. This time he left her with a tidy sum in large, green drafts, drawn on a bank no more than half a day away, and a quantity of gold coins sufficient to carry her through childbirth and beyond. Dolboy's mother got on with her lace making, and his father had no doubt that he would visit his foreign hobbyhorse again.

Such were Dolboy's ancestry and parentage.

Infancy

DOLBOY WAS BORN by candlelight and a howling wind. His first months were the darkest days of winter, when a steely sunshaft lit the airborne dust of his mother's attic for no more than thirty minutes at the middle of each day that was not black with cloud. In the night, while her fingers flew among the bobbins by the wavering flame, he gazed at the corrugations of roof tiles that rippled and clattered as the gale gusted into and out of their world. When there was no storm, the wheezing of the wind rose and fell continuously, while the steady flame stood upright, turning at its yellow point into a black wisp whose jagged dissipation delineated the movement of the higher air. Sometimes he was aware only of the windmoan and the irregular pattering of raindrops on the rooftop two feet from his head, hour after hour, day after day. When he was a man, Dolboy would sometimes still his thoughts and shut out all else to focus his ears on that primeval noise. The sights we see and the sounds we hear before we have thoughts are imprinted on our minds no less vividly for the lack of words to contain them, and may reappear for the smallest part of a second and without bidding, twenty, thirty, sixty years later, so that for an instant we feel secure again, in an original world without definitions.

On summer nights he lay by the open window, listening to the beelike approach of a hundred bombers in formation, crooning with joy when their hum grew to a thunder that filled the sky and made the drinkers roll their peasant eyes heavenward, and his mother speed the bobbins to keep her thoughts from fear. Then gun emplacements in the forest sent whistling shells up pencils of light to pock the gliding belt of aircraft brightly, while the infant Dolboy pedalled the air, and gurgled his delight at this development.

Six months after his arrival, anxious that his father might never return, Dolboy's mother descended into pits of despair, from which the struggle to rise up grew harder each week that she was alone in the world with only her work and her motherhood. She slipped into a dull melancholia which obscured her sense of passing time. Sometimes she would blink, and think it was only a minute since she fed the sodden bundle by her side, when it was a day. Some mornings she would get up from her palliasse, and some mornings she would not. One day she ventured to the door of the vodka house to feel the sun on her face, and saw a straggle of soldiers, aghast and bloody, creeping like grey spiders with their limbs half picked. She remembered her mother, and smiled at their suffering.

By autumn she seemed thoroughly mad, as she ranted in her own language, and people on the road looked up and shook their heads at her wordless baying. In December she sat in an open-flung window high in the roof, like a sea captain in his cockpit, with straw in her hair, and a gale blowing through the icicles of her bleak domain. Dolboy took on a grey hue, and staggered about his mother's queendom, searching the floorboards and

8

crannies for overlooked crumbs. As long as she had money, the landlord came to her door and left it without complaint. But when she tried to pay in remnants of soiled lace, his forbearance evaporated, and she was dragged to a hovel, half brick and half plank, where the alcohol was distilled. This improvement was Dolboy's salvation, since through a trapdoor he had access to potatoes and grain, some half rotten, some half eaten by field creatures, but capable still of sustaining life. And the heat of the distillery could be felt through the wall, in a winter when the tiles of the attic were welded with ice, and soldiers froze in their boots.

It was in this state, one late February day, that Dolboy's father found his mate and his progeny. His expectation of renewed carnality, nurtured through a journey of undreamed complexity, fell flat when he beheld the object of his imaginings. She sat like an anthropoid survival from a brutish era, barefoot in the mud, her demented eyes twitching behind a ragged skein of hair. They regarded each other for a long time, she trying to recall what she had been, he remembering. Her hands roamed about the lap of her black shift, as if searching for her mislaid bobbins, and her lips trembled on the brink of a beseeching cry. But no sound came. At length, Dolboy tottered to her side, his naked legs caked with mud, his bare belly blown big from the raw things which he gnawed. His eyes sat large and limpid in his tight-skinned skull. The traveller's gaze crept to and fro, over his handiwork.

Dolboy's father had his paramour washed and trimmed, reclothed, rehoused, and fed, but still he could not escape the destruction he had delivered to a creature that was already half consumed when first he fell on her. He tried to arrange things busily, to avoid looking at her, but his glance was for ever drawn back to find her practising a smile, or a nod, or half a curtsy, as if she were honouring royalty. Wherever he went, ordering furniture for her lodging, overseeing her resupply of foods, listing her needs to the woman who was to be her overseer, Dolboy's mother followed, ready for the moment when he wanted her again, waiting, waiting, waiting.

A week after he had arrived, Dolboy's father climbed into a deep wagon used for coal, with his bags beside him and the boy in the crook of one arm. Dolboy's shaven head was patterned with red blotches where lice had gnawed, and red circles where worms burrowed. His eyes were underscored by purplish rings, and his belly was still big, but for the first time he was clothed against the freezing air. As the starved horse strained, and the wagon grew smaller, Dolboy's mother clasped herself in the doorway of the vodka house, rocking to and fro, keening in her senseless monotone, as she tried to keep the two beloved beings in view, long after they had ceased to be distinguishable from the shivering trees that enfolded the road.

The journey

CROSSING A continent at war is not impossible: the wrangling with officials at national borders is replaced by frank demands from men with power of life and death in fiefdoms stretching over three fields, from this hillock to the next, from tree A to tree B. An accountant, finding himself in uniform, soon learns the joyous ways of Atilla the Hun, a butcher turns his knife to human throats, but each has his price.

Dolboy's father travelled with letters of authorisation acceptable to the occupiers, and currency readable by the small, dangerous fry who held letters upside-down. Many were suspicious of a polyglot with white half moons to his nails, and a fur-collared coat, and a ratchild at his side.

'What's his story?'

A gauleiter responsible for an area of birchwoods outside Krosno Odrzanskie indicated Dolboy with a sheaf of papers which made no mention of a child.

'His story is: no story.'

The officer looked over Dolboy, and his father, and the impeccable papers, and the folded banknotes. He allowed his head to rock gently forward and backward, as if he might the next instant fall asleep, and without moving his lips, he recited:

'Good, bad, good, bad, good . . . bad . . . good . . . bad . . .'

He was too tired to kill anything, too tired for any event, however ordinary.

'Good . . . Very well. Good.'

In the woods beyond, Dolboy saw people with faces greyer than his own, standing with nothing to do, and skeleton trees against the yellow sky, and men looking down from wooden towers. His father saw his own face beyond the wire, and though he searched it for an alien sign, it refused to resemble someone other than himself. He gathered his son against his chest, and covered Dolboy's eyes as their wagon moved westward.

At night, Dolboy's earliest joy was renewed when bombers seeped like a stain across the sky, probed by wands of light which threw pearly discs on ghost clouds. Not once but many times his father found him at an icy window, his wondering face turned up to watch the explosions of pink and yellow that peppered the thunderous stream. Sometimes his lips moved, as if he were tasting raw potatoes and wheat grains. Sometimes his gaze wandered to the extremities of naked birch, etched on the flickering sky like the hair of a wild woman.

So rich and numerous were the complexes of sense that occupied Dolboy's preverbal brain that it seemed he had been an age on the earth. So slow was the passage of time, so infinitely intricate each new perception. Without the impediment of language, these sensory incursions formed fresh patterns from instant to instant, so that his head filled with a billion permutations every hour, whose sum became his mind. Travelling west he saw a nest of rats in the belly of a dead horse, two hundred geese winging in a perfect chevron, ten gallons of turnip soup, boiling in an oil drum, a mile of bandaged men, dragging themselves one step every two seconds. He saw a field with nothing in it but dead birds as far as the horizon, a forest of spruce, crisped with hoar, fading on every side into blue smoke, and sage-green tuffets of moss underfoot. He saw a city with its components piled in the streets, while its roof timbers lay ragged and torn on their plots. He heard bird flocks, boots on cobbled roads, and iron wheels, whinings through the air and blastings to follow, aeroplanes low and aeroplanes high. He smelled food and gun smoke, horses' urine, food, sawn pine wood, food, ruptured sewers, pigs and chickens, food ... Before he arrived at his destination, Dolboy was already old.

Arrival

DOLBOY'S FATHER had no clear intention when he took possession of his son. He simply saw himself in the half-naked thing, and knew his imagination would not allow him to dismiss the spectre if he turned his back on it. But as he travelled home, a picture of Dolboy's destiny formed in his heart. He was not a parental creature, but from nowhere appeared a vision of himself, visiting intermittently a growing, strengthening child, who would adore his father's wisdom and his gifts. It was a relative of the vision he had entertained of a compliant mistress, enjoyed from time to time in a foreign land.

He had a childless sister in the wooded estates of the Gelderland *Graafschap*, a remote region which the nobility of the Low Countries had sequestered for deer hunting, and the building of castles, with avenues of oak and beech. Even in war it was, for the moment, an untouched, ideal landscape, which seemed perfectly shaped for his unreal tableau. His sister Ineke had become infatuated with the region when she first viewed it from the lacquered black carriage which carried her from Zutphen to a Westphalian folkloric festival at the age of thirteen. Although the land was flat as a millpond, it had been given plateaux of pine, foothills of poplar, mountains of oak, and everywhere you looked, silvery frills of pollard willow along innumerable streams, rivers, dykes and canals. Here and there, from the roof of this arboreal cloak thrust the steely grey towers and turrets of the *kastelen*, which amounted to miniaturised versions of Loire chateaux, rather than structures intended for serious warfare. The *Graafschap*, thought Ineke, was like a warehouse of operatic sets, furnished with living leaves, and herons and kingfishers, in which successive dioramas dissolved and enclosed as you penetrated deeper in their dreamy depths. The remainder of her youth was devoted to searching out a husband with property in this fairy realm.

At the age of thirty, having selected and won the eldest son of a family with three centuries of sound commerce to its credit, and a substantial home (albeit no castle) in the *Graafschap*, Ineke had grown to accept that the granting of her chief wish had precluded the award of any other. She was resigned to being unmusical, socially inept and barren, and never more in her nightly prayers mentioned the possibility that her cup might overflow if just one of these secondary deficiencies were remedied. And so, when her brother voiced his regrets for imposing on her the care of a wretched thing trawled from the belly of war, she closed her eyes in silent thanks to Him, holding her breath for fear that movement of any kind might dissipate the benison.

Her brother developed his apology, but she stilled him, and asked him to repeat his request, this time with her eyes fixed on the blue-tinged face of the tiny being who wavered on the chequered tiles of her hallway.

'What's his name?' she asked.

For an instant he thought of explaining the namelessness of the unspeaking offspring of a speechless madwoman.

'That's up to you,' he answered instead.

'He's like a doll,' she murmured, tight-breathed and unbelieving. She lifted him and exclaimed again. 'He's nothing but feathers. What does he eat?' And she set off to find food, repeating what she had already observed:

'He's a doll boy, so tiny and light. A doll boy.'

And so Dolboy was named.

She returned with a bowl of pink glass, which she placed on a low table of yellow tulipwood. Dolboy bent his head to examine it, and saw stumps of candied angelica, quivering on chestnut purée. He saw candied orange and lemon peels, ginger stems, glacé cherries and petrified fragments of greengage, half submerged or suspended at the surface of the dense nut paste. At its centre, a twirl of whipped eggwhite and cream had been raised to an oblique extremity, like a ballerina's leg.

The opalescent bowl sat on a doily of linen, which also bore a small silver spoon. Dolboy looked up at his father and his aunt. Ineke gestured to the confection, and named it with deliberation, so that he should better remember it.

'Nes-sel-rode,' she enunciated, gesturing now that he should eat. Dolboy looked at the father with whom he had crossed half Europe with infrequent need of a spoon, and his father was no help. Ineke raised the spoon, and mimed the act of eating from it before offering it to Dolboy. Dolboy looked closely at the spoon. It had a finely twisted shaft, as if it had been worked from wires of silver, and its bowl was formed of radiating flutes, like a tiny seashell.

Dolboy's father bent forward, swept the peak off the cream with his middle finger, and licked the finger clean. Dolboy watched, then followed his example, and sat bemused at the sensation of a thing's disappearance, without further aid, when it crossed his lips. It bore no resemblance to anything he had placed in his mouth before. It was something other than food, something which did not need to be consumed to still the spasms of a hollow belly, but was nonetheless compulsive.

He took another portion of the decorative froth on his finger, conveyed it to his mouth, and once more looked from his father to his aunt, and back, with an expression of wonder, while his tongue explored his lips. He took another portion, and another, and when Ineke held the spoon towards him, he gave it no attention, and improved his eating from a single finger by using the flat of his hand to scoop the insubstantial stuff into his mouth. When the egged cream had been used up, and he brought to his mouth his first portion of nesselrode, he started at the changed experience, staring with even greater astonishment at his onlookers, as he discovered the piquancy of the preserved fruits and stems which completed the mixture.

When he had emptied the bowl, he held it in both hands, and scoured its inside with his tongue.

'Nes-sel-rode,' Ineke repeated, with deliberation. Although she knew nothing of children, she understood that a bowl of chicken broth would have better suited Dolboy's needs, followed perhaps by soft-poached egg, forked to a cream with goat's milk. But she sensed that her first duty was to offer him a memorable welcome to her world, and in this she had succeeded.

The little runner

OLBOY'S FEET touched the ground as his soldier uncle tired of his tantrum and lowered him. The circle of surrounding faces closed and looked down, still laughing, still coaxing him to embrace the man who had returned to clasp his aunt like a predator. It resembled a constellation of moons, converging horribly on his fragile planet.

When his uncle returned from the war, Dolboy's ignorant bliss became a tiny dream, which sometimes swam into his consciousness like the fleeting perfume of a lost day spent lying in a summer field.

When his uncle returned from the war, Dolboy's infancy ended. He knew, the day of the celebrations and laughter, the day the encircling faces urged him to accept the ox-big hero, that his world had come to an end, and another world was beginning. Since his father had committed him to the care of his thankful aunt, she had made him a universe in himself, its laws whatever he wished for, its purpose the gratification of his needs. He had come to her like the heavenly gift of a living doll, and in obedience to that sign, she nurtured the propensity until Dolboy became indeed an angelic toy. He was sheltered, pampered and groomed like a child star of the cinema.

When his uncle returned from the war, the days of his ignorant bliss, which had seemed like an eternity, assumed the coherence of a historical epoch. That time of woollen toys, piled until they made a woollen hill, fell into a perspective which embraced his starved infancy, the time before, and his ordered boyhood, the time after.

Once, when he felt that the change from indolence to industry was more than he could bear, he ran away, and at the age of six years might soon have been discovered and returned, had he not fallen into a slow river, which tumbled and numbed him, then buoyed him for many miles further than he would have run, before he was discovered, clinging to a willow root. How he avoided drowning was uncertain. But the experience was not without benefit. He had seen the land outside his home: cows and trees gliding by, and windmills and bridges, and churches and bell towers gliding by, and more trees, and people in the fields, gliding, gliding. He had seen a world less finite than a world of woollen toys, and wanted to be in it. From that revelatory day of hanging in cold water, while a pastoral landscape processed on both sides, Dolboy wandered out whenever the opportunity presented.

To the countryfolk of the area he became known as *'t rennertje*, the little runner, from his habit of trotting along the dirt roads and dyke paths like a preoccupied dog. Wherever he went, he went at a skipping pace, looking about with open eyes, but never lingering. When he went hunting with his uncle, he ran with the dogs to retrieve the fallen hares and woodcock, and the hunters joked that he would one day become an athlete, or a deliverer of parcels. He grew taller and stronger, but instead of leaving behind his childish trotting, he increased its speed, and substituted for his skipping gait a steady, rhythmic stride. The only time he changed his pace was when he left the open roads and made a straight line through dense woods, where no paths lay. Then, it seemed, some primal instinct gained ascendancy, and he plunged with sharpened senses into the obscuring foliage like a Neolithic creature in pursuit of its prey.

His aunt remarked that he was a wonder, because no matter how long he had run, or how far, his skin stayed free of sweat, and within a minute of stopping, his breathing was slow and steady, as if he had just arisen from an afternoon of gentle sleep.

'Dolboy runs as a bird flies,' she told a visiting neighbour. 'It is his nature to speed through life, while we must watch him pass.'

Moths

DOLBOY PLUNGED headlong through a veil of spruce fronds, knowing it would yield harmlessly to disclose another and yet another blue-green wall, secure in the knowledge that the ground beneath his feet would remain soft and flat for five miles, yet alight with the thrill of running full tilt into whatever unseen thing lay beyond the needled curtain. Once he fell over a wild sow and ten striped piglets, which screamed recedingly in every direction, while he paused to reconcile his delight at the surprise, and his fear that he had for ever disrupted a familial bond, ten times over. Another time he ran knee-deep into a nest of giant puffballs, and stood amazed as the destroyed spheres engulfed him in the black fog of a billion spores, before collapsing like soft eggshells on the floor of the clearing they had colonised. And one late morning as he hurtled through coniferous greenery he felt himself captured and suspended in a veil of duck-egg blue, in which he lay with beating heart, until he recognised the silk of a parachute. Cautiously, he unpicked himself from its eddies and cords, following them in every expectation of finding a skeletal fright, rattling in the remnants of a matted uniform. Instead, he found an open harness and an empty boot.

It was while enraptured in this random, irresponsible flight that Dolboy was confronted by the gleaming white and leaf-green summerhouse of the castle of Weisse. Without warning, the deep bed of pine needles over which he flew gave place to tuffets of trembling grass, as the dark woodland opened on a clearing of birch, whose silver stems shone over a sea of foxgloves. And near the centre of the clearing sat a single-storey chalet in the Swedish style, with a fretworked verandah, and a roof of scalloped tiles. Behind it lay more birch and foxgloves, before the wall of spruce resumed.

'At last!' he murmured. For his reckless thudding on the forest floor had been no more than a tremendous gamble: a gamble that before he blundered into the jaws of a leg-severing mantrap he would come upon something wonderful and unexpected. And this was it. He stood at the edge of the clearing until the blood beat quieter in his ears, and his panting subsided to a steady breathing, and then to almost no breathing at all. The singularity of the scene calmed his thoughts until they disappeared and were replaced by a consciousness only of sensory things: the whispering of leaves and branches, the smell of the pine wood, the cool air moving over his lips, and the glimmer of the shining toy house on its lake of purple plumes.

Then the cry of a woodpecker recalled him to action, and he stepped through the grass and the tall flowers until he stood before two broad wooden steps to the verandah. He climbed them, looked in through a window of the summerhouse, and once more drifted beyond the world of thoughts and words, into that other realm. Inside the long room of the fanciful shed lay everything you might expect: a bare floor, painted chairs around a table, an oil lamp on the table, and a wicker chaise longue with a crocheted shawl in pink and mauve. But what entranced Dolboy's senses was the cloud of giant, pale green moths, which fluttered to and fro along the cedar room, some pursuing, some pursued, but never colliding, despite their density in the air.

A half dozen of them had settled on the curtains and the sill, and Dolboy saw that they had downy bodies as thick as his thumb. Their forewings spanned five inches, their hindwings trailed in swallowtails, and in every copulating couple the quivering females bore slender antennae, while their mates had great, feathery horns, to detect and track their chosen vessels. Back and forth the others beat, and when he held his breath he heard the scaly susurration of their hundred wings. It was in the pursuit of just such wonderment that Dolboy had sped through the woods, blindly but unerringly.

As he left the birch glade of the white summerhouse an hour later, he studied the sky to learn the direction in which it lay from his home, and every twenty paces he snapped the terminal shoot of a tree or a bush, tying it in a knot to mark his way, as he had seen hunters do.

'Return of the wanderer,' remarked his aunt Ineke, setting a dish of hotchpotch before him. While he ate, she wiped from his face the blood of tiny wounds which the spruce needles had inflicted as he raced through them.

'There is a wooden house three miles through the woods past the second mill,' he told her. 'I looked in, and it is full of moths.'

His aunt laughed, and told him:

'They don't use it often these times, but I shouldn't think the moths have taken over yet.'

'Yes,' he maintained. 'Moths this big.' He held up both forefingers, and varied the space between them until his aunt was impressed.

'Bats, perhaps. Or sometimes swallows will take to a summerhouse with a broken window.'

'No,' he insisted. 'They were moths. Hundreds of them. Green moths.'

Ineke stopped cleaning the blood from Dolboy's face and laid her palm on his forehead, testing whether his temperature was high.

'That place belongs to the Graaf van Doesburg,' she told him, 'and many years ago I danced there, on the grass, to an accordion band. Every summer they laid out plank tables and gave a party for anybody who chose to go: aristocrats and farmers together, millers, bailiffs, teachers and weavers. Owls sat in the trees and watched. Those people at the castle of Weisse made a noise you could hear in Zutphen, and money was no object. Maybe your moths were the sad souls of all the folk who had joyful times there, and visit to mourn their lost lives.'

Unmoved by his aunt's memories, Dolboy murmured:

'They were real.'

'And so are the souls of the dead,' she answered.

Mirjam

ACH WEEK for a month, Dolboy ran to the summerhouse in the woods of Weisse, and each time he returned home dejected. He grew to regard the clearing of birch trees and quivering grass as a private domain, an addition to the several dells near his uncle's land where nobody but he ever lingered. And after he had looked each week into the wooden house, and found it empty of life, he strolled about the open space, examining its treasures. A wren had nested where a fallen birch presented a haven of knotted twigs and branches. And where the purple blossoms had hung on foxglove stems four weeks earlier, he found now the poisonous green hearts of their seed pods.

When he arrived in the clearing a fifth week, he wandered about, plucking stems of grass and rubbing camomile fronds for their smell, as if they were the purpose of his visit, hoping by his indifference to deflect whatever guardian spirit held moths in its keeping. Still, when at last he looked into the summerhouse its air was vacuous. Nothing fluttered or swooped in the wooden room. But when he looked more closely, he saw that on the table stood a cube of black tiffany, the size of a tea chest. Unable to see it clearly, he moved to a shaded rear window so the dark cube stood between him and the window where he had first appeared. Now the bright background made it translucent, and inside he saw the movement of shadowy wings, quivering in readiness for flight: not a throng of green giants, beating to and fro, but a sign at least, a hint of the magic.

He made a tunnel of both hands to keep out reflections from the window glass, and pressed his eyes against it, willing them to magnify and focus the small movements in the tenebrous block. And his eyes obeyed. They showed him velvety black wings, jewelled with iridescent lozenges, thick, bottle-green abdomens, banded with gold, antennae like the ferns that lined the dyke in the woods. They showed him creatures of midnight-blue, that floated in whatever never-ending, indolent spiral their tiffany prison allowed. They showed him what he wanted them to show him, what he imagined, but nothing of reality.

Dolboy moved around the summerhouse three times, stopping at every window, straining to see more meaning in the infinitesimal movements within the gauzy cube. And just as he realised that he must find some entry to the building, and tested its single door more firmly, a soft voice told him:

'I think you'll need this.'

He turned and saw a fair-haired girl with her foot on the bottom step to the verandah. She was taller than he was, but not by much. She was dressed like a Calvinist, with a dark blue apron over her black skirt and white blouse, and on her head a starched linen cap with turned-up points. Her legs were bare, and she wore the bright yellow clogs which housewives of the region favoured for everyday use. She held up a key.

Dolboy felt the powerful tingling in his ears which was always a prelude to their turning red, which was itself a signal to his face to do the same. Then he felt a tingling all over his body, caused partly by the shame which had inflamed his face and ears, and partly by the strange pleasure of finding himself entranced by beauty.

'I was just looking,' he told her feebly. 'I wasn't going to . . .'

They both glanced at the hand which still held the summerhouse doorknob.

'Here. Let me show you,' the girl offered, stepping onto the verandah and placing the key in the keyhole. She turned her head sideways to smile at him as she twisted the key, and it seemed as if two pins had been pressed into her creamy cheeks, as twin dimples appeared there.

'My name is Mirjam, by the way. What's yours?'

'Dolboy,' he answered, casting down his eyes in expectation of the questions that his curious name aroused. But she only smiled again, and stood back as the summerhouse door gave entry. Dolboy ventured in before her, two steps, and rotated his eyes and his head several times to search the walls, the floor and the roof of the summerhouse, as if expecting the congregation of green moths to be clustered secretly, out of sight from any window. There was no ceiling below the beams of the pitched roof, and Dolboy paid attention to the shadowy angles where its ridge met the walls. That was where he had found wasps' nests and bats in old barns on his uncle's land. But here he found only a shining surface of varnished pine. He looked again at the pin-pricked face of the smiling girl, and she told him:

'This is my lepidopterium.'

She had caught him out, for no matter how much he searched

his memory, he could find no meaning to match the word. And she knew it. She let free a peal of laughter, and told him:

'You have no idea what that is, have you?'

Dolboy shook his head, and sensed an intensification of the colouring which burned in his ears and his cheeks.

'It's a place where you keep lepidoptera,' she declared, laughing out loud again. 'And lepidoptera are butterflies and moths. You needn't mind about not knowing that. Nobody does.' She placed a hand on Dolboy's shoulder to make him feel more comfortable about his ignorance, regretful that her teasing had made him so red. 'Really, nobody could expect you to know. Why should you? Butterflies and moths are perfectly good words.'

At the mention of moths, Dolboy's embarrassment diminished, as if the fair-haired girl had declared that he was not, after all, a lunatic.

'I knew there were moths here,' he blurted. 'I knew I saw moths.'

'Here. Come and look,' she said, stepping to the table with the black cube on it. 'These are cherry silkmoths: *Callosamia promethea*. Can you see them?'

Dolboy saw that the dark fabric covered a spacious cage of wire rods, on whose walls hung several leafy creatures, their wings raised over their bodies like those of butterflies. But their bodies were thick, and some of them had the branched antennae of moths.

'Shut the door and I'll show you properly,' the girl said, slipping a catch at one of the upright edges of the cage. He did as she told him, and when he returned to the table, she gently swung open an entire face of the cube, and the two of them looked in on a score of awakening insects, whose quivering gave way to a tentative opening and closing of wings, as they prepared for flight. When their wings were shut, above their backs, their undersides resembled the mottled brown and grey forms of the dead leaves and tree trunks on which they concealed themselves in their natural state. But when they opened their wings, Dolboy saw that their upper surfaces were a mixture of plum and lavender figures, edged with chocolate-brown. Unlike the green giants he had seen when first he looked into the summerhouse, the cherry moths lacked transparent windows in their forewings, through which he fancied those others might look to left and right of them when they flew. Instead, they bore figures like pink eyes.

'Why don't they fly?' he asked.

'They're warming up,' she laughed. 'They'll not fly till they're ready. Look.'

She placed the tip of her forefinger in front of a moth, so that the creature was forced to hold on to it. Then she lifted it, held its abdomen gently, and launched it like a model aeroplane of fur and dark paper. The moth fluttered involuntarily and clutched at the first thing it encountered: a chenille curtain drawn to one side of a window, where it merged with the fuscous fabric. Mirjam retrieved it and returned it to the wall of its cage.

'If you don't mind waiting a little while, you'll see them fly,' she promised. 'But they have to decide for themselves.'

So the two sat at the table, and as the afternoon grew rosy, the cherry moths became more agitated. She looked at him and smiled her dimpled smile when the first of them winged out of its enclosure, whispered past their heads, and sped the length of the room before executing an abrupt turn and beating back toward them. While they followed its oscillations between the further-

29

most confines of its world, they saw the pioneer joined by other flittering forms, as its fellows decided that the time was ripe, and soon the air was busy with rapid wings. The cherry moths were not as numerous as the green giants, but they flew much faster, and more purposefully. While it was a wonder, he considered, that the meandering giants had not collided with others in their throng, it was equally miraculous that the speeding, plum-coloured cherries avoided battering themselves against the walls, so rapidly did they measure and remeasure the length of the room.

Dolboy and Mirjam watched for half an hour, smiling at each other when an insect, four inches broad, soared past their noses, or settled briefly on her cap. Then, as abruptly as they had elected to fly, the moths settled on the curtains and the walls, paired after the pre-nuptial flight which was the high point and purpose of their insubstantial existence.

'That's it,' she declared. 'Now they won't do anything more.'

'Until tomorrow?' he asked.

'Ever,' she answered. 'The females will lay eggs, of course. But they won't send out any more messages for the males.'

'Messages?' he wondered. 'What messages?'

'The females send a signal, a message that they are ready, and the males pick it up and follow.'

'But why won't they do it again?' He was puzzled. The moths had seemed to enjoy their headlong laps of the summerhouse.

'Once is enough,' said Mirjam, regarding him gravely, as if she too regretted there would be no more messages. He saw that her eyebrows and lashes were a pure, shining silver, like the shining down on her arms, and his attention shifted from the pulsating couples which surrounded them to the girl whom he had disregarded in his absorption. She had elfin ears to match the points of her linen cap, and her nose also seemed to end in two points, as if it had been pressed into the corners of a box. Her eyes twinkled when she caught him examining her, and her cheeks flexed to conjure once more the two sharp-bottomed pits which signalled her amusement.

'What?' she asked him, feeling her hair to see if anything was caught in it. 'What are you looking at?'

'You,' he answered. His embarrassment had left him now they had shared the flight of moths. From the beginning she had spoken to him directly, as if she already knew him and he was part of her world. And as his gaze wandered over the arch of her slender neck, and her fragile fingers, and her amused lips, he felt that he was indeed part of Mirjam's world, and always would be.

His dreaming was ended by the peal of the six o'clock bells, and he imagined his aunt at the dinner table, poised over a tureen, waiting to remark the return of the wanderer.

'I have to go,' he said.

'Come back again,' she told him, and rested her hand on his shoulder as they said goodbye in the doorway of the summerhouse, before Dolboy raced to the enclosing woodland.

The proposition

D OLBOY'S FATHER had no clear intention when he took possession of his child. He had pictured a son who would admire his wisdom and talents, and little further. It was a vision he still nurtured when he left the bemused infant in his sister's arms and returned to his place of business, but it was a vision which grew dimmer. At the next gathering of his family, the rosy cherub spoonfed by his sister did not recall the blue-grey infant he had carted across battlefields. Soon, he considered Dolboy Ineke's child, and his life resumed its old pattern.

He rose at eight every morning, ate breakfast at the mansion where he lived with his parents, amused himself at the piano keyboard awhile, then walked the small distance from his home to the mahogany-panelled headquarters of van Baerle, where he was greeted like royalty by every soul he encountered. His progress from the front door to his office generally occupied an hour, as he moved from department to department, exchanging pleasantries with clerks, accountants, secretaries, transportation experts and the occasional barge captain. Sometimes he would address himself to business, as an *afdelingschef* enquired what volume of coffee beans he should accept, or whether it was time yet to offer on the Russian wheat which freighters still brought to the quays of Harlingen and Den Helder. His reply, almost without exception, was:

'Ask me tomorrow,' and the employee was thrown back on his own resources.

This regal progress behind him, the heir to the van Baerle enterprise would slump in an oversized leather chair, behind a desk devoid of anything resembling documentation, and call for coffee, which was an excuse for his secretary to provide him with the day's edition of *De Volkskrant*. He read from the newspaper in bursts of concentration, rising between them to stroll to a window from which he could monitor the passage of time, on a great gilded clock, to the hour when he might adjourn for lunch in the ancient *wijnhuis*, before it was bombed. If it was a market day, he took his newspaper to a chair in the window, so that his attention might glide without hindrance between reviews of new plays in the capital, and farmers' wives throwing their heads back to swallow whole herring, seasoned with onions.

After lunch he strolled Zutphen's main thoroughfare, with its ten-foot doorways and its twelve-foot windows letting light into living rooms eighteen feet tall, to take coffee at the café *Pelikaan* or the café *Coöperatief*. In the former he would discuss commerce with solid burghers whose lives resembled his own, and in the latter he would lapse into *Achterhoekse* dialect and smoke black Sumatran cheroots with workers in clogs, caps and blue cotton smocks. Here the talk would be of women, in the best of times, and in the worst, of ways to perplex the invader who strutted the golden town in shining boots, and uniforms beautified by eagles of metallic thread, and lightning bolts in black.

'Van Baerle, we have found a way to give your life some

purpose,' one of the foremen told him, while sitting in a street window of the *Coöperatief*. The heir to the van Baerle enterprise joined in the joke.

'What? You think I should stay home every morning so you can have an extra hour to manicure your nails before you start loading?'

The foreman smiled, and maintained the smile for so long that his employer understood no joke was intended.

'So. What will give my life some purpose?' he asked, when the laughter had left his mouth. 'What?'

'Cornelius, how do you think you will look when all this shit is over?' The foreman gestured to the street, where two members of the occupying force strolled at their exaggerated leisure, as if disarming resistance by the use of psychology.

'What do you mean, how will I look? I'll look no better and no worse than anybody else will look. I've done nothing to be ashamed of.' All thoughts of a joke had drained from van Baerle's mind. The foreman went on:

'No, little Cornelius, I don't mean you, yourself. I mean van Baerle, the undertaking.' The foreman had known Dolboy's father since infancy, and employed an intimate form of address without special disrespect. 'Van Baerle continues as if nothing has happened here. You are making profit hand over fist. How does that look?'

'We have done nothing improper. Absolutely nothing.' Van Baerle raised his voice above the hubbub, so that people at the next table interrupted the movement of their cups to their lips, momentarily, and glanced sideways before drinking.

'You say that,' the foreman continued, 'but when this situation has passed, people will ask: "What did van Baerle do during those difficult times? De Kuyper was shut down. De Kuyper himself went to prison, and van Wijnen was shot, for God's sake. Herrema collaborated. And what about van Baerle? Was it possible not to be on one side or the other?"'

In the café *Pelikaan* such a conversation would not have been joined. Businessmen respect each other's philosophy, each other's right of independent action. They respect each other's right to survive. Cornelius van Baerle grew icy.

'What is your point?'

'My point is, Cornelius, that it is not enough simply to act as if nothing has happened in our country. These people won't prevail. They walk around as if they could fight the whole world with one hand tied behind their backs, but they can't. They're spread too thin. They're running out of boy scouts. In a year or maybe two years they will be on their knees, begging us to forget. And what do you think? Shall we forget?'

'No, we won't forget,' van Baerle answered. 'But in the meantime we can only wait, and make sure the enterprise is not destroyed.'

'That's not enough,' the foreman answered. 'People will remember that we survived and prospered. They will remember that you could roam around Europe, keeping up contacts, finding new business even. How could anybody do that, without cooperating?' He raised his hand to still van Baerle's objections. 'All that aside, there is a chance for you to do something worthwhile, something that will demonstrate on which side the company van Baerle sits, and incidentally, something that will give you, little Cornelius, some purpose, some justification for your existence.'

'If it's anything to do with your . . . activities.' Cornelius spoke vaguely, but looked furtively around, as people did when they discussed resistance. 'I can't go creeping about at night with a torch. I don't like heroism.'

'You don't have to be heroic,' the foreman told him. 'Just good. For once.'

The two fell silent and ordered more drinks. Outside, a mellifluous carillon filled the air above the crooked chimneys and towers of the great trading town on the banks of the Oude IJssel river, and a stork floated over the historic concatenation without a single wingbeat. At length, Cornelius resumed their discussion.

'So. What is it, this worthwhile thing that will give my life some purpose?'

'Seizing countries is not the worst thing they do,' said the foreman. 'That's just land, territory. They can't dig it up and take it away, and they can't occupy half of Europe for ever. But they have another project, which you may know about, or not: I don't know. You travel a good deal, but do you keep your eyes open? Do you see what's happening around you?'

Van Baerle waited for him to continue, without answering.

'I imagine you know about Westerbork camp?' the man in blue continued.

'An occupying force likes to keep its dissidents in one place,' van Baerle observed. 'A camp in the woods is not such a bad place to spend the war.'

'This occupying force puts a bullet in the back of a dissident's head,' the foreman scoffed. 'You don't imagine they send real dissenters for a holiday in the woods, do you? And people who go to Westerbork don't spend the war there. They may spend three months, or six, or even nine months there, but they don't ever stay. Sooner or later they're put on a train.'

'Sent home?'

'No, Cornelius, not sent home. Most of the people they have in Westerbork are the same people they've been chasing in their own country for the past eight years: the Goldschmidts, the Neumanns, the Cohens and so on.'

'Goldschmidt is in Westerbork?'

'Not our Goldschmidt. People like him. Westerbork is a holding camp for those people, a railhead. They're winkled out of their homes in the West, stripped of their possessions, classified, and shipped east in their thousands.'

'East of Westerbork.'

'Not the east of our country. East, as far as you can go. To the country outside Berlin and Prague, to the forests between Dresden and Krakow, between Warsaw and Lvov. They're sent to camps buried in the woods, and the intention is that they never come back, they don't survive.'

'They're executed? Why transport them for execution?'

Cornelius waved away the packet of cheroots he was offered, but the foreman lit up and continued:

'They are executed slowly. They are worked to death, while at the same time being starved. So, you see, there is a purpose in transporting them. They have some value, these Neumanns and Cohens, which is to be extracted before their extermination.'

Cornelius fell into a brief reverie, in which he recalled his journey from the east with his infant son, and the grey-faced people he had seen standing behind wire fences, beneath the yellow sky, while men looked over them from wooden towers: those faces in which he had seen his own face, as he and Dolboy trundled westward in their wagon. He had covered his son's eyes and closed his mind to them, but their image persisted. He sighed, and asked the foreman:

'What does this have to do with me? Why are you telling me this?'

'These places are hidden. They're secret. We know only half truths about them: half truths distilled from rumours. And when this shit is over, and these people are on their knees, begging us to forget, in this case we'll oblige. They will have destroyed any trace of what they did there, and when they ask us to forget, we will oblige, because we will have only half truths and rumours as a basis on which to accuse them. Unless, that is, somebody is able to see and to recall their crimes. Unless there is a witness.'

'A witness,' van Baerle repeated. 'There will surely be many witnesses if they're doing this on any scale.'

'If they see defeat coming they will take steps to conceal evidence that they behaved with inhumanity,' the foreman insisted. 'They will eradicate their camps and the people in them. Perhaps some of the unfortunates will survive to tell what happened. Perhaps not. Who can be sure? But if somebody were to go and see these places now, before they are burned and buried, his word would be useful in the time of reckoning to come. And that man is you, little Cornelius. You will be our witness.'

Cornelius was not surprised when the foreman arrived at the conclusion of his lecture. He was no fool. He had heard rumours.

And when the foreman spoke of a witness, he knew he was to be that witness. Even so, he protested.

'And who has appointed you to appoint me? Are you hearing voices now? Do you want my job?'

The foreman looked down, smiling, and shook his head.

'Your job? That's a good idea. I'd like that. I think I could do it, Cornelius.'

Then, after drawing deeply on the remaining fragment of his cheroot, and expelling the smoke in a jet, like the exhaust of a train whistle, he explained:

'People like me – people who can't sit and wait for things to get better without helping matters along – we talk to each other. We exchange news about what's happening in our country. We exchange rumours of what's happening in the forests between Berlin and Lvov, and we agree we need to know with certainty the basis of those rumours. We need to be sure, so that it is not forgotten. So that we don't oblige them when they're on their knees, begging us to forget. Nobody appointed me, Cornelius, and nobody is appointing you. We're telling you that something bad is happening to our fellow countrymen in a distant place, and that somebody who has the means, God knows how, to roam around Europe at will, might consider it a moral obligation to keep his eyes open the next time he travels east.'

Cornelius plucked his upper lip between his thumb and forefinger, while nodding his head.

'And he should travel quite soon,' the foreman added.

Breakfast

CORNELIUS VAN BAERLE did not care much for talk about moral obligation. It was the kind of talk which had visited a nightmare on the continent in the first place. If the foreman had said: 'We can't think of a good argument why you might want to do something so dangerous, beyond the fact that you have the opportunity,' he would have respected his logic. There was absolutely no reason why he should consider venturing into that perilous zone, to poke his nose into other people's business, when he was perfectly comfortable in Zutphen. And yet he felt a curious tingling in his stomach when he sat down to breakfast the next day, and heard his own voice tell his father:

'I have to make a trip again, a journey to the east.'

His father applied the concentration of a surgeon to the task of knifing a perfect oblong from the slice of old Gouda on his plate. Then he pinioned the cheese with his knife, and pushed its free end with his fork, so that it buckled and made either a little concertina, which he skewered and ate, or a cylinder, like a miniature Swiss roll. He believed that ambient humidity decided the outcome. If he secured a run of more than three consecutive rolls, he would look up through the window and forecast certain storms. When he heard Cornelius's announcement, he answered:

'Don't we have enough women in Gelderland?'

'It doesn't concern women,' Cornelius protested.

Van Baerle senior looked at his son, over the top of his eating spectacles. His expression of silent disbelief prompted Cornelius to go further.

'It's something, apparently, I'm required to undertake for the good of the company, for the good of our name. We're doing too well. It doesn't look decent.'

Now his father was intrigued. He interrupted the dissection in which he was engaged, to give the matter fuller attention.

'And travelling east, visiting co-traders and suppliers will dispel that perception? I don't see how.'

'I wouldn't just be doing our usual business. I would be looking out for other things at the same time. Things arising from the hostilities.'

'Spying? You? Spying?' Van Baerle senior was incredulous. 'What in God's name gives you these absurd notions? What have you been reading? I suppose you'll be taking a little radio set and a bottle of invisible ink?'

He ran out of words and gave way to snorts, as his attention wandered back to the remaining cheese on his plate. His response determined Cornelius to insist.

'I shall go. It isn't spying, as you imagine it. I don't intend to note troop movements, or communicate with headquarters. But my witness may be of some value, not least in dispelling the notion that we are war profiteers.'

His father glowered, and clenched both fists as he made a

conscious effort to breathe away his rage. Having succeeded, he smiled kindly at his only son, and told him:

'You know, things have changed since you last represented us. It's more desperate now. Our masters are fighting for their lives. The only movements you're likely to see are the movements of bombs, falling from the sky every night, and even in the daytime now, I'm told. Those bombs won't know of your mission. They won't fail to explode, for the sake of our company's good name. Wait a year, or two years. Then you may travel as you like.'

He knew he was speaking for the sake of the noise. He knew his son.

A week later, armed with his usual sheaf of banknotes and drafts, and with gold coins stitched into his clothes in places where you might expect them, and in others where you would not, Cornelius received from his chief clerk a note from the regional gauleiter, authorising his travel, and prepared to take leave of his father. The old man called him into his office, looked up and down the corridor before closing the door, and then began twirling the combination wheel of his great iron safe.

'I already have what I need,' Cornelius told him.

'Money? Yes, to be sure. But this won't do any harm, either.' He took out a stiff envelope and withdrew from it a sheet of folded buff paper, bearing a crest. When Cornelius glanced at its contents, he felt the sensation of the entire earth moving, while his stomach remained in the same place. It was a note, brief and unconditional, ordering that free passage and all privileges be accorded to its bearer, on pain of displeasing the highest Air Marshal of the Reich.

'So it's true!' he exclaimed. 'What people say! Van Baerle is a profiteer, a collaborator? I can't believe it. It's unspeakable. I don't accept this.' And he threw the useful document on his father's desk.

'No,' the old man answered. 'Van Baerle is not a profiteer, or a collaborator. That note has been in darkness since it was written, seven years ago. It was given to me in thanks for certain items of luxury which I provided this sybarite when I was on business in the east. I almost laughed out loud when he presented it, like some potentate granting favours to a vassal. I never imagined those people would be taken seriously, outside their own country. I kept it as a curiosity, a memento of a meeting with a puffed-up opera buffo. It has never occurred to me to let anyone know that I ever met this man, leave alone avail myself of his safe conduct. But now that you propel yourself into his dangerous world, I don't hesitate to use it. And I beg that you will exploit its authority without scruple if the need arises. I beg it.'

And so Cornelius took his father's portentous *laissez-passer*, and the two men stood and embraced, clinging to each other as if they would never meet again, which indeed proved to be the case.

Another journey

EVEN IN THE rolling green landscape of Thuringa, Cornelius witnessed the new desperation of which his father had spoken: the country folk crawled on hands and knees, searching the broken clay for an overlooked potato, combing the stubble with their fingers to extract the last grain of wheat. From Mülhausen to Altenburg innocuous towns lay wasted, their inhabitants camping stubbornly where once their homes had stood, or dragging salvaged mattresses and sticks of furniture in listless convoy toward no particular destination. He looked one day down a road which stretched to the horizon, transfixed by the spectacle of a thousand people throwing themselves into ditches on either side, like a zip fastener opening, as a fighter plane flew low along its length.

'They do it for pleasure,' one of the re-emerging homeless informed him. 'But if you don't play their game they have their red button. Better to be safe, and look like a fool.'

While he had travelled with some difficulty during the earlier stages of the war, his movements now were intolerably choked with armoured columns and checkpoints, and temporary headquarters in commandeered villas, where he was arraigned to present his papers and explain his presence. More than once he was arrested, and on one occasion was held under guard for two weeks while his interrogation was interrupted by military exigencies. But instead of disappearing like a million others into that absurdity of smoke and accidental gunshots, he dusted down his coat, enjoyed a glass of wine with his erstwhile captors, and resumed his route.

'You can't possibly be a spy, because a spy would have a believable story up his sleeve,' a corporal guard told him, while cleaning from his bayonet what appeared to be a heavy coating of dried blood. 'Anybody who says he's travelling here for the sake of trade is too simple to be a spy. But then again, anybody who would travel here for the sake of trade is no businessman, so maybe you are a spy.'

'What the God-in-heaven does some gauleiter in a cushy foreign posting know about conditions in the world, to give you travel papers now,' complained the corporal's superior, releasing Cornelius to continue his mission. 'You'll never see home again, I promise you that.'

Cornelius accepted that what the officer said might be the truth.

Sometimes he thought of his earlier eastward journeys, filled with lust and expectation. But when he considered retracing that route, whenever desire kindled memories of Dolboy's mother, awaiting him on her knees, the image was overlaid by that of her subsequent form, and he remembered her practising a pathetic curtsy, as she awaited his pleasure. And so he contented himself with memories of the excitement with which he had read each new road and railway sign that marked a diminishment of the space between him and the hypnotic object of his desire, and continued on his other route.

On this other route, six weeks after leaving home, he approached a region which his idealistic employee had designated for scrutiny. Somewhere in beechwoods before the Ore mountains, and on their further slopes (if the foreman was believed), fellow countrymen subsisted on the leavings of the populace, quarrying stone on which to bed a railway line, digging pits and kneeling at their brinks to topple more conveniently in. Did those blameless woods provide concealment for such harm?

Walking the main street of an undevastated village on the first morning after his arrival in the area, Cornelius was unable to overcome an illogical urge which had blossomed in his thoughts, and asked a dishevelled workman:

'Excuse me. Could you tell me the way to the concentration camp?'

Unastonished, the workman ran his eyes down to Cornelius's buttoned boots and back up to his felt hat, decided that this was a man of importance, and with no emotion on his face, pointed out a road running into woodland to the east of the settlement.

'Thank you. And a pleasant day further,' said the visitor, and followed the indicated route on foot. Pursuing the logic of this impulse, would he on sight of a penal settlement ask at the main gate if he might inspect the prisoners? How was it possible that naivety could lead him unchallenged to a site of such secrecy that its annihilation was a priority of the state? Perhaps the workman was complying with that code of rural etiquette which deemed it impolite to leave unanswered a request for guidance, even if the answer was unknown: better to point, in whatever direction, than simply to shrug.

For two miles in the sunny woods, Cornelius drifted with

the birds which made their nests, and awakening bees which reconnoitred earthen banks for holes to house their dynasties. Brambles pressed fresh shoots through the detritus of last year's bracken mat, and boughs of blue spruce were punctuated at intervals by bright new needles of deciduous larch. He decided to allow himself one more mile of this sylvan ramble before he returned to the village in which he had asked directions. Why had he not asked how far? That workman could have obliged with a spurious number to complete his faulty assistance.

Then the breeze which carried the perfumes of the warming forest took on a change. Cornelius continued to breathe in the vapour of resin and pine needles and wild violets, until that other smell, not of the forest and not of spring, insisted on recognition. He sniffed the air and asked himself what he smelled, and the answer was that he smelled the inside of a damp cupboard in which the discarded shoes of many years mounded up, reeking their ancient stink of cheesy feet. He smelled the bedroom of a nonagenarian, dying of cancers. But of course, he smelled no such things. He smelled that combination of old sweat and old dirt on human bodies, to which no other smell is comparable, commingled with the vapours of uncollected human waste.

Between converging trees ahead he saw a barrier on the road, with guards in uniform, and behind it a gate topped with barbed wire, set in a high fence with a similar frieze. The odour of the place restored him from that dangerous gaucherie which led him to ask directions on the street, like a *dummkopf* tourist, and he stepped from the road and into the woods. His senses sharpened as he recognised that the errand he ran was no escapade, and might this minute or the next bring his life to an unexplained conclusion. He glimpsed his weeks of blundering through the arena of war, of standing on a road with one hand shielding his eyes to watch a Lancaster roar over, of waking at the thud of a bomb, and he understood that the charm which had preserved his innocent life was dissipated, now that his journey was over. Now he had broken the surface of that pool which constituted his imaginings. Now he had entered reality.

He trod lightly on the forest carpet, avoiding any wooden thing that might crack and send a brace of pigeons in the air to mark his approach. He heard no sound from the settlement ahead, where he had expected poor ghosts to be bringing hammers down on hard ground, and pushing wagons, to the agitation of Alsatian dogs. The sickly air hung silent as the trees grew thin and then became a fringe, where gorse and bramble thrived. There was a wire fence, such as he had seen before, enclosing bare ground, and an arrangement of long huts, like chicken sheds, raised on piers of brick, with air space underneath. In watchtowers along the fence he saw solitary guards, nodding in the unexpected warmth, and in some no guards at all. The inmates, in loose uniforms, were present in their hundreds, but at first glance seemed to have postponed all other intentions for the sake of a group photograph, so little did they move. Cornelius felt he might have been considering on the wall of a great museum a large-scale painting by a master of the Golden Age, on a theme of indolence. How could so many people do so little, simultaneously?

He considered the situation, while examining the sombre tableau he had travelled so far to view. Of what was he witness? What would he tell that court of later reckoning, to whose assistance his foreman had called him? As he watched the listless prisoners from whom that stench extended, he saw they were beyond the wielding of hammers and the laying of rails. They had the colour of artificial fruit: wax grapes and wax apples in greenish shades. The skin drawn taut over their skulls and claws shone with an angelic pallor. Some held together as they crouched in pairs; others stood distracted, alone or in aimless groups; others lay on the ground, face up, face down, alive and dead.

The silent assembly, Cornelius realised, consisted of those who had no will to speak or move, no reason to do so, no strength, no life, and those who were sunbathing. He watched for half an hour, and nothing changed. That was his witness: that people suspended at the point of extinction may yet enjoy the sensation of sun on their skins, and soft wind from the spring woods.

The camps

OVER A PERIOD of many months, Cornelius van Baerle extended his acquaintance with the conqueror's woodland storage depots, travelling chiefly on foot to the east of Chemnitz and Dresden, then further east toward Lublin and Krakow. The foreman's inventory proved reliable, and each place he had selected for examination offered its own variation on the half-enacted project to dispose of those souls, collected from every corner of the continent, who did not fit the template of the master race's master plan.

As he progressed, the situation of the populace grew more desperate daily. The roads were choked with people. Attacking aeroplanes grew more bold, and might appear at any hour of the day and night, unopposed. His progress grew easier. When he had encountered an army unit two months earlier, he took out his papers and prepared for a long delay. Now the soldiers drove past him without pause, unconcerned by anyone who travelled without a machine gun and grenades. Who cared if he might be a spy? What was there left to spy on?

Sometimes he was surprised to discover other camps, enclosing communities of prisoners with their own uniforms, enacting rituals of authority and rank to keep their structures intact for the time to follow. This was a different category of inmate, writing letters home, receiving Red Cross parcels, eager to call to him through the fence for news which might indicate the time of the end, which they knew to be coming soon. These prisoners of war did not fear the turning of the machine guns inward, the locking in huts to be followed by the dousing with petrol, and the burning of the evidence which those others feared, those unwashed, half starved, with flesh of green wax.

One day in late January, as he walked down a forest road much like the one which had led him to that first camp, in the beech-woods of Thuringa, he saw ahead of him the next camp he sought, and above its gate a moral motto in iron letters. He looked to left and right, deciding which way offered the best covering of trees. Then he noticed that the watchtowers by the gate were empty, and there was no guard on the road. He decided to approach a little closer before striking into the woods, and when he did, he saw that the gate stood ajar, and prisoners in their striped uniforms wandered out, unchallenged. He continued along the road until he faced one of them.

'What has happened?' he asked.

'They've gone,' the bewildered scarecrow answered. 'The guards have taken the day off.' And he drew his thin lips into an expression of pleasure that exposed bloodless gums no longer capable of holding teeth.

Cornelius passed him and walked to the gate, while tottering escapees scattered to give him a wide berth, in case he repre-sented authority, in case he had come to shatter their disbelief. Some of them he stopped to ask again:

'What has happened. When?'

'This morning,' one of them answered. 'We didn't get the chance to kill one of them. They just disappeared in the night, the bastards.'

Cornelius looked up and down the man, who barely had the flesh to stand upright, and saw that the notion of his killing a guard was a figment he clung to for the sake of dignity. He continued forward, against the stream of pallid people staggering to the freedom of the shattered countryside beyond the wire. He had become accustomed to the smell of these places, but when for the first time he stepped inside a long shed which housed the unwanted, his stomach revolted against the stench penetrating the handkerchief he pressed to his face. Inside, like narrow storage racks in a warehouse, stretched long rows of wooden bunks, three layers high, on which lay a spoiled human cargo. Arms consisting of bones and skin projected randomly over the edges of the bunks, like obstacles thrown to hinder his progress down the long alleys. Many of these sleepers had died recently, but one corpse was older. Van Baerle stood before a mattress on which he beheld a mummy, a desiccated creature with skin of brown paper, whose face resembled a wasp's nest, set with teeth.

He had not witnessed all of the things which the foreman in Zutphen had listed. But this he had witnessed.

He walked the length of the building, noticing here and there that a dull eye followed his passage, without any movement of the head which contained it, and hearing from time to time a feeble cough or a moan, or the weakest noise of air, sighing from a lung. Then he stepped out into the sunlight, and looking to see where he should move next, saw a group of soldiers riding along the perimeter toward the gate by which he had entered.

Some were in armoured vehicles, others on horseback, riding at a gallop, and he saw on their khaki tunics, held in by belts, the flashing red of their insignia. They entered the gate and thundered toward him like Cossacks, and he was unable to suppress a thrill that ran through him at the sight of the liberating army from the east. He held a fist in the air and shouted with an emotion of elation which arose unbidden from somewhere deep in his soul. Then, as the horsemen enclosed him, he felt the brief, shocking nausea that precedes unconsciousness, as a heavy rifle butt, swung like a club, crashed against the back of his head.

The van Doesburgs

B UT WHAT OF the green moths, the giant green moths? Dolboy's aunt Ineke listened to the story of his meeting with the silver-haired lepidopterist, and that was her only thought.

'The cherry moths are not like any moths we have,' he told her. 'They have strong colours, and they fly like butterflies.'

'So what makes them moths? Perhaps they are butterflies.'

'No,' he explained. 'They have thick bodies, covered with hair, and antennae.'

He had only just learned the word, but he employed it like an expert. His aunt was bamboozled.

'Antennae? So, you're a specialist now?'

'You know: horns, growing from their heads.'

'Like butterflies have,' she smiled.

'No. These are different.' He reflected for the first time on the distinction, and concluded with scientific accuracy:

'Butterflies' antennae have knobs on them. Those of moths are pointed.'

'But what of the green moths, the giant green moths?' His aunt reverted to her first thought.

'I don't know,' Dolboy admitted, as his aunt replaced the dish which had contained his meal of vegetables with one of spiced apple and cream.

'Mirjam is the daughter of the Graaf Hubert van Doesburg,' she told him. 'There are three children: an older boy and another girl, younger than Mirjam. Sometimes they come to take part in the gymkhana or the August street fairs, but mostly they stay apart. They don't mean any offence; they have everything they need in their own world. But I should find that limiting, for myself.'

'What else?' Dolboy asked, when she came to an end. He wanted to know all that was to be known about the inhabitants of the castle of Weisse.

'The castle is a picture,' his aunt resumed. 'We presented ourselves there when they held their parties in the woods. From the end of the drive it looks like a pretty gamekeeper's cottage. If you didn't know what it was, you would nod and pass by. But the drive is much longer than it seems from the road, and the further you ride down it, the longer it becomes. You see that the trees by which you judged the scale of things are not beech trees like those on our boundaries, but giant plants ninety feet high. Their trunks have been trimmed of branches, so they have the same proportions as our trees, but the bare stems are forty feet tall before leaves begin.

'As you travel along the drive, the gamekeeper's cottage grows bigger, until you see that it is as tall as two normal buildings, and set on an island surrounded by green water. Its smallest face looks to the road, and when you make a circuit of the castle you find that its sides are five times deeper than its front. Your uncle says it is a monument to modesty. They were trying to look smaller than they really were, the van Doesburgs. They have lived there since the Golden Age: four hundred years, and in all that time they haven't once attracted attention to themselves, for good or bad. That's a history you have to respect.'

Aunt Ineke paused to reflect on the record of inconspicuousness, and Dolboy prompted her again:

'What else?'

'What else? Too much to tell in one telling.' It was the formula by which his aunt indicated that she had reached the end of her interest in a topic. Perhaps there was more to tell, and perhaps there was nothing. Dolboy never knew. It was simply a device.

So the next week he ran to see for himself the castle which belonged to the summerhouse in the woods of Weisse. He ran not through the heather that gave way to the birch that gave way to the spruce, but along the dyke that skirted his uncle's two mills, and along the dirt road that gave way to the cobbled road, and along the cobbled road until it gave way to the paved road that carried the carts and the lorries between Zutphen and Winterswijk. On the grass-edged track that followed this road, he settled into his steady dogtrot, breathing deeply and rhythmically as his heart adjusted to its accustomed elevation, dreaming into the future while his resilient body undertook the duty of conveying him to his destination.

Unconscious of processing pines, and the sparse traffic that shared his route, he saw himself gliding in a bottle-green landau, possibly a Mercedes, down a long avenue of beech trees, from which at intervals estate staff bowed and waved to him and his beautiful, silver-haired wife, whose silken scarf streamed in curlicues behind them like the undulations of the sea behind an ocean liner. Their progress slowed to a halt before an ancient but pristine mansion, garlanded with wisteria and clematis, from which laughing children issued, glad to see their lustrous parents home. The eldest of them stepped forward, and opened in celebration a gilded casket, from which, to the tops of the towering trees, dispersed a cloud of green moths.

When he returned through time, he stood at the iron tracery flanking the main gates of the Weisse castle drive. He looked through it and saw, as his aunt had described, a bucolic structure, tiny with distance, at the focus of the avenue of beech he had recently dreamed. He opened a subsidiary gate, stepped in, and held himself to walking pace, the better to luxuriate in the sensation that enveloped him, of entering the world for which he was destined. Half an hour later, having dawdled the extent of the bowered corridor, he stood at another gate of wrought iron, through which he saw an arched footbridge crossing a moat surfaced with lily pads. On its far side a flight of steps led to a divided door of grey oak. The building to which it gave access comprised two high storeys, rising to a steely mansard roof, interrupted by ornately framed windows. The façade was of rosy brick, ornamented with open diamonds of blue brick, and festooned with climbing roses and honeysuckle. While he stood, one half of the sun-silvered door swung inward, and a serving woman dressed entirely in black, apart from her lace bonnet, clattered in wooden shoes over the cobbled footbridge. She had the rosy-cream skin of a child, but when she smiled, her face broke into a complexity of ancient facets and fissures.

'Are you lost, or here to see someone?' she asked. Unaccustomed to receiving questions about his presence, Dolboy answered without pause:

'Mirjam.'

The old infant invited him inside the gate and over the foot-bridge, but left him standing at the doorstep while she click-clacked into the darkness beyond the chequered tiles of the hallway. He had not intended to apply to the castle. He had intended only to inspect it, and to compare it with his aunt's remembrance, but when he was asked the reason for his visit, he spoke what came into his head. He felt no embarrassment that he had set in motion some mechanism that must reach fulfil-ment before he was allowed to retrace his course, over the green water and down the green alley. Its initiation had been uninten-tional, that is to say, it was destined.

Mirjam appeared abruptly out of the velvet dimness, and he saw that she wore half boots of felt, in which she might skate the hallway as easily as if it had been ice.

'Dolboy!' she exclaimed in a surprised way, laughing the twin-kling laugh that conjured her dimples. 'I had no idea who it could be. Minneke said there was a young gentleman who had arrived on dusty feet.'

They looked down together at his shoes, saw that they were entirely coated in road dust, then looked at each other and smiled.

'I was running,' Dolboy told her. No further explanation of his presence was needed. Mirjam asked him to stand inside the door while she skated back into the shadows at the far end of the long hallway, and in a minute she reappeared in clogs. They crossed the footbridge together and took a path along the side of the castle, where the moat widened and assumed a darker green hue, and Dolboy saw that the building was indeed much more extensive that a visitor to the front would suspect. It was also less decorative, and at the level of the water were slit windows, designed, perhaps, to assist in defence against Spaniards.

They took a winding path through false woodland, where the species of the surrounding country were employed, but in an orderly, picturesque fashion, interspersed with exotic specimens equipped with plaques on which their names were inscribed, in the vernacular and in Latin. They crossed by a quaint footbridge of iron, cast to represent wooden branches, a canal where pink water lilies revealed their yellow pistils above a surface of dull, elephantine leaves. From the banks of the waterway on the castle side loomed a canopy of water rhubarb and giant hogweed, while on its other side nature asserted a humbler plan of dock and nettle, and beyond them the woodland of spruce which enclosed the clearing of birch, and the summerhouse in the Swedish style.

The poisonous foxglove seed pods in the grove of birch had turned to brown tinder, which rattled like little drums as Dolboy and Mirjam brushed them. She reached in her pocket and held up a key when they stood on the shaded verandah, and as she placed it in its lock, she turned her head sideways and smiled at him in remembrance of their first meeting. Then the door opened, and he breathed again the resinous air of the cabin, on which something liquorice-flavoured also hung.

'That will be an emergent,' she told him. 'Let's look.'

They crossed to a screen-covered window at the back of the room, where two large moths with banded bodies, and wings patterned in clay shades, hung over drops of fluid on the sill.

'That's what you can smell,' said Mirjam. 'When they emerge from their cocoons they have no wings, to speak of. They are like little sacks attached to their thoraxes. When they have found a place to hang, they inflate the sacks through veins until they reach their proper size. Then they wait until the wings have dried, and when that's over, they let the liquid free.'

Dolboy held his face close to the hanging insects, to see more clearly the intricate patterning of their pristine wings, and their curious odour filled his nostrils.

'These are Robin moths – *Cecropia*,' she said. 'Now two females have emerged, there's sure to be a male out soon.'

'They have begun with their messages,' Dolboy suggested.

'Yes,' she agreed. 'Even a pupa, which is like a nut in a shell, can receive a message when it's the right time.'

They regarded each other and considered this mystery in silence.

'But then, after everything, what happens then?' Dolboy asked.

'After everything?'

'After they have flown together, and the females have laid their eggs. What then? Where are the big green moths I saw, and where are the cherry moths?'

'The *luna* moths? And the *prometheas*? They're here, some of them,' she told him.

'Where?'

She walked to one end of the wooden room, where a tall

60

bookcase was attached to the wall. She reached up and pulled with one finger on the embossed spine of what seemed to be a heavy volume. It came easily free of the shelf, and fell lightly into her hands. As she opened the covers, a crease appeared along its spine, and the book revealed itself to be a box of cedarwood, three inches deep, which contained the impaled corpses of twelve moths, their wings spread uncharacteristically flat beside their bodies. Their colours were faded, but Dolboy recognised in these frozen jade effigies the ghosts of the bright green creatures he had seen jostling in the air of the summerhouse when first he looked in. He had never seen beings stored after their deaths in a regimented fashion, and wondered over the purpose of the practice.

'What do you do with them?'

'Do?' Mirjam smiled, indulgently. 'You collect them.'

'What for? What do you do when you've collected them?'

'You store them,' she answered. 'You list them, label them, and you box them. See: each has a little piece of card under the thorax, on which the insect's history is written. And, of course, you must add crystals to preserve them from mites.'

She pointed to a miniature bag of cotton, pinned in a corner, and held up the box for Dolboy to smell. When he drew in the air it contained, he recognised a camphoric odour he had encountered before, rising from the corpse of a servant who lay two days in an open coffin, dressed in the costume of the region, while village people came in small groups to view the spectacle.

'But what for?' he asked again. 'Why would you want boxes of dead moths?'

'For the scientific record,' Mirjam explained. To that he had no response.

'And what about the rest?'

'The rest?'

'You said some moths were here. Where are the others?'

The two pinpricks reappeared in Mirjam's cheeks, and her eyes twinkled as she confessed:

'I'm not supposed to, but I let them free in the woods.'

'Where, exactly?' Dolboy wanted to run out directly and see the green giants again, swooping through bushes and branches in the full flush of their living colours, without pins through their chests, or their wings unnaturally fixed, as if they were dried flowers. He imagined the green cloud he had seen in the summerhouse, dancing in an expanded mass through the tops of birch and oak.

'I let them free on the verandah,' she told him. 'They went in every direction. Sometimes I see one at dusk. They come to our window lights and feed from honeysuckle. But I'm not supposed to. Father says they could take hold and become a pest, but I don't see how. Most of them die in a few weeks, and even if they lay eggs, they make such a tiny colony. The loss of a few leaves seems a small price for the pleasure of seeing a *luna* come to the window, or a cherry moth over the scented stock. My mother remarks on the "most unusual" bats. They don't make any connection with my lepidoptera.'

She laughed out loud at her parents' credulity, and as Dolboy watched, her linen cap became a cloche hat of a plum shade, and her white collar stretched and billowed in curlicues like the undulations of the sea behind the bottle-green landau in which they rode. He had not intended it, or noticed earlier that Mirjam was that silver-haired bride with whom he glided under arching beeches to his flower-decked mansion. But she was, and he knew his vision was a vision of the inevitable.

The house of irresistible desire

WHENEVER he arrived again at the castle of Weisse, Mirjam greeted him with an expression of surprise and amusement, as if he were the last person she had expected to be standing inside the oak door, though he went there every week. She received him in a conspiratorial way, fetched her outdoor shoes, and took him along the moatside path and over the rustic bridge to the clearing of pale-stemmed trees where their summerhouse lay. The serving woman with the infantile complexion smiled and shook her head as she watched them wander into the woods like Hansel and Gretel. Then she followed them with a basket in which she carried young cheese and herring, with greengages and cream to follow, and sometimes flat cakes stuffed with almond spice, to fill any space, as she said. They sat in the painted chairs at the pine table, helping down their feast with glasses of goat milk, flavoured with cranberries and cooled with ice, and Dolboy thought this was how he wished to live the remainder of his life. The old woman nodded in the chaise longue, waiting for them to finish, and her cheeks looked like two apricots.

One afternoon there was a curious addition to the contents of the summerhouse. As they entered, Dolboy saw on the table a model of the building in which they stood: a wooden summer-house, painted white and green, about a yard long and a foot high. It was a perfect doll's house, a replica with fretworked decoration on the verandah, and separate tiles of wood on the roof, but what made it curious were the windows, which seemed glazed with ruby-coloured celluloid. He admired it from several angles, and thinking it would be impolite to mention the red windows, he complimented Mirjam on her new toy.

'Don't you want to know what it's for?' she replied.

'I suppose you play with it,' he answered. 'With little people and model furniture.' His aunt Ineke still kept a doll's house she had owned as an infant.

'Try again,' Mirjam grinned. She clasped her hands together with her fingers intertwined, and her forefingers resting on the two points of her nose, as she waited for Dolboy's conclusion.

'It's a model. It's just to look at,' he offered.

'No,' she exclaimed, gleeful at his perplexity. 'Didn't you notice the windows? You wouldn't make a model summerhouse with red windows, would you?'

When she saw that Dolboy began to feel stupid, she stopped the game and explained the purpose of the little building.

'It's a mating chamber,' she told him. 'My father calls it the house of irresistible desire.' She laughed out loud. 'Look in the windows and tell me what you see.'

Dolboy bent and applied his eye to one of the ruby panels near the door at the centre of the model, and saw nothing on its inner side. He tried the window on the other side of the door, with the same result.

'Nothing,' he reported.

'Try the ones behind.'

He moved behind the toy house, where smaller windows replicated those of its archetype. When he peered in the first of these, at one end, he saw that the space inside glimmered with jostling mothwings. He looked at his amused companion with an expression of surprise.

'Now the other end,' she suggested, and when he looked into a second small window, his puzzlement increased, as he observed a further gathering of moths, but this time sitting still. It seemed that in the same room, some crowded to one end to struggle with frantic neighbours, while others sat quietly at the opposite end, and all shunned the larger space at its centre. How could that be?

Mirjam was delighted by his bewilderment. When she had enjoyed it sufficiently, she placed her fingertips under the eaves of the model and slightly raised one edge of the roof, which was hinged along its length. Dolboy peeped through the narrow opening and saw that, unlike the room in which they stood, the inner space of the miniature house was divided into three by partitions of plywood. Each partition created a small chamber at opposite ends of the building, and in each was cut a rectangular opening, covered with the same black tiffany that had made a cage for the cherry moths. In one small room rested the calm moths, and in the other those in an agitated state. The larger space in the middle of the structure was not empty, as he had supposed, but held just two creatures, joined end to end, which had lain beyond his view when first he peered in. He looked to Mirjam for an explanation.

'Sometimes you want two particular moths to mate,' she told

him. 'Perhaps they have a special depth of colour, or a variation of pattern you want to replicate. But they don't take an interest in each other. They prefer other mates, who will provide less desirable offspring. They are stubborn, and no matter how much you coax them, they keep to their decision. But if you place them together in the middle of the mating chamber, after you have installed male moths in one end space and females in the other, they no longer have a choice: they feel compelled to couple.'

'Why are they compelled?'

'The females at one end are sending out their messages, and the males are receiving them, through the gauze, and trying to find a way through. Somehow, the pair you chose, the two in the middle, become the agents of the frustrated insects around them.'

'They realise they are lucky,' Dolboy suggested.

'The messages are too strong for them to resist,' she said. 'Their stubbornness is overcome in the house of irresistible desire.'

'But why must the windows be red? Won't it work if they're clear?' he wondered.

'If I shine a torch in to see what they're doing, they are distracted and fly at the windows,' she told him. 'But they can't see red, so if I shine light through red windows, they aren't disturbed, and I can watch.'

Everything in the world of the dimpled lepidopterist was so ingenious and interlocking. Everything had its purpose, each mystery its solution. Perhaps the entire world was constructed so, and Dolboy only needed the guidance of a sympathetic interlocutor for everything to fall into his understanding. Perhaps the recollections of war and infancy which came to him in the night, of riding in a river, of plunging through walls of spruce, dreams of driving with his serene bride: perhaps in some hidden system all of these perceptions fitted logically together, and could be crystallised by the agency of an explainer who would kindly raise the hinged lid, and let him peep inside.

'We are having a party,' Mirjam announced. 'And we should like you to come.'

'In the castle?'

'No: here in the summerhouse, just for children. It's fancy dress: you must come as something from the animal kingdom.'

'Return of the wanderer,' said his aunt, as usual.

Captivity

THREE FINGERS of a delicate hand held a silver propelling pencil upright, by its top. The tips of the fingers slid down the shaft to the metal cone at its further end, raising it and allowing it to swivel until the top of the pencil rested on the surface of the desk. The three fingers then slid down the shaft until they once more held the clipped end, which they raised and allowed to swivel until the point of the pencil rested on the desk, as it had done in the beginning. Then they slid down the shaft to the metal cone at its end, raising it and allowing it to swivel until the top of the pencil rested on the surface of the desk. This perpetual motion was accompanied by a high-pitched tick as the pencil point contacted the desk, and by a lower-pitched tock as its blunt end did the same, in its turn.

Cornelius van Baerle, slumped in an uncomfortable wooden chair before the desk, watched the upending of the pencil until the officer behind the desk judged his attention sufficiently restored to be engaged.

'So, Herr van Baerle. What are we to do with you?' he enquired. It occurred to Cornelius that people speaking to each other in a language which is native to neither of them frequently understand each other better than people using a language which is native to one party. Or to both. 'Your situation is, to say the least, ambiguous.'

'You know my situation,' Cornelius replied. 'I am not a citizen of this country, or a combatant. My papers plainly state my profession, my nationality, and my reason for being here.'

'Although, as you have already told us, this was a falsehood,' the officer of the liberating army interrupted.

'Yes, it was a falsehood. The purpose of my visit was humanitarian. I was here to witness particular crimes of the regime, and that I have done, and was doing when I was captured by your forces. Now I trust you will restore me to liberty, or at least pass me to an authority with appropriate jurisdiction.'

The soldier smiled faintly, and allowed the silver pencil to perform its arc in slow motion.

'This is the authority with jurisdiction,' he murmured, patting the leather holster of a pistol on his waist. 'And it is appropriate.'

He allowed a silence to descend over their proceedings, and continued with the pencil.

'Contact the authority in my region,' Cornelius urged. 'By now it will have reverted to the control of your allies. They will vouch for my position. Speak to the command of the resistance there' – he mentioned the foreman's name – 'and they will confirm the nature of my mission here.'

The officer smiled again.

'My dear Herr van Baerle. That is not how warfare proceeds. Do you imagine I have at my disposal on the battlefield a telephone by which I may place a call to determine beyond doubt that I am attacking the right tank? Must I dial to establish that a village is culpable before I flatten it, or an individual is a paid-up party member before I blow his head off?'

'But this is not warfare. The war is over. You don't have to make those decisions any more.'

'The war is never over. We in our country have been at war for all of my lifetime, and just because this particular enterprise has run up against a brick wall doesn't mean I won't go back and find that same war continuing. If I keep my guard up, I may survive. But if somebody reports that I gave free conduct to a character dressed like a theatre impresario, whom we found skulking around a death camp, I may find myself on a train journey to a camp that makes these places look like ski resorts: if I am not executed, that is. No, Herr van Baerle, my instinct is to have you shot, here and now. Nobody would object.'

'I would object.'

'How many camp commandants and guards do you imagine are at this very moment shuffling meekly in files of refugees, with papers in their pockets to say they did nothing more than their patriotic duty? You think if they're pulled out of the line they won't say the same things as you? "Call this administration. Call that administration. They'll vouch I was nobody."'

'So why the discussion?' asked the prisoner. 'Why don't you shoot me? Why are we talking about it? You know I have a headache.'

'Your case has peculiarities,' the soldier answered, throwing his pencil aside suddenly. 'To begin, you have attempted no convincing subterfuge. You stroll about in your good boots and your long coat, as if you are proud of having avoided the privations which afflict people inside and outside of the wire here.

Clearly you are not the type to make a career as a guard in a place like this, and you are too weak, too reasonable, to be a military man or camp administrator. So, I ask myself, why are you found in such a place? Your story of having travelled here at this juncture, principally on foot, is, frankly, absurd. So, we are left with a simple bourgeois, curious about the ghastly sideshow which has just thrown open its gates, or perhaps somebody of importance, stranded inexplicably. Someone who salutes with one arm raised in the air . . .'

The monologue tailed off, as if the man with power of life and death had lost interest, and allowed his attention to be captured by a passing fly. Then he reached into a drawer, and threw onto the desk an oilcloth folder.

'This is what saves you from a bullet in the head, for the moment,' he announced. He opened the folder and scattered its contents on the desk. Cornelius let his eyes run over the banknotes and the drafts, and over a selection of gold coins which he rightly surmised to have been extracted from the stitched repositories in his clothing. The officer ignored the money, and his hand alighted on the stiff envelope, from which he withdrew the sheet of folded buff paper, bearing a crest.

'To whomever may read this, touching the liberty and right of passage of the bearer,' he read. Van Baerle lowered his eyes as he listened to the words which surely would seal his doom.

'His Excellency, et cetera, et cetera, You Know Who. Air Marshal of the Reich,' the interrogator concluded.

'I have no explanation that you would believe,' Cornelius began. But the soldier interrupted him.

'Save it. Anybody walking around with a *billet-doux* like that in his pocket is highly connected. A backer of the regime. A war criminal, even. If I shoot you, I could deprive my superiors of an important catch. That would not be a good idea. The question of letting you go does not, of course, arise. No. I have only one course: to pass you on to somebody of higher authority, so somebody else can make the decision, and I remain free of error. I may even get a gold star on my report,' he concluded brightly, with a nod of his head which two privates recognised as a signal to seize the prisoner, drag him from the room and throw him back into the guarded cellar from which he had been brought.

The cellar

AFTER SOME DAYS van Baerle realised that he was in the sort of place where it served no purpose to complain about the food. Where his head had been split, the coagulation of blood and hair had formed a protective boss, like that which forms on a pollarded tree, and he had ceased his attempts to mollycoddle the wound, and decided to leave matters to nature. Others who shared his cell appeared to be in worse states, but nobody complained. A beefy man who had served as a guard in the concentration camp was recovering from a beating at the hands of the inmates. Cornelius pictured the event as an attempt by stick insects to thrash a wild boar, but the man seemed genuinely hurt, and where they had been unable to achieve a satisfactory result by cutting his hair with scissors, his victims had torn it by handfuls, taking his scalp with it. In the half light of day which shone through the grating of their cellar, the ex-guard's head resembled an artillery shell, patterned with tufts of bristle, bloody scabs and areas where the skull itself was visible. Cornelius attempted to speak to the man, to learn something about his work, but the deposed warder turned his back whenever another prisoner approached him. After a week, when he appeared to be recovering something of his strength, he was taken outside and shot.

Cornelius was in the company of a dozen other men whose status was not clear enough to merit a bullet. After the scale and randomness of the carnage which had washed over the continent, year after year, it seemed odd that the barbaric liberators should take pains over the fate of such an insignificant ragbag as they had assembled there. Surely matters would be simplified if someone tossed a grenade into the cellar one night? Who would complain?

One of his companions – for that is how we think of anyone, however strange, who shares a fate – believed that now the fighting was largely past, the military needed some other thing over which to dispute and exercise authority, and they were that thing. Their presence allowed the officers to weigh the pros and cons of a problem, to assess each other's contributions, and make decisions where rank permitted. It allowed guards to guard, and non-commissioned officers to make reports on the quality of the guarding to officers who would note their reports and dismiss them. They, the cellar rats, provided a focus which allowed the soldiery to go through the motions of serving a purpose, in the absence of an adversary. Another of the prisoners, who seemed informed on most things, explained that the political cadres, which followed behind the fighting force, and were chiefly concerned with categorising and despatching whatever civilian detritus they could lay hands on, were also charged with maintaining the proper conduct of the troops, according to their ideology. And that ideology was so full of pitfalls that the army officers were paralysed by the presence of the politicals, for fear of making a false move. That was why they, the stranded and imprisoned ones, were neither condemned, nor exonerated.

At length, one of these ideological functionaries, dressed in a blue cap and blue uniform, with red stars on his lapels, took a look for himself at the contents of van Baerle's cellar. He interviewed each man separately, as the officer with the silver pencil had done, and in most cases, like the soldier, drew a blank. Three men suffered the fate of the mauled camp guard; the remainder were returned to continue their discussions in the cellar. But not for long. After a further three days they were woken at dawn and led up into the light, each of them noticing how beautiful was the form of a tree, and following with tender longing the flight of a single house sparrow, in what they took to be their last minutes.

But they were not executed on the spot. Instead, they were marshalled on board an ancient charabanc with whitewashed windows, each with an armed soldier at his side, and driven away from their erstwhile lodging. A diamond of bevelled mirror glass on the fascia near the door of the vehicle was echoed by a grille of woven golden fabric in the same shape, over the driver's seat, from which issued the music of a dance band, interrupted intermittently by the voice of a female radio announcer, listing song titles. The ambience was that of a pleasure trip.

Cornelius managed without any difficulty to rub with his shoulder a patch in the whitewash of his window, through which he soon saw that they had become enfolded in coniferous woodland. He had heard of mass graves in the forest, where the awkward and unwanted were led to be neckshot and bulldozed, and yet he felt no concern for his life. He looked at the faces of the armed men who lined the aisle of the bus, and found no sign of their intentions. They were vessels, who would do what had to be done, and still maintain that blank opacity of expression. And if they did, what then? The number of the dead millions would be amended by ten.

They disembarked at a small railway platform, where a train with closed and barred wagons waited. The officer in charge of their transport exchanged words and papers with the officer in charge of the train, and one of the goods trucks was opened to admit the new arrivals. As they dragged themselves in a line toward the track, the soldier who had accompanied him took van Baerle's hand in his, and wished him good luck.

'And to you too, my friend,' Cornelius answered.

A train journey

THROUGH GAPS in the plank wall of his wagon, Cornelius watched the glorious woods of spring roll by, as he read the names of small towns and large towns, crossing points and halts in the depth of the forest: Jedrzejów, Skarzysko-Kamienna, Radzyn Podlaski, Biala Podlaska, Kobryn, Ivacevicy, Baranavicy, Dzarzynsk . . . They were heading north-east, at a leisurely rate. Sometimes they stopped for hours on end, at no particular place, for no particular reason. People in the wagons shouted to be let out, to attend to their natural functions, but nobody paid them heed. The only time the heavy door slid open was when the guards arrived, once a day, to ladle water into a churn, from which it must be taken in cupped hands by the travellers. Many of them had been in transit for some time, Cornelius imagined, for they greeted the arrival of water like desperate animals, fighting to be first, trying to dip their heads to the surface. In addition to the ten from the cellar, his compartment held thirty or forty others, of both sexes. Although one corner had been designated for their soil, it was not possible in the confined space for people to circulate there, and the urgency of their diarrhoea rendered superfluous any system calling for order or delay. One night, a couple made love, standing among strangers, and the noise of their endeavours prompted others to follow their example.

After five days of travelling in this style, Cornelius and his companions were shooed out of their box onto the tracks of a marshalling yard at the edge of a city. He could see smoke hanging over rows of ruined houses and industrial areas, and the truncated towers of several churches, standing beside hills of rubble and stranded Gothic arches. Behind him, the air of the wagon shimmered with the flight of bluebottles over a dozen corpses. Travellers jumped or fell to the ground along the length of the train, and soon a large contingent was herded to a pen by soldiers of the liberating army. Here they were held until they were completely dispersed by six covered lorries, which required two days to complete the task. The ten from the cellar clung together like survivors of a shipwreck, refusing to be parted for separate transit, as if their existence would be diminished by division. They knew almost nothing about each other, except that they had survived together two experiences of terror, which was more than they knew about anyone else in the world to which they were now committed, and which for most of them would constitute the only world they henceforth inhabited. Thus they found themselves in barracks, lightly guarded but secure, among several thousand other uncertain souls.

The interminable interviews recommenced, as soldiers, the blue-uniformed People's Commissariat for State Security, apparatchiks of various persuasions and even local disposers of the labour market took their turns to run the cornered and unclassified humanity through their question mills. Rumours were rife among the shuffling prisoners about the fate of the men and women who failed to return from interviews, and the fate of those who remained.

After speaking with a few dozen of his companions over several weeks, Cornelius understood the sentiment of the officer who had first interviewed him, that the war was never over. He had thought the man was being rhetorical, but others who shared his captivity assured him that in the east there was a continuing terror, not always for reasons that were apparent, perpetrated on the citizenry by agents of the jovial father of the nation, and that nobody, foreigners included, was free from that shadow. Many of those who did not return from their interviews were passed on for more savage questioning, he was assured: questioning over topics which admitted no certain answers, and accordingly no escape. Ultimately, they would be put out of their misery, or despatched to one of the corrective labour camps which occupied twenty million of the population in life-destroying toil for the greater prosperity of the nation: a prosperity which thus far had failed to arrive.

'Number AUS 715,' called a guard with a clipboard, names having been dispensed with. Van Baerle's companions looked in his direction apprehensively, and gathered to shake his hand. His time had come. He bade the cellar rats goodbye.

Questioning

'S O,' THE COMMISSAR remarked. 'You play the piano.'

'Here?' Cornelius responded, foolishly.

'No, not here. Our piano does not arrive until next week.' The commissar smiled at his little joke. 'I mean before you came here. At home.'

'I play the piano?' Cornelius could not connect his home in Zutphen, that galactically distant haven, with the place where he now stood, before the seated official who at the onset of a bout of stomach acid might order the job lot of them machine-gunned, or consigned for life to an Arctic slave colony. The commissar grew impatient.

'Do you or do you not play the piano? Are you musical?'

'How could you know that?'

'I know it. Is it true?'

'Yes,' he answered. 'I play the piano. If there was a party I would supply the music.' For an instant he looked up from the keyboard where his fingers flew, and saw a room in his father's house, decorated with bunting, in which laughing faces loomed and receded as the dance progressed, and the floorboards shook with stamping, and he scarcely heard the sound of his instrument over the singing, while a dozen children screamed together as they sprinted in a catching game between the lumbering revellers.

'Well then,' asked the commissar, 'will you play for a party here, in the city?'

'What sort of thing?' Cornelius enquired. 'I have no music prepared. I am not familiar with popular or folk music here.'

The commissar interrupted him.

'Do you know "Moonlight Serenade"?'

'You mean the "Moonlight" Sonata? Beethoven?'

'No, no. "Moonlight Serenade." Glenn Miller. Can you play that sort of thing, for dancing?'

Cornelius read music well, but popular music he could play by ear. It was a talent to which he attached no special importance.

'Yes,' he answered. 'I can play American dance music. But I have no repertoire. I should need some preparation.'

The comrade waved one hand in the air to still the protestations, and it looked as if he were waving goodbye.

'We have the drummer, the trumpeter and the bass,' he said. 'They have some sheet music between them, and there are gramophone records. You have until Saturday to prepare. Where's the problem?'

'What day is it today?' Cornelius wondered.

The entertainments officer looked exasperated and told him the day.

'How could you know I played the piano?' Cornelius returned to his earlier puzzlement.

'You don't imagine everybody here, or on that train, was sworn to secrecy, do you?'

The interview was at an end. As he was led from the room he tried to remember the prisoners with whom he had shared stories about home life, life before the war, before the train, before the cellar, and there were too many.

'It's not important,' the commissar called as he left. 'It's not an offence to play the piano. But it could be.'

Music

THE BASS PLAYER of the group was able to play two notes, pum-pom, pum-pom, which he imagined to be the heartbeat of their performance, its bedrock. When the title of the piece changed, he consulted his sheet music once, and adjusted the speed of his throbbing. The other musicians had to race, to keep up, or they must play in slow motion, to remain in time with the decelerated pum-pom, pum-pom of the bassist. Attempts to negotiate variations in his theme were fruitless, as he simply shrugged and indicated that he shared none of the languages they commanded, although he was always the first to shelve his instrument when a cry from an adjoining room arose, sometimes in a Slavic tongue, sometimes in a Germanic, indicating that refreshments were available.

The trumpeter had a military background, and tended to lapse into the rhythm of a march. His flourishes brought to mind a call to action, and to any tune which bore a trace of mawkish sentiment he added an unmistakable echo of the last post. As for the drummer, he was a drummer. Like all drummers, he might start a session of music by acknowledging the presence of his fellow performers, but quite soon he would be elsewhere, following a lonely path, entranced by the ecstasy of his own invention.

'"Drummin' Man",' he announced, and tried to reproduce a flight of crazed cadences he had heard on a Gene Krupa record.

'We are not attempting "Drummin' Man",' van Baerle reminded him, 'because nobody will be able to dance to it. We have to play items suitable for dancing. The drummer looked serious, and nodded his head to indicate that he agreed entirely. Two hours later, having forgotten the interdiction, he made his announcement again, and once more demonstrated what Gene Krupa would have done in their circumstances.

The other musicians looked to Cornelius to provide the melodic thrust of their performance, and took every opportunity to play *sotto voce*, leaving him unexpectedly exposed, like a soloist in a concerto. When he drew attention to these desertions, they said it sounded better that way, and they were right. Even when attempting a piece he had never before encountered, Cornelius was able to make it sound more musical, more danceable, when the distractions of his fellow performers were at a minimum. And so, after three days of rehearsals on the podium of the restaurant where they were to appear on the Saturday, it was agreed that their hopes resided chiefly in him, and they would rein in whatever impulses beat in their breasts, to follow quietly where he led.

Between their bouts of preparation, the performers were kept in the custody of two guards, in a suite adjoining the restaurant. This was a momentous improvement over their barracks lifestyle, even though they had only two beds between the quartet. They were large beds, and they had sheets as well as blankets. Each evening they luxuriated on the beds and armchairs of their domain, awaiting the arrival of palatable food from the kitchens, blessing the parents who had compelled them to persist with their music lessons, or in the case of the bassist, considering if he should extend the range of possibilities available on the instrument with which he had only very recently become acquainted.

On the afternoon of the party, having decided that no further improvement could be achieved from the repetition of their programme, the musicians lounged in their suite for some hours, until a sergeant appeared abruptly, tossed a bundle of dark clothing into the air and called:

'Tog up!'

From the floor of the apartment they assembled four sets of evening dress, complete with starched shirt fronts and cuffs, which they shuffled and exchanged until they contained approximately their various bodies. The drummer and the bassist wore their cuffs on bare arms under their jackets, and their gleaming shirt fascias failed to conceal completely the ragged underwear which was the only covering to which they were accustomed, beneath their coats. They looked each other up and down, comparing the transformations of which a change of clothing was capable.

'What do you think?' asked the trumpeter, preening before the others. 'My usual table, Pierre, and step on it with the champagne.'

'More like:"Would you prefer the pine coffin or the mahogany, madam, and would that be cremation or burial?"' the drummer corrected.

Whatever effect formal dress might have had on the image they presented was to some extent undermined by the fact that three of the group wore shoes which revealed their toes, in varying numbers. But, Cornelius recalled, the podium of the restaurant had at its edge a raised wall of footlights, which would almost certainly conceal this deficiency. Overall, they resembled a coherent group, in need of hairdressing care.

For the purposes of the party, the tables of the restaurant were consolidated to leave an oval space between them and the podium, where the diners might dance. The guests consisted of a mixed party of apparatchiks and men in military uniforms, some with women who appeared to be whores, and others with more heavily-painted partners who were clearly their wives. Unlike the creatures with whom Cornelius had passed recent months, the revellers seemed more than adequately nourished, which did not prevent them from consuming a meal that extended from coarse-grained and pressed black caviar, via salmon, roast pig and game bird, to cheeses and a confection of sorbets and fruit, swilled down with a battery of wines, white, red and bubbling, preceded by vodka, and followed by cherry liqueur.

Although they had eaten some hours earlier a meal which in the barracks would have been judged a feast, the musicians experienced audible yearnings in their stomachs as they played an anodyne accompaniment to the conspicuous feasting. The leg of a bird or a slice of pork would not have been unwelcome. Instead, they were passed glasses of the varied alcohols.

At length, the commissar who had been responsible for their assembly stepped onto the platform, snapped his fingers and told them:

'Pick it up. Give us something for dancing.'

Van Baerle nodded his signal to the others, and they began their programme with 'American Patrol'. The event was going well, Cornelius judged, as he stilled the demands of his grumbling stomach with another glass of champagne. The liberating army knew how to live. They were fun, when they were not shaking up your brain with the butt of a rifle. The gaudy couples gyrated beyond the footlights which blazed up into his eyes, and his fingers danced up and down the keyboard of their own volition, conjuring rather more than they had rehearsed. For a while, the other musicians nodded their approval when they all turned to each other at the end of a composition. But after an hour or two, the expressions of the bassist and the trumpeter grew less wholehearted. At the conclusion of a foxtrot which Cornelius had embroidered with a fast-moving cadenza out of the ether, the trumpeter signalled him with both hands pushing the air downward, to contain his enthusiasm. Yes, he was drunk, but he always played better in that state. In that state his soul visited its requirements on the strings of the instrument with a minimum of assistance from the hammers.

He downed another glass from the row lined at the trumpeter's feet, and noted that the drummer was also glowing with the unaccustomed excitement and lubrication of the occasion. The trumpeter looked apprehensive, and the bassist plodded impassively onward with his pum-pom, pum-poms. Then, without warning, the drummer diverged from the programme, and instead of admonishing him as he had done habitually in rehearsal, Cornelius duelled with him in an assault on 'Drummin' Man'. The trumpeter and the bassist dropped out of the event, and the dancers slid to a halt and stood in astonished pairs. The piano and the drums ran through the jungle and leaped off cliffs, as their operators fixed each other with wild eyes and exchanged demonic grins. Then there was a momentary silence. The silence was followed by uproarious approval, as the intoxicated dancers recognised the savage joy which had visited the occasion, and they resumed their dancing with a new abandon.

Things were going perfectly. The musical week had attained its zenith. Everyone was content. At some hour after midnight, the commissar drew the edge of his hand across his throat, to indicate that the festivities were at an end. At this point, it was agreed, the band would appeal to the patriotic instincts of their captors with a rendition of the Internationale. As they began that rousing anthem, the assembled comrades stood and bellowed lustily, and the sheer exhilaration of the sound engendered somewhere deep in Cornelius's soul an emotion of elation akin to that which had made him shout and raise his fist in the air at that camp of the dead, with the uplifting motto over its gates. But this time he had an instrument through which to express his joy. He extemporised, to begin, then syncopated, and yes, the tune was improved. He changed the time signature completely, threw in quotations from totally unconnected pieces – 'The Blue Danube', the Marseillaise, 'I Got a Gal in Kalamazoo' – and still he had hardly begun. The possibilities were endless.

The other musicians, including the drummer, fell behind, then ceased completely. The upstanding comrades likewise fell silent. The trumpeter covered his eyes with his palm, and eventually, between the glaring bare bulbs of the footlights, Cornelius perceived the glaring eyes of the commissar. When he noticed the effect of his performance, he ended it. Where the podium met the dancing area, a circular space had developed, in which the commissar stood quite alone, as if the other revellers had no wish to be in his proximity. Cornelius rose unsteadily, and before

Fancy dress

ALONG THE CREST of the dyke moved a curious bird. Its feathered arms lay not on its back, as the wings of an earthbound bird are supposed to lie, but moved up and down, not in unison, as they might if it had been attempting flight, but in opposition. Its sturdy legs folded at their midpoints, and also moved up and down, unbirdlike. Its slender body inclined forward, and behind it the point of a dark tail wagged awkwardly from side to side, in time with the pounding legs. Its yellow beak it carried in one hand, behind which fluttered the ribbons that were to attach it to Dolboy's face.

The stork had become his emblem on the day of his father's memorial service. On that grey morning, as they stood in solemn ranks before the tablet on which 'Cornelius van Baerle' had been inscribed as an addendum to the names of the known dead commemorated a year earlier, Dolboy felt his sleeve pulled.

'Look, he's come,' his aunt whispered, and pointed up to the low clouds on which a stork traced effortless spirals.

Before that time, at the end of his bedtime prayer he had reached from the low table where he knelt a framed photograph of a clear-browed, handsome man with a thin moustache, and kissed it.

'Good night and God bless you, father, and soon come safely home,' he recited, every night, from before he could remember. The prayer was for his aunt's sake, for he had no recollection of his father's face. Ineke believed that the supplications of children were more pure, and therefore more answerable than others, and so made her request to Him through Dolboy's agency. Until one day, for no reason he knew, the dear, tearful woman asked him to amend his prayer, and ever after when he knelt, he kissed and murmured:

'Good night and God bless you, father, until we meet in heaven.'

After the visitation of that mournful bird on that day full of mourning, Dolboy was encouraged to attach special significance to the species, and on whatever occasion it appeared, whether he was wandering in the noisy throng of Zutphen's Thursday market, singing at a crowded party, or cruising in the black Opel saloon, his aunt would catch his eye, incline her head and smile wistfully. If they were alone, she would say:

'Look: he's come again. He's watching over you.'

When he told her of Mirjam's plan for a party of fancy-dress animals, his aunt offered no suggestions, but asked his preference. He looked at her with a surprised expression, and answered:

'A stork, of course.'

She smiled and nodded.

His costume was constructed of goose feathers, anchored in a framework of chicken wire, and attached with straps over his shoulders. His arms were separately feathered, with stiff fins extending from each like half-deployed wings. His legs were covered with yellow cotton stockings, and over his hair fitted a rubber bathing cap, punctured with a multitude of backward-facing plumes, to represent a crest. To the considerable nose of a Venetian carnival mask his aunt added a pointed cone of card, as a beak. The effect was suggestive of a stork, rather than definitive.

When his uncle backed up the saloon, to deliver him to the party, it was discovered that the costume was designed exclusively for standing, and precluded the negotiation either of a car door or of a seat. Dolboy looked from his uncle to his aunt, kissed them both and set off at his usual pace, while they stood and shook their amused heads until he disappeared from view.

And so he ran along the dyke, along the dirt road and the cobbled road, to the paved road that he always took to the castle of Weisse, encumbered, but not entirely disabled by his costume. Along the way he saw few people, although a carter bound for Ruurlo stopped to let him pass, so that he might have a second viewing, and a farmer held off from harnessing a horse to call his wife from her kitchen. She stood in the doorway with sleeves rolled to her elbows, and fluid dripping from her knuckles, as she screwed her eyes, then turned to tell him:

''t Rennertje.'

They bared their half-toothed gums to each other and watched him trot on, his elbows reciprocating like feathered machinery, his black tail oscillating unevenly.

A flock of crows took to the air abruptly, like specks dispersed by soap on dirty water, as he legged the avenue of giant beech. And he wondered: was it possible? Might it be possible? He broke his stride to execute balletic leaps, holding out both arms like the arms of his spirit father, the visiting bird which graced that sad ceremony, and soared from time to time above to watch him, and yes, it was possible. He flew. He leaped and he flew.

The earth spun distantly beneath him, and as he threw back his head to see the green canopy above, it seemed he was among the leaves, spinning, floating, until his foot touched the ground and he sprang again, like a stork, a running stork that paws the earth momentarily as its wings beat and it gathers momentum for flight. And so he sprang with floating strides, and eyes fixed in the treetops, until he came to rest, came to earth, at the gate to the bridge to the door of the castle.

The serving woman with the skin of a child greeted him with her habitual kindness, and led him into the dark hall. While he stood, a fox approached him, an upright fox, with a bushy tail he held curved over the crook of his arm, and whiskers painted on his thin, foxy cheeks. Then a badger came, with a dark stripe that began in the middle of his face and ran up his forehead, through his flour-dusted hair and down his back; and next a cow consisting of two people, one upright, one behind and bending, under a cover of cotton sheeting, figured with ellipsoid and amorphous shapes, in black. From the one who represented the cow's rear quarters was suspended a rubber glove, filled with liquid and tied to keep it in. As Dolboy's eyes adjusted to the shadowed light, he discerned an assembly of animals, some waiting quietly, as if they were unsure of themselves, others chatting brightly and confidently as they awaited the arrival of the hosts who would conduct them to the site of their festivities.

The first of them to appear was a boy, taller than Dolboy, and dressed from head to ankle in a suit of rust-coloured velour, with a set of small antlers mounted on his head, and his eyes outlined in black. His footwear had been adapted with sheaths of card, so that he appeared to be cloven-hoofed. His dark eyes sparkled, and he announced himself by throwing both arms in the air and executing a great, stag-inspired leap. Mirjam ran in behind him, laughing like a peal of bells, swooping among them with fluttering hands, to suggest the passage of the silvery moth which the paper-covered hoops on her back showed her to represent. She stopped when she came to Dolboy, and remarked:

'Dolboy. A stork. I hope you won't eat me.'

And turning to the stag boy, she said:

'Ivo, this is Dolboy, the boy who likes moths, the runner.'

'Ah-hah,' her brother exclaimed, 'the lepidopterist's assistant, masquerading as a stork. I imagine you have brought a baby.' And everybody laughed, while Mirjam explained the significance of his joke to Dolboy.

The third of the van Doesburgs was also inspired by insects. She was a fragile child of seven years, with hands like an insect's, and long, slender legs. She too wore wings on her back, but unlike Mirjam's modified triangles, hers were transparent and oblate. Projecting backward from her waist, a brightly coloured cylinder terminated in cardboard pincers, plainly suggesting her role as a dragonfly.

'This is Trixie,' Mirjam smiled. 'I made her compound eyes, but she preferred antennae.'

She brushed the two fronds of fern attached to her sister's headband, which matched those on her own and were strictly not part of a dragonfly's equipage. The small predator raised with great solemnity her tiny hand for Dolboy to shake, and when he did, it seemed she had abandoned it to his care, so inert did it lie in his grasp.

'A pleasure, I'm sure, to make your acquaintance,' she piped, and he could not help laughing at the formality of her greeting. Mirjam joined in, but placed an arm around her sister's shoulder at the same time.

'My little treasure, she is too perfect,' she declared.

Then the servant woman and two others appeared with baskets, and opened the door to carry food to the summerhouse. Over the footbridge and down the woodland path ahead of them drifted the children, talking like a parliament of animals. Along their route, bushes were decorated at random with posies and chains of daisies, and when they arrived, they found the summer-house garnished, inside and out, with swags of wild flowers. Trestles had been set on the verandah, where squares of linen, weighted along their edges, were strewn to protect loaves and cheeses, until the arrival of the perishable foods. Inside, the table and chairs had been moved to the edges of the room, to leave space for games. On the table stood a gramophone, whose handle Mirjam wound enthusiastically, while her brother searched in a box of black discs until he found 'The Laughing Policeman'. He lowered the thorn needle onto its face, and played the record to the end three times, to ensure that everyone present, including the serving women, was forced to laugh.

They ate cold meats and spiced sausages, pickles and herring, jellies and blancmanges, and they drank milk flavoured with wood berries, and a cloudy concoction of ginger, quince and lemon, with ice fragments forming a crust at its surface. Then they played blind man's buff, and musical chairs, and charades, and when they tired of games they ate again and danced in a double ring, the animals in the middle rotating one way, and those on the outside, the other. And at last they danced in pairs, the stag with the rabbit, the fox with the badger, and the stork with the silvery moth, he with one hand on her waist, she with one on his shoulder, and their other hands holding gently together. They circled the wooden room where moths had swooped, breathing each other's breath as they invented polite talk, while their eyes searched each other's face for recognition of the love they wished to see reflected there. Dolboy felt a strange, terrible pang, a fear that his adoration of his perfect partner would not be returned, and Mirjam too felt the tearing of that first adult emotion, that confusion of joy and terror combined. And wherever they circled, entranced, there circled at their heels a dragonfly with a grave, waxen face, waiting her turn.

When they threaded back by lantern light through the darkening woods, Dolboy still held Mirjam's hand, and wanted never to let it free. His aunt and uncle were waiting at the castle, and after he had shed the remnants of his costume, to fit in their vehicle, they drove through an alley of waving hands, which he searched through the glass for that one angelic face, straining until the animated bestiary was engulfed by darkness.

At the castle

THE WORLD of the van Doesburg children became Dolboy's world. After their first meeting he was Ivo's lieutenant and Beatrix's hero; and he was Mirjam's sweetheart. He went to all of their celebrations: to their *Sinterklaas* party and their birthdays. At their harvest supper he carried in the fruit, and when the visits of distant relatives occasioned festive meals, he was included. He wondered why Mirjam's parents encouraged his absorption so absolutely, even after the *graaf* observed:

'To the fatherless child of a hero's son, we must be mother and father both.'

He knew this conundrum applied to himself, and when he asked his aunt for its meaning, she said: 'They are thankful for your father's sacrifice.' The manner of Dolboy's arrival in the region was widely known, and allowed him some notoriety. Even Ivo, who was two years older, and wise about everything and everybody for ten miles around, would ask with envious longing in his voice:

'What was it like, travelling through the war?'

Dolboy could not always say what it was like, especially when the question arrived unheralded, as they were shooting arrows from a bow, or sailing tinfoil boats. When he was alone, and invoked a trance, he could conjure everything that lay in his head: the smells, the sounds and the sights of his infant life and westward journey. And when he woke sometimes in the night, they were there still, all around him, while his mother wailed through an open window at the frozen world. But these things would not submit to translation. He could not frame them as narrative. They were real, but they were his alone. He would answer:

'It was dangerous. There were explosions.'

'And shooting?' Ivo would prompt. 'Did you see people shot?'

'Yes,' Dolboy would answer. And it was true.

'Who? Who did you see shot?'

'Lots of people.' It was true.

'Yes, but who?'

'Once a general, and all of his officers.' It was not true.

'And their horses?'

'Yes, their horses under them.' Not true, again.

Ivo was also impressed by Dolboy's running. If they contested an event in a hundred-yard meadow by the castle, Ivo would burst ahead and win. But whenever they competed over the landscape, no matter which marker they agreed as the turn-home point, Dolboy was always first. It did not seem to him a matter of great interest. He could run at one speed, more or less, all day. People who achieved more speed seemed unable to sustain it, and therefore would inevitably be overtaken. That was the situation, and it appeared to him that no great virtue resided either in running rapidly over a short distance, or slower over a longer one. But Ivo differed, and introduced a succession of friends to challenge and be humiliated by Dolboy's churning legs and piston arms. Once he brought a boy who stood a head taller than Dolboy, outfitted in white shorts and a singlet. He wore athletic running shoes, and made Dolboy wait while he exercised and ran on the spot.

When they set off, the specialist put a good distance between himself and his amateur opponent, but when after five minutes he heard Dolboy's tread behind, he accelerated to maintain his lead. The effort tired him, and soon the relentless noise nagged at his concentration again. Again he responded by spurting ahead. After several repetitions of this shunting, Dolboy cruised beside his challenger. He looked up and smiled at him, and thought they might complete the course together, rather than contest it. But in spite of all he might have learned from the tactic earlier, the other runner speeded up again, and quite soon Dolboy was surprised to see him standing in a bent position, with the heel of each hand resting on each knee, while he wheezed like a dying horse.

'That's my boy,' cried Ivo, as Dolboy rounded the last bend of the canal towpath before the castle meadow, and Mirjam clenched both fists under her chin and bit her lip in excitement as he pounded the last lap home. The runner with the equipment still had an overheated face an hour after they retrieved him, and Dolboy saw him counting out money into Ivo's hand. Later, Ivo passed Dolboy several coins, and told him:

'This is your percentage, your reward.'

Ivo was Dolboy's model. He had dark, almond-shaped eyes, and fine hair that lay wherever he put it on his head, unlike Dolboy's, which billowed as if it were spiderweb, no matter how he patted it down with water. From the side, Ivo's face resembled that of a Greek statue, his nose and forehead completing a straight line, without either ridge or depression, and his top lip curled like an Assyrian bow. He had been away to school, and would go again to improve the French and the German which he adopted whenever he wished to speak beyond Dolboy's understanding. Mirjam pulled a face when he did that, and told her sweetheart:

'He can only say a dozen foreign things. When you know what they mean, you have come to the end of his secrets.'

'Tais-toi, méchante,' Ivo commanded.

The hero's avowed ambition was to be an agent, a spy, working covertly to protect those freedoms recently menaced, and to this end he must add Russian to his languages. Dolboy swore to do the same.

Sometimes Ivo fetched from his room two pairs of leather boxing gloves, and the boys faced each other in their trousers and vests, Ivo circling, while Dolboy tucked his face behind the defensive wall of his big gloves, and rotated on the spot. When Ivo let loose his flurry, Dolboy raised his gloves higher, so that although he could no longer see it, his head was entirely protected from the outside world. After five or ten minutes of this ineffectual flailing, executed while he danced on the balls of his feet, moving his weight constantly from one to the other, Ivo declared himself the winner. If he persisted further, the bout was ended by Mirjam, who caught hold of her brother's elbows from behind, and hung on them until he promised to stop. Although the sport was not fulfilling for Dolboy, it did him no harm, and Ivo frequently exercised to the point of exhaustion.

Wherever they walked or wherever they stood, Dolboy would feel a groping hand attach itself to his, and looking down, would meet the solemn eyes of the littlest of them, with a doll in her other arm, watching his face, studying him.

'You are her shining Adonis,' Mirjam told him. 'She speaks of nobody else.'

'Thank you, Trixie,' Dolboy smiled, and she answered:

'You are my husband.'

They all laughed and cuddled her, and she looked from one to the other, seriously, and wondered why they were amused.

Most of their days were spent in the meadows and artificial woods around the castle, and in the summerhouse which had secured him entry to their world. The summerhouse was their headquarters, and Dolboy was happiest when the rain drummed on its roof, and they were confined there the entire day. He seemed almost to walk in a dream when that long-remembered noise lulled his senses and calmed his thoughts, while he followed with loving eyes his angel in the linen cap. Sometimes they sat on the painted chairs around the pine table and played board games that took them into the realms of frogs and heron, hotels and promenades of the capital city, kings, knights and castles. Sometimes they played cards, with blackberries for money, and sometimes they studied volumes from the bookcase, reading aloud from time to time whatever they imagined to be of general interest.

'*Michiel*,' he enunciated. 'The biography of a mosquito. How, after a lifetime of endeavour, he was invested by the king as a Knight of the Order of Malaria.'

From her favourite work, Mirjam read in her soft, clear voice:

'One can admire to fullest extent the complicated organism, wondrous colouring and miraculous life processes in the evolution of a moth, but that is all. Their faces express nothing; their attitudes tell no story. There is the marvellous instinct through which the males locate the opposite sex of their species, but one cannot see instinct in the face of any creature; it must develop in acts.'

When they seemed to be at an end of everything, she would reach from the bookcase a box of her moths, and recapitulate each species' natural history and mythology, while her audience watched the serried corpses and imagined what their lives had been. As the year drew on, and the days shorter, an oil lamp was lit for them, and they saw themselves by its light, reflected in the black window glass like spirits in another world, while little Beatrix curled asleep.

The year's end came and went, and a second spring to follow, and the summer, and it seemed lovelier each passing season that Dolboy should spend the life between his lessons with ideal companions. He watched Mirjam work with her silken cocoons, with her thick, exotic caterpillars, patterned with stinging bristles and metallic blotches, and he shared with her the flight of moths from India, Borneo and the highlands of Peru. While the grave child at his side reproduced in her drawing book her various visions, Mirjam painted spangled moths on artist's paper, and in breach of her father's edict, Dolboy clambered with Ivo in the topmost leaves of oak to distribute far-from-home larvae in places they imagined safe from birds.

'The summerhouse, the summerhouse. What would life be without the summerhouse?' his aunt mused.

'You're right,' he answered, as if the thought were new. 'It is my most essential place.'

Then, that summer's end, Ivo took his leave, and they were three. Still they passed the weekend hours in their cedar world, sometimes on the verandah, looking out, and sometimes wandering in the birch. But Ivo's flight to French and German had disturbed their equilibrium. They had been a perfect group, one of each: a child, a girl, a boy and a higher being, and his going left them askew. Ivo always had a plan when inactivity threatened. And Mirjam always seemed more perfect, more welcome, when Dolboy had returned to her from some project shared with Ivo: from diving under the green mantle of the castle moat, or climbing like a fly along the mill sails. Now he looked up sometimes from a book and saw Ivo in the doorway, when it was his sweetheart, and a little disappointment dulled his pleasure in her company. A melancholy sense of loss accompanied the arrival of the harvest season.

Dolboy fretted for some distraction from the dissolution of their idyll, and in his impetuousness, begged that he too should be sent away to school. The excitement of bursting on an unknown world might fill the void of his days, just as the thrill of running into unknown woods had often done. And so it was agreed that he should have the experience of being educated in a foreign place. Like his father, and his grandfather, and his grandfather's grandfather, he would attend a boys' school on the offshore island.

Wandering with Mirjam one evening before he left, he saw the moon reflected on the surface of a pond, and above the water two wraiths, two green, swallow-tailed wraiths hovered and swooped over its reflected disc.

'My *luna* moths,' she murmured. 'They don't understand that what they want lies far away, and in another direction.'

Jazz

FAR TOO EARLY, on a day he felt he might die, when his head radiated pain in anticipation of the next pulse of blood, sixty times a minute, and the flesh of his entire body was in some horrible, infinitesimal motion, Cornelius van Baerle was encouraged from the bed he shared with a stinking exponent of drumming. The drummer slept on while Cornelius dressed, but the other musicians lay motionless and awake, wondering if their fate would be lumped with his. With their eyes, they bade him farewell for ever as two guards led him away.

He was returned to the barracks, and kept standing outside the door of the commissar's room for an hour, during which time he begged his Creator many times to be taken before a firing squad the next moment. But his self-inflicted torment would not be so readily extinguished. When the commissar's door eventually opened, he was prompted forward to stand before a desk where that powerful man sat drinking tea from a glass, while disputing with an aide who stooped at his side paragraphs on sheaves of papers, and attaching his signature to various orders. When the junior officer swept up the papers from the desk, squared them sharply on its surface and retreated from the room, the commissar still seemed preoccupied, and scribbled at something Cornelius could not see, whistling to himself a tune which consisted more of air than of sound. It seemed, almost, that he rendered the Internationale.

At length the commissar placed with great deliberation his pen on his blotter, so that it lay parallel with an edge, and centred on it. He held his palms flat together in front of his face, as if he were praying, with thumbs and forefingers touching his chin and nose while he regarded the pianist.

'Do you know who was present at our party last night?' he enquired, softly. Cornelius shook his head and winced at the error.

'The Party Secretary,' the commissar went on. 'That is the Secretary of the Party of this entire socialist republic.' Then he bellowed:

'Orderly!'

An orderly skidded into the room, and the commissar barked at him in Georgian, a language of which van Baerle had no knowledge.

'And do you know what the chief concern of the Party Secretary of this republic is?' the organiser of the dance enquired. Cornelius shook his head again, as the orderly returned with a tray bearing two glasses of dark tea. 'Jazz,' the commissar remarked. Cornelius was uncertain what this betokened, and remained silent. The explicator indicated with a wave of his hand the glasses of tea on his desk.

'Take a drink, man, before you die standing. You look like death warmed up.'

'It was the champagne,' Cornelius murmured. 'Champagne on

an empty stomach, and the excitement of playing.' He sipped the tea.

'Yes,' the commissar continued, 'he is mad about jazz. To such a degree that he has equipped his own band, complete with instruments and uniforms. The bloody works, in fact.'

Cornelius was still unsure where this narrative might lead. The commissar ended his uncertainty.

'Anyway, he asked me to deliver you to his custody. After seeing your performance last night, he has a job for you.'

'Another party?' Cornelius wondered.

'Possibly.' The commissar shrugged. 'Anyway, you're off my hands. And think yourself lucky for that.' Cornelius did not doubt the judgment. The commissar snatched up his pen afresh, committed a scrawl on a document, sealed it in an envelope, and bellowed again for attendance. Cornelius was led from the room to the same vehicle which had delivered him, and this time, accompanied by only one guard, was conveyed through the dereliction that had constituted a glorious mediaeval city no more than four years earlier. They proceeded through a region where rampant flower gardens flourished within a shattered grid of masonry, where once suburban walls defined their boundaries. Here and there a house stood spared, or lightly shrapnel-pocked, as if that biblical angel of death had discerned an agreed sign over its lintel and passed by. At one such they stopped, and van Baerle was handed in and signed for like a parcel.

The custody of the Party Secretary was immediately more congenial than that of the commissar. Cornelius walked unaccompanied over carpets to a quiet room, hung with tapestries and heavy curtains, into which the window light sank irretrievably, saving his eyes, and his head, from its assault. He sat in a voluminous armchair, closed his eyelids, and attempted a breathing exercise designed to combat nausea. More tea was proffered, this time in a Dresden cup, and he was joined by a fat gentleman in an Italian suit, whose purple jowls he half remembered from the previous night.

'So, you like jazz,' the comrade suggested.

Still unaware whether his situation was hazardous or safe, van Baerle nodded in a manner which he imagined to be beyond interpretation.

'What's your favourite piece?' the new arrival asked.

'My favourite piece?'

'Your favourite jazz number. Go on, try me.'

Cornelius searched the attic for a jazz title, any jazz title, and came up with:

'"Egyptian Momma." Jelly Roll Morton.'

'You know my baby is terrific, though she's a hieroglyphic,' the Party Secretary sang out immediately. He held up both palms toward his prisoner, fingers extended, and made them tremble as a nigger minstrel might, baring the whites around the pupils of both eyes to complement the effect. Van Baerle was almost certain that Jelly Roll Morton had never performed in that style, but his interrogator was delighted with himself. Still grinning broadly, he hurried from the room, and Cornelius noticed that he wore immaculate dove-grey spats over gleaming brogue shoes. Two minutes later he returned, holding in the air a black acetate disc, which he conveyed to an elaborately fretworked item of furniture in a corner of the room. He raised the lid of the piece, placed the record inside, cranked a winder vigorously, cocked his head and stood with one finger raised. Within a second, the air was torn by a savage, sandpaper cry:

> *You know my baby is terrific,*
> *Though she's a hieroglyphic . . .*

Cornelius winced from the assault, but consented to hear the piece out. He could hardly do otherwise. And before the needle had arrived at its endpoint, he found himself delighting, in spite of his pain, in the rambling advances and retreats of Jelly Roll's fingers across the piano keyboard.

'Give me another,' instructed the most important man in the republic, raising the arm of the gramophone from its operational state. Cornelius was ahead of him now, and without hesitation offered:

'"Creole Love Call." Duke Ellington.'

The Party Secretary virtually swooned. He clasped his hands together, closed his eyes and rolled his head gently from side to side, emitting a wordless, crooning lament, in imitation of the melody that sounded somewhere in his head. Then, as before, he disappeared briefly from the room, returned with a record, and sat once more with his eyes closed as the air grew rich with the sound of the actual thing. Cornelius lolled in his deep chair, and followed in the subfusc tapestries that contained him a narrative of warfare, surrender and enthronement, all on horseback. The soft room was beneficial to his condition, and the music heavenly. He noticed, as it drew to a close, a tear roll down the distracted comrade's cheek.

'Now let me ask you a question,' the jazz fan suggested, as he returned to the world. 'What do you know about the Jack Band?'

Cornelius ruminated, but knew from the beginning of the rumination that it would be unfruitful.

'Nothing,' he replied, eventually.

'Quite. And why should you?' his host reassured him. 'The Jack Band was founded by Eddie Rozner, a Jewish trumpeter, born Adolf Rozner in Lvov, who went to New York in thirty-three to play in the Bauermann Jazz Band. He was an admirer of Harry James, and grew a moustache to match Harry's.' This was a dossier the comrade had memorised. 'He made the mistake of returning home to Berlin five years later, and fled east for his life within six months. He got as far as Minsk. And that's where he is now: right here.'

Cornelius had no response to this news.

'I set him up,' the Party Secretary resumed. 'I got him instruments, sheet music, musicians, uniforms – not military uniforms, you understand, but something that made them look speedy. And they are all here, even as we speak.'

This time a response was called for, and Cornelius expressed his surprise and admiration, but was unable to suppress the question that followed those emotions:

'Why didn't they play at the party, if they are here? That would have been ideal. We who appeared were a random group.'

The politician enunciated his response slowly, deliberately, and with venom.

'Because. Some. People. Don't. Like. Jazz.' He hissed the words. He implied heathenism. 'They say they can't dance to it. Can't dance to jazz? Can't bloody dance to jazz? Well, if anybody can't dance to jazz, he can't dance to anything. He deserves to have his legs cut off, that's all.'

He calmed himself, and Cornelius reflected that some people, people who did not like jazz, would be well advised to overcome that aversion if they planned to pass much time within the jurisdiction of this administrator. He sensed the man was capable of a greater range of emotions, and ancillary actions, than he had displayed in response to Jelly Roll Morton and Duke Ellington.

'Anyway,' the plump man resumed brightly. 'I'm putting you in the band.'

'Me?'

'That's right. You're with Eddie Rozner now. They lack a decent pianist. You fit the bill nicely. I like the way you played last night: you had range, you had versatility, you had enthusiasm. That's what we need: enthusiasm. How can you rebuild a fucking country if you don't have enthusiasm? You and Eddie will get on like this.'

He locked the second finger of his right hand over the first, to illustrate the closeness of the bond that Cornelius and the admirer of Harry James would share, and waved in a perfunctory way as he paraded his wonderful shoes and expensive suit into another part of the miraculously preserved building.

Eddie Rozner

EDDIE ROZNER'S moustache, of which the Party Secretary had spoken, amounted to mirrored letter Ls, lying on their backs along his upper lip, with their feet ascending to his nostrils. It consisted of very little hair, and a great deal of black pencil.

'Another life saved by jazz,' he remarked, with irony. 'Let's hope it sticks.'

Cornelius had been driven once more through the ravaged city, and deposited this time in an area of boarded-up pawn shops and butchers with nothing for sale. Half-starved people, who had been treated to alternating bouts of savagery at the hands of defenders, invaders and liberators alike, hung around the streets as if they expected, in spite of all evidence, that something good would turn up. It was possible to read on patined posters adhering to the district's walls announcements of events scheduled to take place four years earlier.

The band was billeted in a ruined theatre, whose stage, dressing rooms, wings, safety curtain and orchestra pit remained intact, while of the auditorium there remained no trace. With the curtain lowered, and reinforced in part with tarpaulins, the performance area was moderately weatherproof, and the dressing rooms and service chambers, annexed as living quarters, habitable. Here the members of the Jack Band passed their days in rehearsal and their evenings in philosophical debate, complicated by the lack of a common language, while awaiting their next command performance.

'What do you mean, if it sticks?' Cornelius requested elucidation of the maestro's introductory remark.

'Don't take any notice of me,' Rozner advised. 'I'm not a paid-up believer.'

'Believer in what?'

'Tomorrow. Providence. Religion. Human kindness. Everything. I'm a cynic.'

'So what did you mean by it?' van Baerle persisted.

Eddie sighed and enacted that universal token of the realist, the shrug with the upturned palms, the what-do-I-know?

'What I mean is: enjoy what's been given, and play as if your life depended on it, because it does. You can play the sort of thing we do, I take it?'

'I don't know,' Cornelius answered. 'I've never heard you perform.'

The jazzman had been taking his morning coffee when van Baerle was delivered to the theatre, with instructions from his escort that he should be co-opted. The members of the band were elsewhere in the shell of the building, and not expected to rehearse until the afternoon. Eddie took down another cup, and poured a drink for his new pianist.

'Enjoy your coffee,' he wished. 'Then I'll introduce you to the piano. In the meantime, do you mind telling me how you came to join my band?'

Cornelius recalled what he could of the previous evening's antics, and asked if he might have his drink refreshed.

'What do you think of it?' asked the band leader. 'When did you last taste coffee that wasn't made from chicory? So, you made an impression on Daddy Sergei? That's a good start. The man would sell his grandmother for sausage meat if it meant he could spend an extra ten minutes in front of a jazz band. He's a fanatic.'

Cornelius described the quiz to which the Party Secretary had subjected himself at their meeting, and Rozner recognised it.

'He could have gone on,' he said. 'He has the biggest record collection in the country, and he knows everything in it. Did he cry?'

Van Baerle confirmed that his patron had been moved by the 'Creole Love Call'.

'It's genuine,' said Eddie. 'He will shed a tear of real emotion over ragtime music, while at the same moment signing an order for a thousand of his fellow countrymen, whose only offence was to be captured by superior forces, to be shipped to corrective labour colonies for ten years, just in case they were infected by contact with humans of a different political colour. And it's not just soldiers. Those other unfortunates: the poor sods in the pyjama camps. The same precaution applies. It's out of the frying pan and into the fire for them. All aboard! Next stop Siberia.'

He made the sound of a train whistle, and gave a bitter laugh at the thought of the jazz fan's contradictory nature. Then he reverted to the prospects of his newest member.

'Well, let's see what you can do,' he suggested, rising from the oilcloth-covered table where they sat. 'You're lucky in one respect:

they had a good piano in this place, a Bechstein. I have it tuned, and believe me, Rubinstein would be delighted to play Chopin on it.'

The two men negotiated a web of stairways, corridors and connecting rooms until they stood on the boards of the former Luxor Theatre, where Cornelius discovered that the piano which his imagination had outlined was unavailable. Instead, he was confronted by an instrument which had been coloured white, in household paint, some time before a wave of shrapnel swept the area, rendering the Bechstein, on superficial inspection, the close relative of a Dalmatian dog.

'Never mind the way it looks,' Rozner declared. 'Just hear the tone. Go ahead: help yourself.'

He was right. Cornelius tried a few chords, and liked the Bechstein from first acquaintance. He played 'Für Elise', the softest music he could remember, followed by a barely audible 'Moonlight' Sonata. When Eddie placed the score of 'Saint Louis Blues' on the music stand, he played that softly too.

'Is the headache no better?' the maestro enquired, 'or do you always play like a mouse?'

Cornelius begged to be excused, and Rozner consented, leading him up a staircase at the back of the stage to a room with a red plush settee, and little else in it.

'This is where the last pianist lived,' he told him. 'And don't ask what happened to him. You don't want to know. Just make sure your head is well enough to entertain noise by this time tomorrow. I'll expect you at rehearsal then. In the meantime, rest and be happy.'

The Jack Band

THE MOST IMPRESSIVE feature of the Jack Band, on first meeting, was its size. Van Baerle had expected to rehearse with a gathering not much larger than the scratch combo in which he had last featured. Instead, when he arrived on the boards of the Luxor Theatre the next day, he was preceded by twenty others, and ten more followed later. The Party Secretary had mentioned the Harry James band, certainly, but one could hardly have hoped that a superabundance of musicians would be available in a nation struggling, without evident success, to rise from its knees. Then again, Cornelius amended his reflection, manpower did not necessarily entail efficiency, any more than the commissar's assembling of a dance-band quartet had guaranteed that all four of its members were capable of playing more than two notes.

But he need not have worried. Eddie Rozner arrived, chatted with everyone who cared to engage him, handed out scores and told van Baerle to join in where he felt able. Then he stood before them with a trumpet dangling loosely from one hand, while with the other, the fingers of which were poised as if holding an invisible teaspoon, he made a tiny, swift sign of the cross, and sang out:

'A one, two, one-two, one-two.'

The tatterdemalion throng, which looked as if it had been dreaming in thirty different directions simultaneously, focused its attention with miraculous speed to engender a wave of synchronised noise. It seemed as if its members had studied ways to present the appearance of indolence and inattention, while practising secretly a unity and precision of purpose. Cornelius was so impressed that he felt able immediately to join the commotion, and after forty minutes had warmed up sufficiently to interject a solo. Without taking their instruments from their mouths, several wind players nodded in his direction as he allowed them back into the piece, and when they took a pause, Eddie laid a hand on his shoulder, and told him:

'Nice solo, Corny. I like your playing. I'm glad you can make noise when your head allows.'

They met every afternoon to rehearse on the permanently curtained stage. Sometimes they swayed like wind-blown wheat when the fabric billowed inward in a gust from the world beyond, and when the days grew short they played in hats and scarves and coats. It was quite soon clear that van Baerle fitted Eddie Rozner's scheme like a hand in a glove. The new member gave his attention completely to learning his role, and only occasionally, while riding the spotted piano on the swell of the Jack Band's trumpets and trombones, did he wonder at what point his status had changed from that of suspected backer of the destroyed Reich, protégé of the deposed Air Marshal, to that of guest musician. The answer was that it had not, and that somewhere in the office of the barracks commissar, or the Party Secretary, reposed a dossier in which a course of action hung suspended, like a guillotine, but only so long as he swung and syncopated in an approved manner.

The band played every Saturday and Sunday evening in the city, a vehicle calling at a side door every Friday for the Bechstein, and a tuner finding work each Saturday morning, restoring it to pitch.

'Sure, there are plenty more pianos in town,' said Rozner. 'But do you want to learn a new one every week? Trouble? What trouble? I don't hear anybody say he doesn't need the work.'

Their appearances alternated between two venues which had survived the recent barbarities: an assembly hall with potted palms some years dead, and the extensive dining area of the city's largest hotel. In each place they found the same faces, the apparatchiks and gentlemen in military uniforms, feeding themselves too lavishly for such famished times. Sometimes van Baerle fancied he saw the commissar, regarding him through tobacco smoke, checking if he fulfilled expectations, anticipating his recall. And at every performance he saw the Party Secretary, Daddy Sergei, wallowing in saxophone riffs, and standing to clap with both hands above his head when Rozner performed his party trick of playing two trumpets at the same time. The Jack Band was good by any reckoning; in the circumstances of the time they were remarkable, in their black trousers and gold-piped scarlet jackets, with their baker-boy caps to match.

On weekday evenings, Cornelius would lie on his red sofa, smoking cigars he had stolen from the hotel, or sharing a glass of vodka with his fellow artists, who drifted through the warren of candlelit chambers like the ghosts of long-dead thespians, detecting indications of tobacco, sniffing out alcohol, sensing food and the occasional woman. They exchanged their stories, compared their prospects. Most of them were Jacks by choice, having joined when the most important man in the republic first took up Eddie, before the war. They received wages, which were two years in arrears, and they were free to resign and take their talents elsewhere. It was a notional freedom, since in the vast geographical tract of the union of republics, not one other of the many orchestras and bands played jazz, and that was their enthusiasm.

Cornelius mused frequently over the boundaries of his own freedom. Might he, for example, write home a letter explaining his circumstances, reassuring his loved ones that he would return when certain questions had been settled? The others lounging in his room looked at him with amusement.

'You are making a joke, tovarich. Correct?' observed one.

'You don't think that would be permitted?' Cornelius asked the room.

'For you to write is permitted, certainly,' the man answered. 'For you to take a rope and hang yourself from the top of the stairs is permitted too. It amounts to the same thing, but the second course puts you to less trouble.'

Van Baerle wished to know why his suggestion was outrageous.

'Do you imagine we have a postal system here which kindly sorts the mail to pigeonholes and sends it round the globe? No, my dear Van, our postmen work in reverse. A letter addressed to a foreign destination is traced to its source, and its source is asked to explain what imperfection it finds in our world, that it must communicate with that other one, that corrupt world beyond our perimeter.'

'But I am of that world. I am a foreigner,' Cornelius protested. 'I would not be reaching outside, but reconnecting. Surely that is permitted? Who is harmed by it?'

A Slavic trombonist joined in.

'Don't even talk about it, Van. We all know each other here. But if you lose your job tomorrow, you will search your memory for every word we have spoken, to discover who seemed most the Judas. Don't talk about it, then when it happens you won't have our names on your mind.'

'Is it such a bad idea?' van Baerle persisted.

'You don't want to find out,' advised the first. 'Believe me. You have a job here. It's very little, but you enjoy it, and you eat. Only when you don't eat, and you don't enjoy splitting frozen timber in the forest, or digging coal on your bare knees, only then will you remember this job, and say a prayer to wake up in your past life.'

They fell silent to consider their careers for some minutes. Then the trombonist told him, quietly:

'Lucky it's just us you're speaking to.'

Cornelius paid attention, and waited for him to continue.

'Whatever you do, don't get into conversations of that kind with our colleague Ulrich.'

'Ulrich?'

'The second soprano sax: big fellow with a face like a raw turnip.'

'I know him, of course,' Cornelius answered. 'What's wrong with Ulrich?'

'What's wrong with Ulrich, my friend, is his job,' the Slav went on.

'His job as second saxophone with the greatest jazz band in the history of Minsk?'

Van Baerle's reply evoked no amusement in the stony faces which formed a ring around the red settee.

'No, Van. His job as agent of the fucking *Narodny Komissariat Vnutrennikh Del*, the People's Commissariat for Internal Affairs. Don't trouble to ask Ulrich when the Post Office makes its next pick-up for your home town, or you'll be delivering it yourself, on foot, via Siberia and the Arctic gold mines.'

Van Baerle saw this was no joke. Another of the group joined in.

'Look at the streets outside, Corny, and you'll agree we're a lucky crowd. We have very few responsibilities. Okay, we don't live in great style, but we enjoy life. Some of us, people like you, have in the back of their heads the thought that another life goes on in a place they have left, and it is only a matter of time, of sorting out the paperwork, before they get back to that place. Then everything goes on again as normal. As before. But others of us, people like me, know that ideal place no longer exists. Mother is no longer baking cakes for our return. We don't have that other possibility in the back of our heads. This is our life. This. Maybe we're lucky to see that reality, whereas you seek to console yourself with the delusion that this interlude is a reversible mistake. Life may be a series of interludes, but none of them is reversible, for sure. Life never goes on as before. Accept that this – this creeping around a ruined mausoleum, this dressing up like chocolate soldiers to play for pigs, these weekends of making Eddie Rozner's dreams come true, these afternoons of making happy music – accept that this is your life, my friend, and enjoy it while you may.'

And so Cornelius did.

School

IN THE SECOND summer of Dolboy's schooling, a teacher informed him, on the occasion of a famous victory, that he was a failure.

'You will never fit into society,' he fumed, 'because you think first of your own wishes. Society accords such people a lifetime of displeasure. You have failed before you have even started with life.'

The cause of the teacher's anger was the school's team race, an event in which forty boys, representing four teams, competed over half a mile. While the boys milled and elbowed two laps of a course around a meadow by the school, an enclosure of ribbon was set up, a pen which only ten boys could enter before it was closed. The team with most penned members won a silver chalice, to show in its case in the assembly hall, on which its name would be inscribed, to join a repetition of inscriptions. Dolboy examined the revered chalice and read:

'Venus. Venus. Jupiter. Saturn. Saturn. Mars. Saturn. Mars. Venus. Jupiter. Saturn. Mars. Jupiter. Venus. Mars . . .'

He was two years younger than the oldest runners, and not expected to be there when heads were counted in the ribboned box. Boys of his age and size ran the second lap with one eye on the pen, and when they saw it closed, whether they were near or far away, peeled off from the track to dissolve in the crowd. They disowned the further proceedings, and were in turn disowned. The teacher of his team explained their function at the line.

'You little boys, stay back from our runners. Keep their paths clear. But if you find you block a runner from another team, there's no harm in that. I don't say positively that is your aim' – he winked, while all the boys laughed at his innuendo – 'but if it happens, there's no harm done. Start slow, to let the runners clear, and stay together as a team, so everybody sees our colour as one block, united. Good luck, Saturnians! Next year you may be runners in your turn.'

It was a contest of conflicting goals. Two or three Saturnians were accounted runners, while all the others served to make a show of unity. But if it was their hope to send as many Saturn boys as possible into the pen, the man's advice must be misguided, Dolboy thought. If everybody tried to win, their number in the end enclosure would be more than if they lagged in solidarity with their slowest boys. Which was more import-ant: aiming for the prize or seeming a united group? His inno-cent analysis went no further. Their captain, standing tense with one toe on the line, turned with a last command before the gun:

'Nobody to run off the track, no matter how far back he is. Start slow. Save your strength to finish all together.'

But Dolboy had a different scheme: start fast to clear the ruck, then hold a steady pace. And so he did. He could not outrun the seniors in a sprint, but as they focused on a longer haul, and took a slower stride, he ran a wide route round the throng and spurted clear.

'Hold back, van Baerle, hold back!' He heard the teacher shout. And having made his effort at the start, he had no choice but to obey. He could not maintain a sprint indefinitely, and felt his heartbeat speed to overcome the deficit his effort had created in his reservoir of energy. He breathed unusually hard, and felt his legs grow heavy. Soon the tread of big boys sounded close behind, and one by one they passed, his captain having breath to call:

'Bloody fool, van Baerle.'

Possibly he was. But he was clear of the milling makeweights, and he had space. Soon his heartbeat steadied to that accustomed pulse which carried him so often through the woods and fields of home, looking for his summerhouse, or racing for Ivo's entertainment. His breathing settled, and his legs grew lighter. His effort was behind him. Although he trailed a string of bigger boys, and could not hope to sprint again, he could at least maintain his pace to finish well.

One lap completed, and strategies revised to overhaul a sprinting rogue, the leaders slowed until their work was drudgery, and the four hundred yards remaining looked like a mile. But Dolboy had achieved his equilibrium, and skipped brightly forward, *'t rennertje*, down the dyke path, along the cobbled road and on to the paved road in his mind. He overhauled the rasping leaders, one by one, the boys who ran this distance once a year. He ran and forgot them, on his way to the iron gates, and down the avenue of giant beech to more gates, his tread unfaltering, his speed constant, while arms around him flailed, and heavy legs grew heavier. Dolboy didn't see them on his way, where people craned and shouted, he didn't see the ones he passed, and looked around surprised when he arrived, and the iron gate was a ribboned pen, where boys leaned in to slap his back, and the team teacher delivered judgment on the course his life would take.

'I'm sorry, sir,' Dolboy answered. 'I just kept running, and nobody would stay in front.'

The teacher looked at him with disgust.

'Idiot!' he snorted.

The team captain, fourth man home, joined in.

'This is the team race, van Baerle. Where's your bloody team? And why aren't you with it?'

Dolboy, unable to comprehend the disapproval he attracted, answered:

'They lost.'

The teacher and the captain focused speechless hatred jointly on his head, and Dolboy melted into the crowd, to join the other makeweights.

A week after he had won the race he was not meant to win, Dolboy was called to another teacher's room.

'Van Baerle,' the teacher said, 'it seems a shame to me your effort in the team race should go unrewarded. Perhaps you did not understand the purpose of the race, the strategy employed, according to tradition. But that should not overshadow your achievement.'

He was right. Dolboy did not understand a race in which competitors were designated in advance to lose. The fact that they lost together, as a team, did not disguise the futility of their enterprise.

'Sir, why don't they just let senior runners in the race?' he asked. 'They are the ones who decide the outcome.'

'But then it would not be a team race, Dolboy, with representatives from each year.'

Dolboy had a further suggestion.

'They could let senior boys start at the line, the next year could begin fifty yards forward, and the youngest further still in front. That way, everyone would have a chance to win.'

'A handicap?' the teacher mused, then changed his course. 'The team race, Dolboy, is as much for us, your teachers, to see what you're made of, as to secure a result. Perhaps the strategy was not explained enough beforehand.'

'Oh yes, it was explained, sir. I just didn't understand it.'

'Dolboy, don't trouble any more over the race: it's complicated. Beside the chalice, there is no prize for winning, but I have something here for you, to mark your effort. To remind you of your run.'

The teacher produced a slender package in brown paper, which Dolboy unwrapped to find a model glider kit.

'Thank you very much, sir, but you needn't have.'

He recognised the gift as something from the man, something original, outside the structures of the school.

'The fact is, Dolboy, I think you have a particular talent for running. A boy from your flight, two years down, has never reached the pen before, let alone reached it first. Yes, you can run, Dolboy, and more than that, you have a feel for strategy: sprinting to the front gave you your chance. Don't you agree?'

'I did it to get clear, sir.'

'Precisely. It placed you in the open. After that, you just had to keep to steady-ahead. But what a steady-ahead! You never varied: that's what wore the others down. You don't flag, Dolboy. You are relentless.'

He was mistaken. Dolboy was not relentless. He was simply comfortable, while others weren't, when moving at a certain speed. Unlike others, when he walked it was with effort and restraint, as if his body must learn new mechanics and deliberation, when all the time it seethed to launch him at his natural pace. Nothing would exhaust him more than to pass a whole day walking. At every corner of every corridor of the school, in red on white, a notice hung, to remind him of this imposition: WALK. DON'T RUN.

'Sir, I just like running,' Dolboy answered.

'Yes, of course,' the teacher smiled. 'That's essential. But you need more than that, Dolboy, to be a famous runner.'

'Famous?'

'You need discipline, strategy, strength: you need training. Turning up on the day and winning all hands down at a place like this is no problem for you. But what would you find if you went outside, to compete in a championship event? What would you find then? You would find boys who had prepared. Relentless boys, like you, who wouldn't gasp when you ran past, but would force themselves on. To run with those gentlemen, van Baerle, you must train yourself to be what I believe you are intended to be: an athlete.'

Dolboy was unsurprised by the teacher's declaration. His talent was something which he had categorised as signifying no great virtue, and yet he knew it situated him beyond the ordinary. It was something with a purpose, whose function was to place him in a plan, as yet unclearly seen. He was glad the teacher thought him something special, not because he valued praise or favour, but because he welcomed someone as a co-conspirator, someone who felt, as he did, that he had a role, a hidden goal, for which a special preparation was required.

'The first thing we must do is find your distance,' said the teacher on the following Saturday, when Dolboy had consented to be trained. 'Set off when I say, and see how far you go before you flag. Ready? Go!'

Dolboy started at his single pace, and kept it steady round the field. When willow and alder whispered past, he saw instead the big boys from the previous week, hauling their weight toward the pen, spurting past despite their plan, to overcome the upset he had made. On his second lap he saw them once again, groaning, it seemed, leaden and ashamed as he skipped by. He ran a third lap and a fourth And then the teacher made him stop.

'That's far enough at that rate,' he warned. 'Are you more or less run out? How do you keep the same speed? Have you trained to run before?'

Dolboy said that where he lived, in country as flat as a bread slice, it was normal to run. To walk wasted time.

'But how far do you run? How far before before you must stop?' asked the athletics enthusiast. Dolboy shrugged.

'I don't know, sir. I never had to.'

'Does everybody run there?'

'Oh yes, sir. Running is quite normal.' And truly, he had never noticed that people in the *Graafschap* walked, unless incited by Ivo.

'Judging by your pace and stamina, I'd say you'll make a distance runner one day,' said the coach. 'But now you'd better train for something less. There's no event for you to run beyond two laps at your age, although when winter comes there's cross-country, for boys a little older. That's a longer course. Yes, let's set our sights on that. Think of the team race four times over. Could you face that?'

Dolboy thought of the space between his uncle's second mill and the castle of Weisse, and he smiled. Then he set off, still at his one, steady pace, and ran the laps, while his co-conspirator, his helper who knew the structure and the scheme of things, stood counting on his stopwatch his amazements.

Jealousy

HIS INTERESTS redefined by daily talk with older boys, his body changed to some half-way, overflowing thing, energetic with desire, Dolboy sailed his glider on the morning air while in his mind he turned time backward. She lounged beside him in the summerhouse, leafing pages in a book. They all were in it: moon moths, cherries, emperors and hawks. His hand reached out to touch their coloured wings, and found instead the downy arm, the silver-covered, downy limb she let him hold, she let him touch, she let him. Whatever held his interest held it briefly, until it shattered to admit those dreams of redirected history, meetings with his love that tilted arrow-straight to one conclusion: she let him. His hands crept everywhere that she allowed and told him nothing, because they had no record of such things. They told him only words, and smells and colours: things that hands don't know. And then he saw her simple smile, and was ashamed to borrow it for pleasure.

Arriving home on holiday, Dolboy pre-empted his aunt's greeting at the door.

'Return of the wanderer,' he announced, standing among baggage.

'But where is he?' she wondered, with eyebrows lifted. 'I don't see my doll boy any more. Where has he gone? And who is this smart fellow?'

They held each other, and Ineke patted Dolboy's back. They went together to a pretty room containing tall cupboards inlaid with marquetry, and a window screen of tapestry, and on the chequered floor a table of yellow tulipwood. They smiled like intriguers, enacting the customary ritual of his homecoming. She left him there two minutes, then re-entered with the bowl and spoon, and placed them on the table, as in the beginning. Dolboy closed his eyes to let his senses run while tasting nesselrode. When he had finished, his aunt propped against the empty bowl an envelope, outlined in silver, and addressed to him.

'You're hardly back and people want to borrow you,' she laughed. 'That came this morning, brought by hand. I knew the woman, Minneke; she told me what it was.'

Dolboy was invited to a party marking Ivo's attainment of a certain age: not yet his seniority, but something reckoned worth a printed card, with pie-crust edges. Ineke shook her head and smiled.

'Every year is a milestone at that age,' she told him. 'Let him enjoy his glory while he may. The milestones will be millstones soon enough.'

This time there was no fancy dress, no gathering at the summerhouse for party foods. His uncle drove him there, his skin glowing from the brisk towel, his hair brushed flat, his suit immaculate, his shirt and shoes agleam.

'What's up, Dolboy?' Ivo greeted him. 'Don't you run any more?'

Dolboy laughed and shook hands with the godlike creature,

whose ideal features had resolved in almost manly forms, where last they had been soft and mythical.

'Oh yes,' said Dolboy. 'I still run. Do you have any opponents inside?'

They crossed the humped moat bridge and climbed the steps to the oak door, with arms around each other's shoulders. Down the hallway they tripped, and into the birthday chamber, a spacious hall, with all the trappings of antiquity, and garlands and balloons beside. Dolboy saw nothing of this. His eyes pictured one thing only, and until that thing appeared they dreamed it. Mirjam, Mirjam, Mirjam, sounded the blood in his ears, until she stood there, and it stopped.

'Dolboy!' she exclaimed. 'Let me look at you.'

She held both arms outstretched, to take his hands, as if they were partners in a country dance, leaning back to examine his appearance.

'You're so shining and fresh,' she laughed. 'You look as if you were made today.'

Dolboy did not know if this were a good thing or a bad. Was he too polished? Was his hair too disciplined? He gave up thoughts about himself and swam in her silver radiance: her hair, her face, her arms, her legs grown long, her body rounding where it never did before. He felt the tingling in his ears that made them red when first they met, and then the same sensation in his face, while in his stomach grew a fearful void. Yes, this was love, the same love he felt two years before, dancing storklike, with a pale moth in his arms.

'What? What are you looking at?' she asked him as her cheeks flexed to conjure again the sharp-bottomed pits which signalled her amusement.

'Your dimples,' he answered. 'They haven't gone away.'

'Of course not. Did you think they would?'

Yes, he did. Neither did he expect to see again the pixie points in which her nose concluded. He had never seen such features in an adult, and felt, without invoking reason, that they were properties of childhood, and would surely fade with passing years. He told her:

'No. I just forgot them.'

This was a lie, for he remembered everything. He brushed his hand the wrong way through his hair, to lose his pristine look.

'Now you seem more like yourself,' she said. 'You have the colour of a runner, and a windswept look. Now I see it's you.' She squeezed his hands, and Dolboy felt completely happy for a second. Then another boy appeared, handsome in his scaled-down dinner suit, and Mirjam linked her arm through his, and looked up at him as if admiring everything he thought or did.

'This is Udo,' she explained, 'Ivo's best school friend. He's come to stay with us the summer, while his father rearranges Borneo.'

Udo was a perfect match for Mirjam; they made a pair. His sombre suit and formal air offset her lightness and her sparkle, providing it a frame and backdrop. Each of them evinced a replica of adulthood: an embryonic diplomat with hair that stayed in place, and by his side his dazzling wife, her waist pinched in, her chest divided down the middle.

'Couldn't he do it before the holiday?' Dolboy enquired, surprised that any task should occupy a parent while his child was free. They laughed, and Dolboy's redness was revived.

'The fact is,' Udo graciously explained, 'I do believe he could have. But then he would have had to find some other cause to stay away. He can't stand kids. He says they should be put away until they're twenty.'

They all laughed again, and Mirjam was so delighted that she clung to Udo's sleeve and nestled on his bicep. Udo looked down and accepted her adoration of his wit. That pang, that void of love that Dolboy had experienced in his stomach, and believed could not be made more piquant, was surpassed. There rose in him the worst of fear and loathing in one shape. Though it was new, his senses were familiar with its ancient ache, as jealousy uncoiled from sleep, the creeping pang of hatred and foreboding in one skin. He gazed on Udo's ideal form, and held himself from murder.

'Trixie has been asking for you all day long,' said Ivo, leading forth a sister wrapped in gauze and tinsel who had become more grave and miniature than ever. She resembled now a stem of white asparagus, on which a midget's face was fixed, and when she handed him her hand, as at their first meeting, it seemed she had no further use for it. It was a gift in perpetuity.

'It's a pleasure to see you again, Dolboy,' the little creature crooned, with undisguised emotion, and Dolboy saw that her devotion was undiminished.

The party was a wall of noise and motion in which he could discern no sense. Dancing followed food, and still the wall stood everywhere he looked in front of him. His senses spun when Udo and his love slid past, while Trixie clung and silently adored. They danced, and everywhere they danced the wall gave way to show the shining pair, Udo and Mirjam, gliding like angels of love through echoing halls and corridors of laughter.

'I believe he could have,' smiled Udo. 'I believe he could have.

Can't stand kids. While father rearranges Borneo. Can't stand kids. Look as if you were made today. Should be put away . . .'

Jealousy possessed him. He did not know or understand it. It was a new and terrible sensation that consumed him. His face and ears were uniformly red. Everyone was looking at him. Everyone was laughing. How could he have hoped that he, that he and Mirjam, that she . . . ? It was absurd, just too absurd. The silver pair slid past again, and breaking from his minuscule admirer, Dolboy thrust himself, chest to Udo's chest, and shouted:

'Yes, but can you run? Can you? Let's see you run.'

Udo was perplexed by this enquiry. He faltered, then supposed he should compose an answer.

'Run? Well, let me see. Run now?'

Mirjam saw that Dolboy was enraged, and laid a hand on his shoulder. The hand she laid on his shoulder when they danced, when they loved, as she now loved Udo. He was the centre of attention. Everyone had stopped to see the scene. What should he do next? What? His anger and torment had only one recourse. He turned and ran.

He plunged through the hallway, tore at the door, flung it wide, and threw himself down the steps and over the bridge. He ran not as he had run before, but in a self-destructive spasm. Something in his stomach, in his chest and in his head gave rise to energy that knew no other exit than a flailing epileptic motion. Destruction was no corollary of his effort, but its aim. He ran a raging pace between the moonlit beeches waving overhead like shadowed hands, urging him toward the line. He ran until his legs became some strange and trembling things, some things unwilling, that they never were before. His chest seemed

A great honour

WITHOUT A SHADOW of doubt, the most significant engagement ever to feature on the Jack Band's calendar was a summons to appear in the capital of the entire Union, at a glorious and famous theatre normally reserved for extravaganzas of the state ballet company. The republic's Party Secretary, familiarly referred to by his protégés as Daddy Sergei, delivered the command himself, one day when Eddie Rozner and a smallish crew were toying with a tune by Fats Waller.

'Make mine an ice cream, mister, and bring one for my sister,' he boomed correctly and destroyed the atmosphere. 'Not strictly jazz, my friends. Not strictly jazz. But hoi, who's counting?'

He strode onto the stage of the former Luxor Theatre, immaculate in navy silk, with shoes of crocodile, and when the jammers turned and paused, he ordered:

'Carry on. Don't stop. Let's hear it through.'

They played a little further, but they struggled. The interlude was not intended for consumption. At length, the visitor addressed the leader of the band.

'My dear Eddie, a great honour comes your way. This could

be the start of something big for jazz, a breakthrough for our music. If the imprimatur of the Party is bestowed upon the form, then yours could be the father of a hundred bands, the leader of the people's jazz.'

Eddie Rozner wasn't sure he wanted a great honour. The thumb and forefinger of his right hand wandered to and fro along the crooked sticks of his moustache.

'What honour?' he asked. 'The people's jazz now? I thought they weren't supposed to like it.'

'You can't suppress the emotion of joy, Eddie. That's what people feel when they hear our music. And it's what they need right now. Holy mother-of-God, it's music from the people to begin. How can they not be right to like it?'

The message bearer was mistaken on more than half the scores he cited, in a nation where the suppression of joy, when it had not been the direct goal of policy, had been its incidental by-product for centuries. What the people chiefly craved at that moment was food, and a reassurance that they would not be dragged off in the night. But politicians are often so buoyed up by words, they lose track of their relation to reality. Rozner recalled him from his flight of idealism.

'What honour? Father of a hundred bands? How's that?'

The most important man in the republic took a letter from his pocket and read aloud:

'In response to your letters dated January the et cetera and November the et cetera of the previous year et cetera, I am instructed by the office of the Chairman of the People's Commissariat for Culture' – he paused and looked at everybody present, individually – 'to order a performance of the orchestra

140

of which you wrote, to take place on such a date, et cetera, and in the following place.' Again, upon naming the elevated venue chosen for this exercise, he examined every available face for signs of gratitude, and found none.

'You wrote letters about us?' Rozner winced.

'And the outcome was good. This is an honour.'

'Don't we do enough in Minsk, that we have to drag ourselves to Moscow?'

'Relax, Eddie. Relax. It's a good thing. Who hears you here? The same old crowd. They'd show up if we had a gypsy band attempting Wagner. They don't appreciate your style, your swing. Now, if you're heard up there, who knows what lies in store?'

Eddie Rozner did not share the enthusiasm of the Party Secretary of Byelorussia for this unexpected engagement. He liked routine. He enjoyed spending five days a week tucked up with a small army of musicians. Twice a week he showed his face, and that was enough. He didn't wish for any more attention. He was suspicious of receiving anything for which he hadn't asked, especially when it was an honour, some thing you didn't want, but someone thought you ought to. His players felt the same. They watched in silence while their leader wriggled. But wriggling was in vain. Daddy Sergei executed a sharp gesture in the air with both hands, and exclaimed:

'Well, no more. It's fixed. I'll let you know the details soon. Meantime, be prepared to play a session of four hours, say five, for safety. So. Congratulations, all!'

He turned to leave, but had a further thought.

'Include a version of "Little Brown Bear".'

'"Little Brown Jug", you mean. Glenn Miller,' Rozner corrected.

'No. "Little Brown Bear". It's a Georgian folk song. Never been played as jazz before. This will be a first.'

'"Little Brown Bear"? Why stop at Little Brown Bear?' Rozner enquired. 'What's wrong with "Troika Bells", or "Horseman in the Snow"?'

The gleaming comrade turned to leave, beaming broadly, with one finger raised in admonition.

'You artists: you'll be the death of me. I swear, I love the lot of you.'

The preparation of a five-hour programme was no great imposition for the Eddie Rozner band; they produced two such every week. Neither was a journey of three hundred and sixty miles a major undertaking. But nobody could be found among them who was grateful. For some the train ride was a poignant prospect: they had travelled before to the rhythm of clicks in rails, and arrived where they would rather not have arrived. Others had grown attached to their quarters, their food, their girlfriends. Like Rozner himself, they were suspicious of change; they preferred their routine. In general, their response to the honour was: 'Better the enemy you know than a friend in a strange place.'

For Cornelius van Baerle the upheaval was unwelcome for this reason alone. He had been clubbed on the head, thrown in a cellar, transported to a country where his life hung by a thread until he played a piano, and now he enjoyed the stability and variety of his life. On any day he might stroll the interesting remnants of the ancient city in the morning, play the afternoon away on a near-perfect Bechstein, and lounge in the evening with convivial friends over a variety of stolen alcohols. At weekends, dressed in his drummer-boy jacket and cap, he was guaranteed a decent meal of left-overs, more alcohol, and an occasional back-room encounter with an overblown lady who swore she was unmarried, but always asked him to speed up their business so she was not missed. On the whole, his life was satisfactory: an enemy he knew, and for all his curiosity about the onion domes and parade squares of that city to the north-east, he would rather have stayed in the half-ruined shell of the former Luxor Theatre in Minsk, thank you.

The reluctance of its members notwithstanding, the Jack Band entrained for the capital four weeks later, and for eight hours endured a glum landscape enlivened only by the passing of Smolensk. They played cards half-heartedly, and drank half-heartedly, and though the guard told every traveller who they were, no one thought they could be other than a funeral group, bound for an important burial. As evening came, and anxiety replaced their desultory mood, they crowded at the windows to see the lights of suburbs and of monoliths, and flags, and statues striving gloriously by floodlight.

Six ZIS saloons, like shining pachyderms, stood waiting on the street outside the Byelorussia Station, and canvas-covered trucks for all their instruments. They packed inside and rode in convoy down broad streets, the lorries with their odd-shaped cases close behind. Arriving at the Hotel Aragvi, they found that buildings in the capital displayed unnecessary headroom: the lobby, corridors and bedrooms all had space for separate floors, or mezzanines at least, above the areas ever reached by guests. Cornelius lay and gazed above his bed, to where encroaching shadows hinted at a ceiling, or infinity.

The next day they were allocated rehearsal space: the hotel

seemed to have six areas big enough to play in. They retrieved their instruments, Cornelius was given a piano, and they took up where they had left off two days earlier. Everything was more or less as it had been, except that their quarters were richer, and the food, and they were not allowed to stray outside. Ulrich, whose secret role had long been undermined, disappeared overnight, to be replaced by oblong men in overcoats. Rehearsals for the big event went well, and on their third day there, Rozner announced the solution to a problem which had been occupying him:

'"Little Brown Bear" is "Sharp Sue", give or take. I checked the tune in a songbook, and the melodies are more or less identical. We play "Sharp Sue", and nobody is going to argue. Let's give it a go.'

They all flipped through their scores until they arrived at the title they had played sometimes before. Cornelius followed the line of the melody and searched his imagination for something concerning bears, to replace 'I like your outfit, Sue, that's really something new.' He could find nothing, and simply replaced Sue with Bru.

One day they were allowed to familiarise themselves with the stage of the famous theatre where they were to play, travelling across the city once more in escorted convoy. There was a profusion of red curtains in the theatre, and more gilt curlicues than they were accustomed to face. But the place held no surprises overall. The Jack Band filled the stage, although it was twice as big as their rehearsal floor at the Luxor Theatre. That accorded with the universal law of dance bands: a group expands to fill whatever space is free. Had they been allocated the Dynamo football pitch, they would have filled it.

The day of the great honour came round, and instead of considering their patron's dreams about the people's jazz, or the imprimatur of the Party, or the fatherhood of a hundred bands, Cornelius and Eddie Rozner and all their fellow jazzmen dreamed of Minsk, the train ride back, the curtained stage, the ruined rooms that were their homes. They had tired of the Hotel Aragvi's sepulchral halls and corridors, its distant ceilings, and of the capital they had scarcely seen.

At four in the afternoon, much too early, they took the ZIS saloons to the theatre, to be in place by six, which was in turn an early start for jazz. Their audience expected promptness, they were told. The blank-faced cohort of the People's Commissariat for Internal Affairs was reinforced, till every member of the band appeared to have a shadow. Van Baerle's protector was an obelisk, a monumental man who tapered to a point. Twenty minutes before the performance was to start, a bassist who had temporarily slipped his escort returned with strange news.

'Prompt, you say. Well that's a joke: the place is empty.'

'What do you mean, empty?' enquired the leader of the band.

'I tell you: there's not a soul out there.'

He had looked through the stage curtain, a habit of performers, who like to see the faces of their public secretly, to read the auguries.

'Maybe they let everybody in at the last minute,' said Rozner. 'Everything seems highly controlled.'

'It's dead out there,' the bassist insisted. 'No lights, no ushers, no nobody.'

Eddie consulted his wristwatch.

'There's time,' he decided. 'And what's the difference if they come in late? We don't have any further plans tonight.'

Five minutes before the hour, they were marshalled from their rooms to places on the stage, and when Rozner stepped forward to inspect the crowd, his watcher placed a palm against his chest and shook his head. Rozner regarded the impassive helper and quoted to him the words of the Party Secretary of Byelorussia:

'When you hear our music, you will be unable to suppress the emotion of joy.'

The comrade raised a forefinger to shush him.

Another of them looked up from his watch and sliced the air with his arm, as if it were the starter's flag at a motor race.

'Begin,' he instructed, and Rozner faced the band as the curtain rose, and made his tiny finger mime.

'A one, two, one-two, one-two,' he sang, before placing his trumpet to his lips, joining the glorious eruption of his signature tune, "Cotton Club Days", and turning to confront an empty theatre. He faltered momentarily, and then played on, indicating with one hand that business should proceed as usual. Cornelius played with both eyes off the keys, searching for signs of life beyond the footlights, and finding none he glanced at Rozner. The leader nodded for continuance. But when the piece was over, instead of waiting for applause he walked into the wings, while silence swathed the auditorium, and saxophonist conferred with trumpeter, and trumpeter with drums.

'What's the idea?' Eddie demanded of the comrade impresario who had ordered curtain-up. 'Why are we playing when nobody's come yet? We can't play to any empty house.'

The man looked agitated, and pushed Rozner back on to the stage.

'Keep playing,' he snapped. 'Follow your programme, as agreed. I'll tell you when to stop.'

Rozner returned and addressed his team.

'I don't know what the game is, but let's carry on. Since nobody has arrived, treat it like rehearsal. Imagine we're on stage in Minsk.'

He resumed his place, announced the second number, and Cornelius found that with little effort he could sense the blistered Bechstein of his Luxor life. Any anxiety he might have felt about the famous place in which he found himself was dissipated, and his fingers flowed about the keys as he relaxed and dreamed into the moment. They roved their repertoire an hour or so, and while he played and sometimes stared into the dark, Cornelius saw a vision. A flame rose up, a yellow flame. It rose and fell, and by its light he saw a face, its upswept eyebrows wild, its black hair springing with unnatural density along its brow, its eyes like burning beads, its thick moustache like satyr's thighs on either side. The flame-lit, pock-marked thing looked like the very devil, lit by fires of hell. And then it sank in darkness.

Rozner's request for an interval after two hours was resisted, and the band played on to the silent theatre, to Nijinsky's ghost and to Diaghilev's. They played the catalogue from Ellington to Armstrong, they touched on Reinhardt, toyed with Woody Herman and Glenn Miller. Then Rozner signalled their request piece: 'Little Brown Bear', and they played 'Sharp Sue'. In the seconds' pause that followed, while Rozner sought his next direction, the hollow of the velvet rows beyond the lights gave echo to a sound: the beating of a single pair of hands. The lonely noise was reinforced, but only to a small degree, and when the jazzmen searched the gloom, they saw a private box in which a coterie of silhouettes applauded, while cigarette ends glowed and died. Silence resumed, and they played on. And then at ten, the chief of their attendants called a halt.

'That's all,' he rasped. 'Pack up and leave.'

'Did you see him?' the musicians whispered, while they packed their things.

'Him?'

'The father of the nation, uncle Joe.'

'He smoked a pipe. It lit his face from time to time.'

'Was that really him?'

'Hurry!' said a member of the *Narodny Komissariat Vnutrennikh Del*. 'That is no concern of yours.'

What a life!

ESPITE repeated requests that they should be allowed to return to their headquarters in the desecrated temple of the former Luxor Theatre, Minsk, the musicians of the Jack Band were detained, without excuse, in the nation's capital. None of them ever rehearsed on that gusty stage again, and with possibly the odd exception, none of them ever set foot again in the remains of that ancient city. The dream of Daddy Sergei had been fulfilled: the saviour of the nation liked his music, the imprimatur of the Party was obtained. Eddie Rozner's band became an example, if not the father, for many more, if not a hundred; and Eddie was the undisputed leader of the apparatchiks' jazz, the Party functionaries' jazz, if not the people's. He would one day be among the four richest men in the country, riding the capital in a Packard with armoured glass two inches thick, formerly the property of that gentleman with the moustache, who smoked his pipe while deciding if jazz were good or bad: good, bad, good, bad, good . . .

But for the moment, Fate had other plans. The Jack Band was transferred to suites at the Hotel Metropole, where they became the resident entertainment. Every night they played for the socialist aristocracy, immaculate in suits of silk and mohair, their wives in sable wraps. Here, as the jazzmen strayed from Ellington to Basie, and their leader blew like Harry James, vast quantities of the richest foods were consumed, and couples drifted like animated ice floes round the giant ballroom, while an occasional shriek of laughter indicated that a drunken reveller had toppled into the ornamental fishpond at its centre. Meanwhile, the Party Secretary of Byelorussia cursed himself for writing letters, and put on another record.

'What a life, my friends! Who would have dreamed two years ago of such a life,' laughed Rozner, while he and his musicians consumed at one sitting a month's rations for a battalion of infantry. 'What a life! Enjoy it while we may. Eat, drink and be merry, for tomorrow we die.'

For more than a year the Rozner band played at the Hotel Metropole, and when its bubble burst it did so without warning, and absolutely. One night after midnight, Cornelius was woken in his bed by members of the People's Commissariat for State Security. They didn't announce themselves, but he recognised who they were, and bade goodbye in an instant to his life of comfort and pleasure. He bade goodbye to playing jazz.

'Come with us. We have some questions to ask,' said the agent with the paperwork. Cornelius raised no objection. In such circumstances it was useless to protest. He pulled on his coat, and suspended for an instant the passage of time, while he looked around the room where he had enjoyed an interlude, an inter-mezzo of pleasant talk and card games, of cigarettes and vodka. Then it was gone, and his life was a different life.

The dark street corners flew past, and without looking, he knew the direction they would take. But no, they did not ride to 2 Dzerzhinsky Square, but headed further out, to Lefortovo jail, for registration and reception. He looked down empty streets on either side, across the greatcoat breasts that flanked him, and puzzled over what he'd done. He'd scarcely ever left the Metropole, he never discussed politics, never sold anything illegally, though food left every day from the hotel tables for the black market. He searched for his offence, and found none. Why him? Because it was his fate.

It was also Rozner's fate, and that of his band. Cornelius was escorted through a granite prison arch into an antechamber, its brick walls smooth with frog-green paint, and there he glimpsed a negro, a saxophonist brought over with a couple more when Eddie left New York. The jazzman made a fatalistic face as he was led away, and van Baerle shrugged and tipped his head to say goodbye. His details registered, he asked the charge.

'You will be informed,' the jailer-clerk replied, and he was led out at the same time that a member of the trumpet section entered.

'Hey, Corny,' the man called, 'were we really this bad tonight? I thought we played okay.'

The entire Jack Band sat in jail, and every day they said a prayer: 'Here, and not the Lubianka, please, not Dzerzhinsky Square.' For some the prayer was answered; for others it was not. Although they never met, the members of the band passed messages, absurdly, through their interrogators. The man whose task it was to break down resistance to a confession of guilt in Rozner's case, and in van Baerle's, was a fan. He'd heard them play, and when he was shut up with either one of them, his first order of business was to pass greetings and news from the other.

Then followed a cigarette, a discussion about great jazz bands, and ultimately, and with regret, his pleadings for an admission of guilt.

The charge in both cases was of spying, and attempting to communicate with foreign powers. The interrogator flipped the pages of van Baerle's dossier and informed him:

'In Minsk you discussed foreign postal communications with co-accused.'

Then he switched from his official voice into his private, and asked:

'Why would you do that? Surely you would have some system organised, some secret way to get in touch?'

'Exactly so,' van Baerle replied. 'If I were a spy, I would not be making enquiries about the Union's postal services, would I? I would have some secret system of communication.'

The comrade switched back to official mode:

'So, you deny it?'

'No. I discussed foreign postal communications. I wanted to write home.'

'Say yes, you deny it,' the man advised, in private vein.

'Put what you want,' Cornelius told him. 'Put what you think best. You know I'm not a spy. I spent the last twelve months in a hotel. What am I supposed to have spied on: bed linen? Menus?'

'Did you ever see Louis Armstrong play?' the interrogator wondered.

'I've never been to America. I've told you this before,' Cornelius answered.

'Louis played in Europe all the time. You never saw him at the Hot Club de France?'

'I never played jazz until two years ago. I never went anywhere to listen to jazz.'

'Is that possible: to go from nothing to the Eddie Rozner band so quick? You must be a natural.'

'I always played whatever I was asked,' van Baerle recalled. 'I have that ability.'

'Sign your confession, please. It's best. You'll sign it in the end.'

'What confession? I don't recall making a confession. How can I sign it?'

'You will,' the confusing man observed, with confidence.

If Rozner and van Baerle had been bona fide spies, they would have been questioned night and day, beaten and tortured, and eventually led to an execution chamber far below the dog-kennel cells of the Lubianka prison. There, while two men held their arms, a third would have put a bullet in their necks at point-blank range. As they had not been so despatched, it was plain that they, like several million others, had been falsely charged. They would be punished for having become entangled in the system, but not necessarily by death, not by quick death. One day van Baerle's interrogator entered with a serious face.

'Eddie Rozner has confessed to spying,' he reported. 'And you must do the same.'

'What's wrong?' Cornelius enquired.

'They've waited long enough. The word's come through: if you don't confess you're to be shot. Believe me. Please, believe me. I don't think you're a bad man; you're not a spy. But you will be shot if you don't comply. Sign a confession, and you may receive a sentence that leaves you alive. Refuse and you will be shot, this week, possibly tomorrow.'

Cornelius needed no convincing. He knew that people were disposed of there without much thought. The paper was produced, and he signed.

'What did we do wrong?' he asked the comrade, not for the first time. 'We were the very darlings of your leaders.'

'Jazz has been declared decadent.'

'He liked it, the boss. It received his imprimatur.'

'That was before. A dynamic society changes. If you like jazz now, you'd better keep it under your hat.'

Eddie Rozner was sentenced to ten years in a corrective labour colony, two of his negro immigrants disappeared for ever into the slave camp of Vorkuta, three more musicians were worked to death in the Arctic gold mines of Kolyma, two were executed after torture, for no good reason, and van Baerle's destiny, like Rozner's, was to be committed for ten years to the custody of *Glavnoe Upravlenie Ispravitelno-Trudovikh Lagerei*: the GULAG.

Brooding

OLBOY PASSED a summer of melancholy. For the first time in his life he had tasks to complete: exercises in arithmetic, books to be read, poems to be learned, compositions to be completed describing highlights of his holiday, and the life of a penny. He placed a penny on his desk for inspiration, and wrote:

'The life of a penny is a brown life. It comprises years or centuries of lying in dark pockets and dark purses, emerging into brightness only briefly, when some interesting person's interesting life requires small change. But however long the succession of interesting lives, the penny sees nothing of them but dark pockets and dark purses. It is, after all, only an object. Its history is determined at its making. Its destiny is to rub along with other coins until its face value is no longer readable, and it is thin and worthless. At this point it is taken by the bank and melted down. Its life has been one of dark pockets and dark purses.'

This offering was not what his language teacher had in mind when he set the subject: either in its content or its length. It was a topic which had been set many times before, and yielded wild adventures. The possibilities were without limit: every aviator, sailor, criminal, sports hero and detective had money in his pocket. The passing of a penny from one to another of them allowed endless flights of fancy: the fortunate coin could one minute attend the unmasking of Jack the Ripper, and have every expectation, the next, of being present at the first ascent of Everest.

Dolboy's interpretation of the theme was indicative of his devastation. His life seemed now to be divided in two parts: life before Ivo's birthday party and life afterwards. The life before was brightly lit and full of hope. Anything might happen in that life: an educational journey in the waters of a large river, flight in the treetops of an avenue of beeches, love in a flock of moths. But since that hideous celebration, Dolboy's life was changed, his dreams were leaden-footed things that nowhere held a place for hope, that nowhere shone with silver hair and dimpled cheeks. The love he thought was true and sure, though undiscussed, was gone, and in its place betrayal, exercises in arithmetic, and compositions on unwelcome topics. The only thing that strangely pleased him was his repetition of 'dark pockets and dark purses'. Something of its sound chimed with his mood, and he could not foresee the completion of his second topic, Highlights of My Holiday, without its further use.

When he arrived home flushed from Ivo's celebration, his uncle, dressed ready for the drive, looked up from his newspaper with an expression of surprise. His aunt, likewise, stopped her needlework and sat to look, her eyebrows raised to ask the question. Dolboy, with his shirt neck open and his hair inflated, looked from one to the other, hopelessly. Nobody spoke, but meanings were exchanged. Why home so soon? Some upset made you run? Please don't ask the reason. We understand: no explanation asked.

Aunt and uncle looked at each other, and concurred: no explanation asked.

'What will you drink?' she enquired.

The melancholy season dragged its time out, while Dolboy lived and relived the monstrous dance, and searched for reasons. Perhaps this was some punishment for borrowing her in fantasy: that fantasy in which his hands crept everywhere, and she allowed. God will punish boys who use their bodies in a certain way, their chaplain said. What their imagination construes, God perceives. It will be as if those things you think, you do in actuality. So think only goodness, and if other thoughts intrude, read from this book (he raised it, black with gilt embossing) and know that you are saved. But when those other thoughts arrived, it was too late for books.

Sometimes his escape was running. Dressed now in proper shorts and vest, he paced the tracks and roads he knew so well, by dyke and meadow, mill and riverbank. He faced the walls of spruce again, and sprang through fir and heather. Stronger now, and tall, he legged the woodland lanes where deer looked up and froze, then leaped in arcs into the bramble. A farmer's wife paused by her door to shade her eyes and watch, but had no words for him, who had replaced the little runner. Somewhere, in some obscure recess, he knew his destination. No matter how he bent his route, and twisted from his course, it led, he knew, to one location, and when he blundered out of shadowed woods to brighter birch and foxglove, his surprise was counterfeit. And as before, that first time when he found the summerhouse, his thoughts grew calm and disappeared, and in their place his senses played: the white toy shone beyond the purple spires, and white stems all around, whose leaves swished in the wind, while scents of sun-warmed pine suffused his indrawn breath.

Why did he go there? To watch until she came again. To wait and be forgiven, start again his dream of love. Or see her grown beyond his reach, reshaped, half woman now, with Udo by her side. His suffering was revived and sharpened. But each time he arrived, each time the birch and foxglove framed his dream, both hopes and torments vaporised. He closed his eyes and time ran in reverse. Recent weeks became the future, time that had never been, and on the step she stood, dressed like a Calvinist in blue and black, her linen cap with turned-up points, her twinkling eyes, her dimpled cheeks, her downy arms and legs . . .

'I was just looking,' he told her. 'I wasn't going to . . .'

'Here. Let me show you,' the girl offered, stepping onto the verandah and placing the key in the keyhole. 'Let me show you. Let me show you.' And she did.

'Just looking,' he told her. 'I wasn't going to . . .' But he did.

All his thoughts and all his days seemed to lead to one conclusion: a carnal consummation flawed by ignorance, a blundering quest through limbs and lips and breasts to that intangible target zone, that nothingness, that maddening vacuity. Why did he return to the summerhouse? Because his imagination led him to hope a thousand other courses might be taken when she came again, to be enchanted by their meeting, and each one led to pleasure.

At early eveningtime one day, he left the fringing wood and stood to get his breath. And while he did he glimpsed a girl, a figure with fair hair, dissolve into the painted house. He stepped through the grass with stealth, half paralysed by indecision.

Should he go on, or back? Should he voice regrets and be forgiven, or enter with reproaches? He saw her smooth his hair, in either case, and press his hands against her breasts. But would she? Which course was best? First he would look in, unseen, and hope for indications of a tactic.

He trod carefully behind the house, and peeped. The three small windows lay in shade, and elder partly veiled them. Behind the leaves he raised his head until he saw the room. The fair-haired girl was someone whom he knew. Her wooden clogs sat neatly on the floor, while she stood barefoot on the table. She held her shoulders back, her face thrust forward like a figure-head. Below her, looking up, knelt Ivo, a pilgrim at a shrine. It was a girl who worked around the house, a helper at their parties. She had yellow hair in ribboned plaits, and the upturned nose and high cheekbones of farm girls from the region. She broke her pose and bent her head to focus on her hip, where seven buttons were unloosed. Her skirt fell to a dark embattlement around her feet. She stepped deliberately out of it, with pointed toes, and paused while Ivo gaped, entranced, then hooked her thumbs into the waistband of her drawers, and eased them by degrees down to her knees, raising each foot in turn to free them. She kicked the garment clear and stood bare-buttocked, pouting on the head of her admirer. Although her face and arms were tanned, her other parts were pallid as a root from being covered. They shone until her upper half merged into the shaded room, and she became a glowing trunk and legs in isolation, like some object of education, brought to its plinth from a delightful land.

Ivo watched, and Dolboy watched, and the girl stood and watched. After a little while Ivo walked around the table several times, his eyes consuming what she had uncovered. Then, while she remained motionless, her hands at her sides, he clasped her with both arms, his cheek pressed to her belly, and kissed the yellow wad, the crinkled yellow focus of her groins. She let him. She underwent the adoration with a smile, and kept her feet together, and her knees and thighs, because she had been paid for nothing more.

Dolboy's breathing tightened, and blood crept to its destination. He saw two shallow dimples, each above a buttock, and two more behind her knees. He saw her flowing calves, two upturned toes she flexed, the swooping flesh above the yellow hair, the full-to-bursting thighs, and knew that all of this comprised the thing he would hold dearest in his life. Just one improvement could be made. He substituted for the piggy nose and yellow plaits a softer face with silver hair, half closed his eyes, and let his hand conclude its curious work.

The prodigy

THE CROSS-COUNTRY season soon came round, and Dolboy's name was entered in his school's yearly race. His training had been simple. Like the beginning of the team race, a cross-country start was a mêlée, and a sprint was needed to clear the crowd. But he must not sprint so fast or so far that he was spent, and easily passed. The teacher who had presented him with his prize glider made him begin at speed over different distances, to see which gave him an advantage that was not entirely lost when he slowed to recover. The same procedure was repeated while he ran, to find how often and how far he could accelerate to clear a knot of boys, or arrive before others at obstacles like stiles and narrow paths. His only other practice was to run four hundred yards further than the course, to build up stamina.

'A wind can make the distance seem much longer,' said his trainer. 'Or ice. Or mud. In conditions less than perfect some run out of steam, and wonder why. If you have trained for something longer, you'll go on. A calm, dry day will be a bonus.'

Other boys were enlisted to assist in his training. They played fox and hounds together. Three set off, the foxes, and after several minutes Dolboy followed, like a hound. When he caught them too easily, they ran in relays: one at the start, and two more stationed round their course, to take up fresh. This made it more a race, but still he overhauled them, one by one. They ran on undulating ground, with streams to cross, and fences. His foxes plunged downhill flat-out, enjoying some relief, but Dolboy kept his pace and watched for ruts and rabbit holes, and when they faced an uphill stretch, he liked that best. The ground seemed nearer at each step, and easier to reach. He kept his pace again, and climbed like a machine, while his helpers faced their nemesis. Whenever he saw an obstacle ahead he accelerated, sometimes to get there before his opponent, sometimes to overtake an imagined group who blocked his path in future time, when he was let loose to demonstrate his speciality.

In class, like other sportive boys, he was indulged, allowed some leeway. If he gave a wrong answer, or failed to deliver a completed exercise, a teacher reprimanded him more gently than he scolded other boys, as if acknowledging that a genius for athletics must displace some lesser skills. His teachers took an interest, as they did with team boys in the ball games, and spoke to him in personal asides, in tones they never used with those whose role it was to constitute the crowd.

'Did you run yesterday, Dolboy?'

'Yes, sir.'

'Despite the rain?'

'Yes, sir.'

'And how is it going? Are you making progress? The rest of you get on.'

'Yes, sir, thank you, sir.'

They seemed almost to curry favour, because they knew he would be famous, and they could say: 'I knew that boy.'

His language teacher handed back their compositions, and singled Dolboy out for praise. He read aloud from Highlights of My Holiday, to demonstrate to all the function of imagination in such an undertaking. The narrative concerned a boy who ran, and ran obsessively, through woodland that blinded him to paths ahead, until one day he found a magic place, a clearing of delicate trees and swaying flowers in which he saw a summerhouse.

'Notice how the third person is employed,' the teacher observed. 'The topic is highlights of "my" holiday, and yet we find the author once removed. Later we will discuss the advantages of this device. Meantime, I think we know who "he" is, don't we?'

'Dolboy,' moaned the class in unison, and Dolboy made his head sink deeper in his neck, and took himself to somewhere foreign, somewhere distant from his shame at being singled out. He heard the teacher's voice, an echo far away, while he was otherwise engaged in dressing as a stork and riding in an open landau with his bride, and watching nighttime bombers overhead in pencil beams of light, until at last, despite his flight, despite his concentration, the teacher's monologue returned while he grew redder:

'There in the gloom, a boy with eyes like almond nuts admired a captive trophy on a table. He reached and stroked the lovely thing. The cockatoo, chained by one leg to its perch, blinked blue eyelids, and accepted its master's touch.'

The class groaned, and Dolboy groaned inside himself. Why

had he rambled so poetically? Why had he not simply catalogued a ridiculous journey by steam train to a beach of silver sand, with donkey rides, and ice-cream cones, though he had never been there? Why had the teacher betrayed his silly, softer self?

'A cockatoo. Who would have guessed such a conclusion?' the teacher wondered. 'But was it simply a cockatoo? Did it perhaps signify some other thing? Who knows?'

A boy put up his hand.

'A dog, sir. He might have meant a dog. There's a cocker spaniel that sounds a bit like a cockatoo.'

Other boys joined in.

'Timbuktu, sir. Perhaps the bird is a clue to where it's taking place.'

'A carrot, sir. He made it a parrot, which sounds like a carrot. You just have to work it out.'

The boys were playing one of their favourite games: enlivening a dull moment with facetious answers bearing a sufficient resemblance to bona fide answers as to preclude punishment. Dolboy had himself enjoyed this diverting tactic many times.

'That will be enough.' The teacher returned the class to reality as another boy twisted in his seat and cupped his hand to tell Dolboy:

'A cock or two. He stroked a cock or two. He's a homo.'

'I said enough.' The teacher's tone grew harder. 'What do you say, Dolboy?'

Dolboy mused for an interval in which he saw himself stand to report the highlight of his holiday: his stealthy creeping to the summerhouse, the blonde girl's falling clothes, her shining flesh. (He looked around and saw astounded faces.) And then the kissing of that golden part. All breathing stopped. Every eye focused on him, waiting for more.

'Well, yes, sir, I suppose it could have been a carrot: that does sound like a parrot.' He chose the path of comradeship. The teacher had offered him the chance of crossing to his side, to seriousness and adult thought. But Dolboy chose the other path. The gleeful boys erupted in a riot. They howled and hooted, banged on desks. He had remained with them. He played their game, and hoped the teacher understood. They exchanged glances through the noise: the teacher's spoke of resignation, Dolboy's said: 'I'm sorry.'

A cross-country race

THE OUTCOME of the school cross-country race was not a matter of great uncertainty, as it often had been in previous years. The boys turned out to see by how much Dolboy won. Some walked into the countryside to find an open stretch, where runners might be watched approaching from afar, and slowly growing small again across a field. Where fences, stiles or streams were crossed, a crowd of watchers stood to wait for muddy accidents. Others stayed in school. They saw the start, then settled to their comics and their books until the shout went up the sports were back, and then they cheered the winners home.

A favourite place along the course was a brook between steep banks, which in the summer idled round large boulders, and in the winter drowned them. If the weather had been dry, a foot of water bubbled on the stony bed, but after rain it boiled in turmoil to conceal the rocks below. In good years runners might slide down one bank, set foot on a rocky island in the stream, and cross to carry on. In bad years they would flounder. Sometimes the race was put off till a safer water level held. The most desired state for watchers was a water flow that promised falls, but did not absolutely guarantee the victims were swept out to sea.

When Dolboy ran, the rain had fallen for three weeks, and water in the stream had three times passed the danger point marked on a post set in the bank. And then one day a senior boy delivered round the school a folded note, which teachers read aloud in every class, to say the time had come to run the race: the mud was no worse, the water level lower. Dolboy felt a thrill when a murmur crossed the room, and boys turned to signal their encouragement with upthrust thumbs.

'Dolboy!' they called. 'Dolboy!' Until their calls became a chant.

His starting burst was regulated not to take the lead from older boys with much more strength, but place himself beyond the pack, and close behind the leaders. When this was done, he found his pace and kept it. If he came to someone's heels, and ran in muddy backspray, he sprinted for a while, until he found clear space. If a fence appeared with two boys in between, he burst ahead to reach it first. The clay built up on shoes and legs, the blood on brambled thighs, and Dolboy gained until three other boys, three athletes, stayed in front. The first two reached the brook and leaped into the water. A raucous shout rose from the crowd when one fell headlong while the second waded through. They scrambled up the other side and crossed to open ground, while Dolboy neared the obstacle.

The banks were built up to a ridge, which made a runner rise before he plunged down to the stream. The third man rose, then disappeared below as Dolboy closed.

'Dolboy! Dolboy!' chanted his supporters, and as he focused on the gap between the crowds, the cheering touched an instinct that had lain unroused. His old indifference disappeared, and in its place a fierceness sprang.

'Dolboy! Come on, Dolboy! We want Dolboy!'

The repetition of his name spurred his excitement, and he broke into a sprint instead of slowing when he ought. They cheered him wildly to the bank, and when he was ten strides away his body had a sudden whim, and varied from his plan. The shouting grew, and then a silence fell. The torrent beating on the rocks, and treetop rooks were heard, and nothing else.

The runner in the water course paused in the awful stillness, and saw above a soaring shape, its rigid limbs extended. One leg reached forward, one reached back, the arms stretched out like birdwings. It seemed to hang immobile for a while, then sailed on to the ground. On both sides of the stream, heads and eyes moved with the arc that Dolboy made, deerlike, to reach in one balletic step, one unpremeditated bound, from bank to bank.

The silence broke, and gave place to a roar. The two ahead looked back to see the crowd break from the stream and run into the muddy field to keep abreast a little while and slap the back of their pursuer. They glanced at each other, and each saw a puzzled face, and felt uneasy. They struggled on, and soon they trailed a leader dry from head to knee, who seemed to fly over the dense ground, who seemed invincible, and was.

'A spectacular strategy, Dolboy,' remarked his trainer. 'You appear to have practised it to perfection.'

'It just happened, sir,' Dolboy answered.

'One day,' said the teacher, 'you will be famous.'

'Famous, sir?'

'Your name will be in all the newspapers.'

'Thank you, sir.'

The teacher smiled, and touched the hero's shoulder.

'No, Dolboy. Thank you for visiting us mortals.'

Another train journey

WHILE HE SAT in the Lefortovo jail, it occurred to Cornelius van Baerle that our perception of time as something finite, which falls into conveniently equal fragments, was a figment of our placement in the universe. Since we found ourselves on a planet that rotated, and in the vicinity of a bright light source, it appeared to us that time was an endless succession of illuminated packages, and that packages delivered prior to the last spin into darkness made up a separate, historical time, apart from that which we expected on the next rotation of our orb: the days of future time. If, say, our planet ceased its spinning, or found itself a great way from the sun, we should see more plainly a continuum, and know there was just one time, and therefore no time outside of man's imagining.

But then, in endless light or endless dark, would we employ the ceaseless passage of events to conjure what we seemed to need: the ordering of things? One ever-present belt would not suffice. That which has occurred and that which is yet to come call out for differentiation. Since time, then, was a construct of the human mind, would time pass slower when events were few? And if the earth spun twenty times a day, would time pass faster? It followed that would be the case.

His speculations on this theme began when he turned his attention from the career of a spider with which he shared his cell. He had no books, no window to look through, no other human to engage now that his sentence had been determined. He had electric light, continuous light, unending day, with no event for punctuation other than the emptying and replenishment, twice daily, of his cavities.

Would his sentence of ten years seem longer in a cell, in spider land, than in a work gang in the forest or the mine? What occupied his time ten years ago, and how fast had the years passed in between? Would repetition of that interval, without freedom, prolong the passing years, or make them speed? Perhaps, he wondered, thoughts might be another way of quantifying time. In that case, if he made his mind completely blank, would there be time? Are cretins unaware of time, and is that bliss, or hell?

Cornelius could be forgiven for such flights in spider land. He had nothing else to do, or say, or think. The artificial, endless day slipped past, the endless, empty brightness. And then his metaphysics was curtailed. He left his cell one morning after dawn, and went to something else. Two guards led him away. He passed five doors along a corridor of stone, and wondered who was in them. Did this one hold a colleague from the band, the trombonist who had advised acceptance of their life in Minsk? Was that one Eddie Rozner's? He smiled and conjured Eddie's slick black hair, his one-two one-two, and his motto from the Hotel Metropole: Eat, drink and be merry, for tomorrow we die. But Cornelius had a longer wait for death.

He joined a group outside the jail and waited under guard. A truck arrived, and took them to a station. A special train had been arranged, the sort of thing he knew: a train of trucks with wooden sides, no windows, and a bar that swung to hold a sliding door in place. Other travellers had already been loaded. Cornelius saw their eyes and fingertips through slits as he walked past. The party from Lefortovo was locked in to share each other's breath and fearful looks, though no one spoke a word. No questions were asked: their time for ten years, fifteen, twenty-five, was at the state's disposal, and where it might be passed was no concern of theirs, and no one knew.

The group was different from the crowd he travelled with to Minsk: there were no women and no children. There were no older folk among them; they all looked good for work. Their wagon opened once a day, for water and black bread. The days were warm, the nights were cold, the season seemed autumnal. Then names were passed from truck to truck of rumoured destinations: Ussolski, Sverolevsk, Karganda, Tobolsk, Ivdel, Korkutsk, Norilsk, Yakutsk, Chukotsk, Sev Vostochni . . . The country held so many possibilities.

The passage of a thousand miles of woods and level ground revived van Baerle's theoretical vein. His days were filled with passing scenes, and people stood on every side, and still time disobeyed the laws he postulated in his cell, where nothing changed. Time still ran slow, though every second some new space skimmed by. Though every day he spoke to fellow men, the hours crawled. Since time passed more slowly when events were few, and speeded up with change, his days should fly. The world he saw go by was but a single thing, he mused: one landscape, one frieze of forest and of grass. The villages that came and went were all alike. The bundled people stood and stared in every place the same, as if at night they were transported down the line to furnish an illusion. And the men on every side were like one man, one face, one fear. His law held good.

A new home

TEN DAYS after he left the capital city of the nation, Cornelius van Baerle and his beard arrived in the settlement which was to be his home for the rest of his life, and wondered how such an extensive land mass could be considered one country. He saw from his wooden transit a range of low hills, the rim of a large clearing in pine forest that stretched from horizon to horizon, prefabricated factories with chimneys delivering smoke in a variety of colours, and windowless log huts, like chicken coops, that filled the spaces in between. There was no fence, no guard posts with machine guns, raised on stilts. The forest was their perimeter.

The door was flung open, and they were cursed out by men in uniforms, with rifles on their backs, and dogs like wolves on leads. This much at least was familiar. He and his group formed a line, and when their names were tallied, they marched at double speed from the railhead, outside the zone of industries and huts, to no-man's-land: the open heath before the woods. Their escort flung two shovels on the ground, between the fifty men, and bawled:

'Dig in!'

The new arrivals looked around, unsure what they should do.

'Dig in? What do you mean?' one of them asked.

A guard approached and smashed a fist into his face.

'If any of you bastards had served a spell in the beloved army, you'd know what dig in means. Now: dig fucking in!'

A prisoner who had the bad luck to be in the proximity of a shovel began to dig.

'Pick that up!' the comrade guard ordered another newcomer, who took the second shovel nervously, and began to chip the heather-knotted ground, while watching how the first man worked. The guard watched both until he judged the moment right. He drew a hissing breath through a cigarette fragment pinched between the nailtips of his thumb and finger, examined the stub to see that it was done, and ground it with his boot into the earth. He let the smoke out with a whistled tune, then held his rifle barrel like a punt pole in both hands and crashed its other end into the backbone of a shoveller, who fell to the ground and moaned.

'I said dig in!' the comrade guard repeated. 'Not dig for fucking coal.'

The shovel lay unwanted.

'Pick that up and dig in!' he screamed.

While most prisoners hesitated, one stepped forward confidently, marked an oblong on the ground with the shovel edge, and in ten minutes had excavated a grave, twelve inches deep. He handed the implement to another, and murmured:

'That's deep enough, believe me. I was in the beloved army.'

The tools were handed round, and when night fell the queue to dig a home was smaller. Cornelius lay in his sandy cavity and shuffled until it fitted, rested his head on one arm, and pulled in fronds of heather for more comfort. Having ensured that the criminals worked according to instructions, the guards left them to their labours. A multi-coloured glow lit up the vapours from the factory blocks, bright clouds moved across a harvest moon, and close by Cornelius heard low voices and the striking of a blade into the ground. He smelled the heather and the earth. The progression of time at its proper pace had resumed.

The next day at dawn, a group of men with dogs moved among the trenches where the new men lay, kicking and stamping late sleepers into awareness of their situation.

'What! You think you're on holiday?' the boss man shouted. 'You'll be in the ground soon enough, you lazy bastards. Two days' work will finish half you lot. Now, get down there and eat. You've got ten minutes, then we start. By the time we're through you'll love these pits. You'll think of nothing else all day but getting back to lie in them, you lazy scum.'

The night had been cold, and the prisoners wrapped themselves in their arms, and rubbed their biceps as they trooped in silence to the indicated zone of activity. There they filed through a small hut in which they were each issued with a tin bowl containing a faintly coloured barley gruel. Fragments of cabbage and potato swirled in it, then settled to its bed. The ration was completed by a pellet of black bread, torn from one loaf into however many pieces were required by the party. The food orderly made his calculation on sight, and when he revised it as more men appeared, the pellets were reduced in size. Here was a lesson, van Baerle observed: take breakfast at the head of the queue, while demand was uncertain.

While they stood outside and scoured their bowls with bread, their waiter appeared in the doorway of the hut and told them:

'Keep the bowls. That's all you'll need. No bowls, no food.'

Cornelius examined his bowl. It was a homely, brown and pewter-coloured thing, five inches wide, with a flattened base and a rim that in places was folded over in a lip, and in other places was sharp enough to shave with. Its surface was pitted where its sides and base formed a less accessible margin, but for the most part it was worn smooth by use, over several dozen dents and hollows. It was a bowl which had experienced many vicissitudes.

As promised, the guard who had addressed them earlier reappeared in ten minutes.

'And don't let me ever see a bowl still out when I come back, else you'll lose it,' he warned. 'Eat and be ready for work in ten minutes, or you'll have nothing to eat from tomorrow. Now, let's see: what have we got?'

He strolled among them like a connoisseur, and without a command the prisoners formed an approximation of a line, and held their shoulders back, demonstrating how ready they were for discipline. The disposer of their lives arrived in three minutes at a series of decisions on which their mortality would depend. He herded them until they formed four groups, and told each group its lot.

'You crowd are for timber, you for road and rail. You arseholes work magnesium, the rest are good for nothing more than paint.'

The first two categories were self-evident, but the manufacture of magnesium and paint were mysteries to all but the guards.

Each man wondered if his designation were a good thing or a bad. Van Baerle was selected to work in timber. On the one hand in the forest you have fresh air, he thought, but on the other, snow and heavy work. He and ten others were taken to be equipped with axes and saws, then trotted at double speed down a rutted track, along which in the opposite direction passed a constant traffic of men, harnessed in teams like horses, straining to haul pine trunks over the muddy surface.

The new contingent of which van Baerle formed a part was too fresh and strong for this variety of drudgery. Its members brought muscle with them from the outside world, which must be used to good effect before it sickened and melted. Only then would they be considered for draught work. To begin, they must fell trees.

The scene of their engagement was frantic with excess labour. The face of the swathe that was being cut swarmed with men. Where trees were down, a dozen climbed with axes in their branches, swinging till the stems were smoothed. Before they had completed their task the haulers were already passing ropes around the trunks, securing them with iron staples driven in the wood. And while these teams disputed the proprietorship of timber, the fellers swung and sawed in pairs behind them. At intervals their efforts reached fruition, and they leaped clear with a shout. Every man glanced up to find the falling tree and act accordingly. Five or six standing trees were under attack at the same time, so prisoners on the ground must stay alert for tumbling beams every ten or fifteen minutes while they worked. When a delinquent pine trunk creaked, wavered, then leaned over them, they scattered like insects if they were able, or cowered like mice if they weren't.

The felling pairs were split to let the new men learn their work. Cornelius faced the base of a pine and saw that his partner, standing opposite, did not welcome the arrival of a novice. The big man swung to sink his axe into the bark, and when he jerked it free, Cornelius took his turn to do the same. But when he pulled the shaft, the head stuck fast. His partner swung again and bit a chip of wood to set it free, then raised the blade to swing again. He had a rhythm, and Cornelius must learn to match it. Twice more he tore at his embedded tool as his partner's looped downward through the air. With his mouth still set in a hard line, the giant raised his eyes an instant, and murmured:

'Don't hit so hard. We're only trying to chip a wedge.'

They alternated on, and when the bite into the bark was deep enough, they took a saw and placed it in the wood. Each of them took a handle at the end of the long blade, braced himself against the trunk and bent his back. Again the big man set the rhythm.

'Don't push,' his iron face advised. 'Just pull. Imagine you're rowing a boat.'

Cornelius looked across at him, and saw that though his mouth stayed hard, the skin outside the corners of his eyes was crinkled with a grim amusement. They pulled the jagged instrument ten minutes to and fro, until the expert glanced above.

'Two more and then look out,' he called.

They made the cuts, cried out and then stood clear. For two seconds all work ceased. Every face turned up to see and, calculations made, turned down again. The tree fell where it should, but when the trunk broke from the fibres of the stump, it gave a kick into the air that would have killed a cow. His partner spoke again:

'You never know for sure which way it goes,' he said. 'Stay well clear and live.'

They moved on to another tree, and then another. Cornelius thought himself strong, but after an hour of work, he trembled in every muscle. Where the saw-hold crossed his hands the skin grew red, then rose in soft, fluid-filled domes. The blisters burst, and he looked at the raw flesh which still had a whole day to work.

'Let the axe fall by itself,' his teacher told him. 'Don't waste your strength to pull it down. Just lift and let it fall.'

Each time they chopped, a spray of sap flew in the air. Their hair and beards and faces glistened where the tiny droplets merged, and hung in sticky beads of resin. Each time they sawed, the sawdust rose and joined the gummy film until the two men became the coagulated essence of a tree: their eyes shone like knots behind the veil of woody scum suspended from their brows; their mouths resembled moist chestnut buds in dust-choked thickets; their arms were scaled, like pine bark, where wood chips clothed the gum.

'Make a bandage,' the big man advised. 'Tear a strip from your shirt and wrap it round your hands.'

Van Baerle did as he was told, and wound lengths of fabric round each trembling hand. The binding eased his pain. He chopped and sawed on through a dull ache now, that varied to a sharper throb when he pulled on his end of the instrument. They moved on to another tree, and then another. They moved on until Cornelius lay on the saw handle, and contributed nothing to its motion as it thrust and was withdrawn, and thrust again through sappy wood.

'Just hold. Don't pull against me,' called the Trojan. And Cornelius held, while the saw worked on. They moved forward, and Cornelius quivered every time he raised his anvil-headed axe and let it fall. Sometimes he raised it once to every two his partner hit; sometimes he let it fall and struck his partner's axe. When he paused and leaned against a tree to stop from fainting, a guard approached and punched him in the back.

'No sleeping on the job. Get on,' he shouted.

'Keep standing. Just hold and keep standing,' said the old hand. 'Soon we'll take a rest and you'll recover.'

And so they killed another tree.

After three hours of felling timber, Cornelius and his partner were allowed ten minutes in which to attend to their bodily functions, eat a fist-sized ration of black bread, and drink from a wooden barrel an unrestricted quantity of water, covered and flavoured with pine needles. Then they resumed the nine-hour portion of the day's work that remained. After a further three hours they stopped for the same refreshment, complemented with two spoons of boiled millet pap, and a slice of sausage made from a horse. After a further three hours they enjoyed an interval in which they took their last nourishment of the day: a ration of black bread and cold potatoes from a bucket, washed down with water. A further three hours of work remained before they were trotted, at double speed, back to their holes in the ground.

At every moment of the day Cornelius believed he could not lift his axe once more, or grip the saw, or stand a minute longer. Then, as the sun slipped below the crest of the encircling pines, one man from the new brigade let out a gasp, clutched at his chest, and fell like a sack of grain. A guard bent down to see his face, then ordered two workers to drag him clear. The fallen prisoner moaned at intervals for an hour or more, and then lay still. From then Cornelius knew he must go on. At the end of the day the corpse was stripped, its clothing shared, and it was slung on an ox-cart and returned to camp for a registration process that began with a bayonet thrust through its heart, to ensure the prisoner was, for certain, in the condition described on the ticket attached to his foot.

The men who returned to their newly dug holes in the heather bore some resemblance to those who had left in the morning, but they were also changed. Their eyes stared from faces ghastly with the memory of what they had endured, and the imagination of its repetition over one more day. Its repetition over a period of years was beyond imagining. Coated with the wood fragments and the dirt of their labours, they fell silently into their pits, and into unconsciousness.

The forest

LONG BEFORE they had exhausted dreams of warfare, concentration camps and cattle trucks, the tortured novices were returned to the present day by a further visitation of boots. It seemed as if their guards crept up on them to guarantee a sleeping target, and stamped among the groaning forms for sport. Van Baerle stood up, and in the silver light that lit the autumn mist he saw a regiment of goblins rise from their terrestrial holes. They groped around, half blind, and bent with aches, while dusty earth fell from their heads and coats, and more stayed on them. Cornelius looked down himself, and when he beat his clothes to lose his dirt, he saw his hands were made of sand. He brushed them with his fingers and the sand remained, set in the layer of stiff pine resin that clotted his entire surface. The hair of his head and his beard had become solid forms: he pressed his hands to his head, and his hair resisted, so he could not make contact with his skull. All around, prisoners examined their sand-caked bodies, and imagined their sand-caked faces.

One man's eyelids were stuck together by the gritty glue, and the more he tried to free them, the more his eyes filled with the stinging compound. He bent and tried to tease his lashes loose, but soon his groping gave way to an angry rubbing, and his moaning grew into a frustrated rage, in which he howled at the hopelessness of his state until a smiling guard felled him with a blow of his rifle butt. As the rest of them were driven like cattle to their breakfast hut, Cornelius looked back to see the guard break the blind man's head until its contents lay scattered like a dish of macaroni on the ground.

They swallowed their bread and gruel, and trotted at double speed, their clothes flapping stiffly with the weight of gummy earth, to resume their new careers.

'So, you like the work. You want to carry on.' Eynarr, his partner of the previous day, greeted him with a slight wrinkling of the skin outside his eyes, and looked him up and down. 'If I were you, I'd cut my hair. And make myself an apron like this one.'

Van Baerle watched him don a greatcoat, backward, so it hung open behind. Through the middle buttonhole he had looped a string, whose ends he drew round to tie at the front. The collar had been stripped from the garment to prevent constriction at the throat, and a vent in the hem had been lengthened to make a slit that ran up to his groin, leaving two flaps of fabric on the front of either thigh. Otherwise it was just a coat, reversed. The expanse of material which had once enclosed shoulder blades now formed a breastplate, stiff with sap.

They resumed their work, and the aching which had suffused his body since he woke turned into pain, while new blood seeped through the rags that saved his hands.

'Work as slowly as possible, without attracting attention,' Eynarr told him. 'Keep it steady, and they won't complain.'

But to van Baerle, the metronomic thudding of the axe seemed impossible to sustain, and the saw moved like a mechanical shark to greet then pull him in, greet then pull him in, greet then pull him into the wood. He grasped its tail, and looked with desperate eyes at his comrade. The other nodded and sawed on. When they stopped three hours later for their first bread and water, Eynarr took out a bottle, poured a pool of tea-coloured fluid into his palm, and wiped it on his neck and face. As he followed with a rag, his face shone through, the gum dissolved. He handed the petrol bottle to van Baerle, who did the same.

'Get yourself a bottle and I'll show you where to find this stuff,' the big man offered. 'Shall I relieve you of that hair?'

'Now?'

'It won't take long.'

Van Baerle's hair, which reached down to his shoulders, had seemed no hindrance till the day before, but now it formed a helmet. His partner drew a clasp knife from his coat and folded out a sharp-edged blade. He made a cut into the skein above the forehead, then sliced down either side. He sawed, moved round the dirt-filled mass, then freed it in one piece and raised it like a fibrous crown. Cornelius regarded the gritty wig, and considered it might make a wild bee's nest, or a pigeon's. He ran a palm over the irregular bristles of his scalp, and nodded at the improvement. Then a guard announced the resumption of their labour.

'Survive a month and you'll survive two years,' Eynarr told him when they stopped again.

'Two years? I'm here for ten.'

'Nobody works longer than two years in the forest,' said Eynarr. 'After two years everybody retires.'

'Retires?'

A new school

OLBOY CHANGED schools. And his fame went before him.

'So you're the runner,' his new games master said. 'Do you do anything else?'

'Sometimes I jump,' Dolboy answered.

'Jump high, or jump long?'

Dolboy considered for a moment, then answered:

'It depends what's in the way, sir.'

On his first day at his new school he sat calmly in his seat, with exercise books on his desk, and his mind open to receive the unknown world that lay before him. He had begun to see that the beauty of natural things, of woods and fields, and moths, was echoed in a realm that man had made, of words and images and music. Now, he thought, his education would seem sweet, consisting of these things. The next instant the door burst open from a kick, and swung to smash against the wall. A man whose hair stood in wings on either side of his dome thrust in with his gown flowing out behind, and two dozen books under each arm. Without interrupting his headlong progress, the master kicked backward with one foot to strike the door, from years of practice, as it rebounded from the wall, and sent it crashing shut.

The boys gasped and tittered at this virtuoso entry, until the master slammed his volumes down and screamed:

'What's funny? You!'

A stick of chalk flew like a tiny arrow from his hand to strike a boy who, laughing to his neighbour, had failed to discern that the master's intention had not been humorous.

'Well? What's funny?' Mr Hendriks screamed again.

'Nothing, sir,' the target boy replied.

'So why are you laughing?' the master barked, and without waiting for a reply, since none was expected, he threw a textbook at the boy, and ordered:

'Get out you idiot! And don't come back until you've copied chapter ten, in ink. Get out with you!'

He threw another stick of chalk to help the entertained one on his way, and swept the class from side to side with wild eyes, as if seeking a further challenge. This was a procedure he adopted with every new group of boys he encountered, and it established beyond any ambiguity the nature of his relationship with them, and ensured that the boys remembered it accurately over a period of years. Once, when no one laughed at his entry, he threw the chalk anyway, and as the boy who sustained a white dot on his cheek denied he was amused, the master simply added to his script:

'Don't argue, boy,' and then sailed on to: 'Don't come back until you've copied chapter ten.'

Chapter ten was the longest chapter in *The Geography and Geology of Venezuela*, a work which remained in Dolboy's possession for a further five years, and which he was never once called upon to read. Its purpose was entirely punitive.

The new school was an obstacle course of rules not known

about until you broke them. Dolboy imagined his foreignness increased his vulnerability, but the system did not recognise such distinctions; its opacity applied to natives and immigrants alike.

'What day is this?' a prefect screamed at point-blank range.

'Friday, mister,' was Dolboy's innocent reply.

'It's Founder's Birthday, stupid boy,' the youth screamed on, and waited for a response. None came, and he continued:

'And what don't we ever do on Founder's Birthday, stupid boy?'

Dolboy searched his mind and drew another blank. The agent of authority remedied his ignorance.

'We don't dress as if we're going to the bloody races, stupid boy!'

'What do you mean, mister?' Dolboy had never seen a horse race.

'The jacket, stupid boy! This is a black jacket day. And lose the rainbow tie. It's black and white. Everything must be black and white. Write out one hundred times: "I must not be a stupid boy on Founder's Birthday", stupid boy, and bring them by tomorrow.'

Dolboy liked the red, green and gold stripes of his new school tie, and never suspected there might be occasions on which it was taboo. Who was Founder, and how old was he? Why did he enjoy such influence in the school?

Acting on the brainwave of a classmate, Dolboy fixed three pens in tandem with elastic bands, and spaced them with two rubbers. He dipped the three steel nibs in three inkpots, and scrawled his punishment in triplicate, a scratchy, blotted text, but undeniably 'I must not be a stupid boy on Founder's Birthday', one hundred times. The prefects expected subterfuge, and tore impositions into shreds without a count. He joined a queue of punished boys outside their hut, and listened while each prefect met his victim with ingratitude.

'Next time it'll be three hundred ... Can't bloody spell ... Late again ... Learn to write ... What's this? Your granny's will?'

When Dolboy's man came to the door, he heard:

'Jesus! Who wrote this? A bloody spider?'

The policeman rolled the pages into a tube and tried to strike Dolboy's head with it, but Dolboy ducked and ran.

Another day a messenger approached at morning break and summoned Dolboy to the prefects' lodge, where an elongated senior appeared, holding a rugby ball.

'Observe, sprog, the behaviour of this solid,' he instructed, and set the ball down on its pointed end, so it fell over. Dolboy observed.

'Well,' the prefect demanded. 'What do you see?'

'Something which is not a solid, mister. It's filled with air.'

'Impertinent sprog! Take one hundred lines: "I must not be impertinent to my betters." Now, let's say this form is solid. What do you observe of its behaviour?'

He stood the ball on end again, and again it fell over. Dolboy could not resist a further cleverness, and answered:

'Mister, it's drunk.'

The prefect made his face look stern, and hissed:

'If any jokes are to be made, I'll be the one to make them, you horrible sprog. Make that imposition two hundred lines. Now shall we go on? I'll ask again: what do you see?'

Dolboy shrugged, and took a course he hoped would spare him further punishment.

'Mister, a pointed ball can't stand on its ends.'

'Precisely so, impertinent sprog. This ball is designed to fit under the arm of a runner. If the runner wishes to kick the ball he must drop it, point first, and punt it once. He must not attempt to dribble it around the field like a football, as you were doing. If we had wished to play football at this school, instead of rugby, we should have supplied ourselves with spherical balls.'

A small group of Dolboy's companions, who had gathered to watch, smothered their laughter as the prefect continued in the vein of elevated sarcasm with which such appointees customarily addressed lesser life forms.

'Now, if you wish to play football – and you may wish it: some people do – I suggest you take yourself off to some place where it is the practice. In the meantime, if you decide to remain here, write one hundred times: "I must not treat a rugby ball as if it were a football." And never, never, never let me see you dribble a ball on these fields again, you horrible, impertinent sprog.'

The knot of Dolboy's friends could not contain their laughter further, and howled in unison as the superior being placed his hallowed ball under one arm and retreated to the sanctum of authority.

The selection of clothing, then, was to be approached with caution (though there was little enough scope for variation), and the treatment of game balls. Why was there no list pinned on a board, in which these strictures featured prominently, Dolboy asked himself. If such a list had been compiled, it would have been extensive, and it would have saved him pain during his first attempts to eat meals in that secretive establishment.

The food there had an odour unlike that of any he had smelled in kitchens in his own land: it gave off the musty air he remembered breathing when he turned over a log in the woods. The dining hall was impregnated with the vapours of burned puddings and meats. Its panelled walls yielded a thousand remembrances of ancient cod, and onion pies, while eminences in niches up above held in their marble nostrils memories of Irish stew. Its tables bore the patina of sauces spilled on gravies spilled on custards.

The boys filed in silence into the hall, a master said grace, and within an instant of amen, the refectory was filled with the tumult of five hundred boys shouting to each other from table to table, shouting to each other at closer range, and shouting for the trouble of it. One-tenth of them milled about to carry plates between the hatches and the tables, while the tiny garrison of masters chosen for the day patrolled serenely, with hands clasped behind their backs, as if oblivious to the uproar.

Dolboy felt sick when first he entered that chamber of odours. When the hatches were flung open and their steaming vapours issued over the battlefield, his nausea was magnified, and when he was presented with the solids responsible for the miasma, he rose at once and ran outside. A prefect found him bending over a trickle of fluid which his stomach had thrown up in protection.

'Come back inside at once,' the officer ordered.

Dolboy shook his head, and spat to clear the remnants of his bile.

'Unless you're sick, come back at once.'

This time Dolboy nodded.

'Yes, I'm sick.'

'In that case report to the sick bay. You can't just funk a meal and walk away.'

The next day he performed again, but this time he was ordered back and given water.

'Nurse says there's nothing wrong with you,' the prefect told him. 'You have to eat.'

His stomach heaved at every delivery it received of Pom, a mashed potato substitute, helped down with water. Nevertheless, he cleared a small space in his portion, and laid his tools down side by side, considering his duty done. But when the servers cleared the plates before a second course, they left Dolboy's in place. The plates of sago came, with decorations of diluted jam, and when the servers came and cleared again, Dolboy was left with two unfinished portions at his place.

'What's the trouble here?' another prefect asked.

'Please, mister, I've finished,' Dolboy said. 'I can't eat any more.'

The other boys at his table cheered and laughed at his delicacy.

'Mistaken in both particulars,' the prefect told him. 'Clearly you have not finished, since there is food on the table. And by deduction you can eat some more, since you have hardly eaten anything yet. Every plate must go back clean. Eat up before I come again.'

'Why must I, if I am not hungry and I don't like what I'm given?' Dolboy wished to know. 'Why must every plate be clean?'

'Because it is the rule,' the prefect answered.

The rules again. Where were they written?

'But I didn't know that,' Dolboy tried.

193

The boys all laughed again as the prefect strolled on his round, and one of them made Dolboy an offer:

'I'll do the sago, for sixpence.'

'What do you mean?'

'Give me sixpence and I'll eat your pudding. If it gets any colder it'll cost more.'

Dolboy handed over a coin, and his neighbour took his spoon, lowered his chin to the level of the table, and consumed the lumpy slop with a continuous, shovelling motion. When he had finished, Dolboy had a question.

'How much for the other?'

The eating machine surveyed the cold Pom, the gristly stew, the yellow paste of Brussels sprouts and made his calculation.

'One and six the lot,' he offered.

Dolboy considered this a deliverance. He handed over more money, but instead of eating the cold mess, his helper reached into the pocket of his jacket for three folded brown paper bags. He checked that no authority observed, then scraped Dolboy's food with a knife into one of the bags. This bag he placed into a second bag, which sagged and showed damp spots before he placed it in the third. For security he wrapped the soft lump in a handkerchief, and placed the whole collection gingerly in his pocket. The prefect returned after several minutes and examined the clean plates. He looked at Dolboy's face, and at the faces of the other boys, then ordered:

'Very good! Server: take these plates.'

'He knows you didn't eat it,' whispered the boy with the fat pocket. 'But he doesn't care where it goes, so long as every plate goes back clean. Now you know, you can bring your own bags tomorrow. Everybody does.'

'It's like Oliver Twist in reverse,' one of the others observed. 'Please, sir, can I not have some more?'

They all laughed and filed out to kick a pointed ball in an approved manner.

Race strategy

AFTER HIS FIRST sports day at the school, Dolboy's identity was redefined: van Baerle the fussy eater became van Baerle the runner. The athletics supervisor of his junior house had been advised he was a gem, and at its trials Dolboy qualified unchallenged for the three events available to first-year boys: a hundred-yard flat race, eighty over hurdles, and a two-hundred-and-twenty-yard sprint.

A hundred yards race is like the flutterings of a butterfly. You take a breath and hold it. You're off! You give your body over to a paroxysm. And then it's past. No strategy is called for. You flail the hardest you can flail, and there's an end of it. Dolboy won the race for boys his age. A hurdles race is similar, but tiresomely scattered. Dolboy won. The furlong sprint is like the hundred yards: you run your fastest all the way, but have a longer time to fade away. Dolboy won the event, and reflected that he did not enjoy these ephemeral explosions. There was no time in them to feel his body's perfect functioning, no time to match the beating of his legs and heart, no time to think. He much preferred to look around and breathe the scents of nature as he sailed along a landscape course.

He had never been beaten in a running race, and it never

occurred to him that he ever would be beaten. Running was his quintessential locomotion, it was his nature and his lifeblood, while others turned to it from time to time, and then they walked. The little runner, *'t rennertje*, had trotted hours on end, day after day, and but for the interruption of his studies, he, the bigger boy, would do the same. It was his special quality that marked him out from others. He ran. So, when he stood at the start of the junior school half-mile race, and looked from side to side on boys who shaved, he felt no fear.

An athlete chosen by his house as one of two to run the race had bruised his foot, and must drop out. Others of that year had run already and were exhausted. The year below held hardly any prospect, but one year further down was Dolboy, the cross-country star.

'It's much faster than cross-country, you realise, no steady jog,' the master warned his last resort.

'I'll do my best, sir,' Dolboy promised.

He tried to construct a strategy based on his old teacher's reasoning about cross-country, but there seemed nothing tangible to cater for. With only eight boys in the race there was no crowd to clear, no stiles or narrow paths to gain before another, and no chasm over which to risk a limb. The course was flat and clear. His cross-country plan had been to start off with a sprint. He followed with a distance at a quieter pace, until his heartbeat steadied and he had the breath to sprint again. It worked across the countryside, so why not use it here? He decided on a set of sprints and recoveries, without regard to other runners' efforts. A thousand miles eastward the same strategy occurred to Vladimir Kuts, and one morning soon, Dolboy would listen with his fellows to a radio broadcast of the ten thousand metres final from the Olympic Games, in which such wild tactics, the commentator said, amounted to suicide, before the great Kuts murdered opposition.

A ribald cheer and hoots of laughter rose when Dolboy burst off from the gun as if he ran the hundred yards again. The athletics master shook his head, then screwed his eyes and rubbed his palm across them. When Dolboy slowed, according to his plan, five runners thudded past and drew ahead, more as a demonstration of contempt than as a tactic. He counted out the distance on the track that he should rest, then burst into his second sprint. Three glanced aside, surprised that he should come again, and saw him pass, but two in front resisted. The instinct of the undefeated urged him to hold his speed until the others flagged, but from his training he remembered that his lungs would heave if he passed fifty strides, and he would have too long to wait before he breathed again with comfort. And so he slowed, and counted on, and waited.

He burst again, and again the two in front responded. At the third attempt he overhauled the second boy and ran beside the leader, while the soprano screaming of his contemporaries registered their delight that an upset threatened. Their joy faded to a moan when Dolby's sprinting distance was covered, and he dropped to a slower pace again, while the other pulled ahead. The watchers thought Dolboy's effort had been eccentric, but remarkable. If he trailed home now, in second or third place, he would be a hero. If he dropped out, he would be remembered.

But Dolboy was busy with a different calculation. His last sprint would be in the straight, with seventy-five yards to the tape. He prepared himself not to slow this time, to keep his place at the other's shoulder without thought of any other outcome but victory. He set his jaw, and summoning his determination to remain unbeaten, burst again, like Kuts, into a sprint.

The tunnel of boys along the home straight resounded with a tumult of discordant voices shouting names, while arms and fists and programmes urged the runners on, but Dolboy heard only a monotone, a background boil of sea on shingle somewhere past his breath and pounding feet. The crowd leaned in to cheer, and Dolboy clenched his teeth and watched the bobbing line. The two ran side by side for forty yards, then Dolboy's rival turned to look at him. He saw the face of someone who would not be beaten, someone who was determined beyond reason to persist, and to prevail. He saw the mechanical motions of Dolboy's piston arms and piston legs, and he faltered. Then he yielded.

When he had passed the tape and taken twenty yards to stop (abrupt halts were a cause of strains), Dolboy trotted back to shake hands with the boy he had beaten. The boy sat on the ground, with hands clasped round his knees and his head hanging down. He looked up and extended his trembling arm, and Dolboy felt a new emotion: pity. The humbled creature screwed his face with pain to catch his breath, and in his eyes were tears of shame. Why had he, who ran for pleasure, been so insistent on victory? When motion in itself was so delightful, why must he employ it to secure another's pain? The structures demanded it: a hierarchy must exist in every sphere, so those who were to lead might stand apart from those who followed. Boys must learn that beating somebody less fitted was not

Sex

DOLBOY WAS an impressionable creature. On his first day at his new school he had felt a fearful thrill as he joined a file of new blazers standing before the ranks of older hands in the great hall for morning worship. The murmuring which had accompanied their assembly gave way by common consent, and at no apparent signal, to a silence which prevailed until the headmaster and the head boy strode to the podium and together began to sing the school hymn: 'I Vow to Thee, My Country'. They were supplemented immediately by a great wave of five hundred voices, whose particular reverberations of bass, baritone and tenor made the backs of Dolboy's hands contract and tingle. It was not his country they were vowing to serve, and he was devoid of religious inclinations, but for no reason he knew, the noise of so many boys' voices shaking the windows invoked in him a swell of emotion of which no other sound was ever capable. When at the beginning of the second verse an organ joined the fray, the assault was irresistible. Dolboy would have enlisted without hesitation, had a recruiting sergeant appeared to take names.

And at the end of each year, when boys like him embarked on a sea voyage to their homes, he was scarcely able to maintain his composure as the school assembled to beseech the Almighty to secure their safe passage. His throat constricted on the mere recitation of its words:

> Eternal father, strong to save,
> Whose arm hath bound the restless wave . . .
> Oh hear us when we cry to thee
> For those in peril on the sea.

How could He not respond positively to a request couched in such noble phrases, and given voice by such a plangent choir? Dolboy took ship on the black North Sea, convinced that safe passage could not be denied him.

As his former teacher had foretold, his name appeared in newspapers. 'The National Junior Cross-Country Champion,' the headmaster declaimed, and held the shield aloft while the five hundred cheered, and Dolboy walked to the platform to receive their praise at morning prayers. Despite a variety of misbehaviours in the next few years, Dolboy was never again asked by a prefect to write out impositions, because of his status as an athlete. Among the plankton cloud of junior boys he shone as one whom everybody knew: van Baerle the runner, van Baerle the famous one.

In spite of his status, however, he was not content, having decided that it had been a mistake to acquiesce in his confinement to an establishment populated almost exclusively by males. Females of any age or state were cause for feverishness in that unnatural fraternity, the mere suggestion of a female. He was not alone among the pupils in picturing in its liberated state the buttressed bosom of the nurse who diagnosed and dosed their illnesses. As the sturdy woman bound him for an injured rib, he stared in defiance of every distraction to memorise the jostling flesh that made her tunic animated. And he joined the queue of inflamed boys willing to pay a coin to keep for one day a stocking, guaranteed to have been removed by a prefect from the leg of the school secretary. The authenticity of the relic was in doubt, but it was a stocking, it was not new, and its foot smelled of a foot. The thing had been in intimate proximity with female flesh: whose flesh was neither here nor there. If you drew it on your hand and closed your eyes to kiss your knuckle, it was transmogrified into a bony instep.

The school stood on the ancient floodplain of a river, where every year the landscape drowned, while cattle gathered on small knolls, and farms lay like islands in the mist. The town to which the school belonged extended across a ridge of tired sandstone, with the tallest church spire for two hundred miles, and several buildings still displaying cannon holes, with shot inside, from the civil war three hundred years before, by which date the school had already celebrated its centenary.

Each Saturday, privileged boys were allowed three hours of liberty in the town. There was nothing to do there but moon around the newsagents and market stalls in groups, and conclude with tea and cakes, but it was a reprieve from institutional life for those judged worthy of reward: the prefects, sportsmen and top five academics in each class. Van Baerle the runner qualified. He began to dream, not any more of purest Mirjam, but of the girls he saw in town: the tough and ruddy market girls, who teased the fancy boys with promises there was no time to keep;

the pouting waitresses; and girls who went to school themselves, and looked for romance in his category. In dreams their possibilities were fulfilled, their promises redeemed.

At length, the knot of friends he drifted with forsook the shops and market stalls, and marched each week to the upstairs room of a faded restaurant, where only twenty years before a band had played for *thés dansants*. Now, between the art deco pillars of this elongated chamber, powdered women sat at wicker tables topped with glass, engorging cakes in intervals between bouts of buying hats, and teenage schoolgirls gossiped over hours-old pots of tea.

The ritual of communication between these tantalising creatures and the boys of Dolboy's tribe was elaborately wasteful of the mere chink of free time they enjoyed each week. Groups of four or five boys and groups of four or five girls huddled over tables with their backs to the world, until, as if to confirm some observation made by one of them, the girls of some group would turn in unison to inspect the backs of boys at a distant table, or the boys would interrupt their conference to focus on a female clutch. This connection between platoons having been established, tentatively, it remained to be determined which individual in either group sought the approval of an individual in the other.

A messenger was despatched: a sign that he or she was not personally implicated in the quest. If the girls went first, their representative enquired if any in the boys' group admired girl A. In place of a direct answer, the boys returned a query of their own: did any at the girls' table admire boy B. If this was a match, the messenger returned with confirmation; if not, she asked if any there admired another girl, girl C, who had responded to the naming of boy B. By this formula, nobody suffered outright rejection, the beautiful ones secured the pairings they desired, and the others had the pleasure of being linked, in theory, with members of the opposite sex remaining. In practice, it was time to return to school.

After many months of this courtship quiz, the names of certain boys became attached to those of certain girls. They might speak briefly to each other, or exchange notes, and older boys would even walk ten minutes with their loved ones in the town. But the rule forbidding contact, like all others in that ancient institution, was no less binding for being unwritten. It was understood. Accordingly, like most forbidden things, contact was all the more desired. It must eventually occur. And this is how it did:

A sportive girl, reporting that her parents would be absent for the day, declared her home a space where boys and girls might meet the following week. The boys talked every day of what they planned to do, and Dolboy half believed the girls would let them, as if the distant signalling of their Saturdays concealed lascivious natures, waiting for release. But when the day arrived, the girls proved what they had appeared to be: five strangers who seemed inviting from across a room. Like the mothers they had seen receiving guests, they asked who wanted tea, and handed sandwiches and cakes around. And then they sat, all ten, and joked and chattered as if no subject were further from their minds than touching hands, and touching lips, than touching anything.

With two hours gone, the awful realisation dawned that they had wasted time in nervous niceties, and couples grew abruptly amorous. Each pair was allocated private space, and Dolboy joined his chums in frantic compensation for their earlier reserve. He found himself on a settee, with a view of flooded fields extending as far toward the horizon as the mist permitted, and a girl with eyes that shone as if they too were flooded, but with drops of glycerine. His partner, Valerie, reclined on a cushion with a seraphic smile.

There were candytwist candlesticks on the oak mantelpiece, and on the sideboard a pewter teapot, jug and sugar bowl, from Liberty's. Valerie had stopped talking, and lay before him while the minutes ticked toward five o'clock. The afternoon light was failing, and the room was filled with shadows from the licking fire. A flowery perfume rose from Valerie, her skin glowed with excitement, and her breast rose and fell gently beneath an oatmeal-coloured sweater of angora wool.

Everything was soft and perfect, and Dolboy, whose dreams brimmed with carnality, wanted only to stroke her fine hair and kiss her cheek. But all around, he knew, the other boys and other girls were devouring each other, creating stories to be elaborated for months to come. Like a moth in Mirjam's mating chamber, her house of irresistible desire, he felt compelled by an atmosphere of enveloping lust to act. He kissed his partner's mouth and felt her clutch him with unexpected strength. Her hands wrapped the back of his head, and their kissing became one kiss that would not end.

This was Dolboy's first sensation of joy in the arms of a girl, and it would have been enough to fill his dreams for an entire year. But more was expected of this expeditionary force. He must return to headquarters with a rewarding report. Expecting to be repelled, he cupped his palm over Valerie's angora-clothed chest, and still she kissed him. He fumbled next between her shoulder blades, and she reached back to loose the catch and let him in. She smiled her glycerine-washed, angelic smile, when Dolboy touched, then held her breast, and as they kissed and pressed their bodies close, it seemed a rhythm grew, until he shuddered in her arms, and still she kissed and stroked him.

Mirjam was his ideal form, his soul's partner, but Valerie could claim the status of a landmark in his memory.

The convict

A S DOLBOY'S FATHER cut more trees, his bloody palms grew scabs. The movement of the axe shaft polished them, and when they cracked, the skin beneath was thick, like burnished horn. His hands, which had been soft and supple, became two brackets, hooked to grip the handles of the axe and saw. He walked with his arms hanging loose, and his fingers curling inward, like an ape's. His body grew less smooth as the layer of fat between his skin and muscle was dissolved. His muscles hardened, but did not increase to fill his looser skin: for that you needed food. He seemed to be another self, a sinewy, tougher thing, that moved like snakes beneath his rags. His pine-stained face grew thin, but there the skin shrank too, to hold the prominences of sharpened nose and cheeks, his narrowed lips, the sockets where his desperation gleamed. His stubbled head was covered by a pirate cap of cloth, set by the resin to a hard, neat fit, and across his chest his breastplate was the jacket of a dead man, reversed and tied with string. He had become a convict.

With Eynarr, the other half of his machine, he sliced through the forest face. The obstacles of timber fell on either side, and they chewed forward through the stems, working wordlessly in unison, as if they shared one brain. As the guard had foretold in his first days at the colony, Cornelius thought often while he sawed and chopped of those moments when he would lie in his hole in the ground, and pull the heather over him, and see the clouds and stars above before he slept. That pause in watchfulness and fear, that idleness that measured minutes seemed like a benediction, and the smell of sand and heather heavenly.

Like others of the sleepers in the earth, he excavated here and there to make his burrow fit his shape. He changed the oblong to a diamond hole, for comfort when he lay on his side, with knees drawn up for warmth. He brought from the forest sheets of bark to place above the heather when it rained, and kindling for a fire. Although they were condemned to have no time of their own, the groundlings lit fires when they returned from their labours, and sat for an hour to warm themselves, and drink decoctions of leaves and roots which they had found in the woods. Sometimes they brought back mushrooms, a dead bird, or an animal to roast on a spit. For those who had only water for their supper, the swallowing of digestive juices summoned by the smell of meat was tormenting. For those who ate, enjoyment was diminished by encircling eyes, and lips and tongues that moved to taste the morsel in imagination.

Now that the prisoners destined to die from the first shock of heavy labour had done so, the survivors devoted themselves to securing sufficient food, warmth, and rest, to continue in life. Their struggle was unequal. The amount of energy they consumed in the pursuit of timber, or in making roads, was more than they could secure from their inadequate rations. The deficit was made good by the consumption of the muscular tissue with which they arrived. Their quest for warmth and rest was no more than an attempt to slow the rate of attrition, to delay the dissolution of their bodies.

As the days grew short, Cornelius sat by his fire at night and held his hands in the flames without feeling any pain. When frost thickened on the ground, he scraped the embers of the fire into his trench, covered them with sand and heather, lay down himself, then pulled a layer of fronds and bark sheets over. As he dozed in the smoky sandwich, and felt his chamber warmed by the smouldering fragments, he thought he could imagine no greater luxury. And then he devised one. He remembered handwarmers which country folk had used in his childhood: tins of hot charcoal, with nail holes in both ends, which workers tucked inside their coats in winter. When they grew cold, they put the tins in loops of string and whirled them round until the charcoal sparked, then wrapped them in a sock and cupped them in their hands. Cornelius scraped around the huts to find a tin, which every morning he filled with charcoal from the ground beneath him. At night, before he spread the embers in his bed, he placed one glowing fragment at the centre of his tin and blew until the charcoal lit. He wrapped it in a cloth, then wrapped himself around its heat. He woke at intervals to turn, and when he did, he remembered his tin of heat, and blew into the punctures of its ends until its glimmer lit his tomb and warmed his hands to help him live.

When snow came, it seemed less cold at night. An insulating layer built up above his hole, and the wind no longer lifted his roof of bark. A dry wind blowing from the Arctic was to be feared more than snow: it froze the ground like iron, and people in it. Cornelius soaked the rim of his pit when the wind blew, and held his barks in place until they froze fast. Sleepers whose coverings had blown away were lifted out like planks in the mornings, and stacked on a cart with two prisoners between the shafts instead of a horse. When it snowed, their sleeping ground looked like any other cemetery: a field of cocoons, whitely blanketed. The guards arrived with poles to probe the ground, and the even hummocks heaved and gave up a gaunt regiment in rags, with frozen earth for decoration. Where the cocoons remained unbroken, the men with the cart delved for their cargo.

The numbers sleeping in the ground diminished. Some perished: admitted to themselves the odds against them were too great, and gave up in the night. Others were rehoused, not by a camp administrator, but by someone who knew where death was looking next. Eynarr, van Baerle's partner in the timber gang, informed him one day:

'I know a place where somebody will die tonight. Do you want his bed?'

Cornelius knew he could not survive an entire winter in the ground. His embers warmed the earth an hour or so, his tin of charcoal served to heat his hands and chest and nothing more. Before spring came he would lose his toes to frostbite, and his feet, and with them his life.

'Of course,' he answered.

'When we go back tonight, come with me,' Eynarr said.

There was no weather but a blizzard judged unfit for felling pine. When the snow blew in a white wall two strides before their faces, the citizens of the punishment colony huddled around stoves in their huts. Some sleepers in the open ground emerged and joined the men who clustered round the oil-drum fires, while others turned like pupae in their tombs and waited for another day. In all other conditions work continued. When rain fell in a sheet, the haulers of timber floundered on hands and knees to keep their tree trunks in motion over the mud slick that snaked from the treeline to the sawmill. And when the wind swayed the ice-heavy conifers until they shrieked and toppled of their own accord, the foresters worked on. They worked to keep from freezing where they stood, and broke the ice to drink.

On such days the timber resonated at a higher pitch under the stroke of the axe. As Cornelius and Eynarr struck the brittle trunks, darts of frozen pine wood flew and scored their cheeks, and they moved like zombies on their stiff legs to swing their mechanical arms. On such days, when a cry rose from the tree fellers, the numbed trimmers and haulers paused to look up, and murmured a prayer. Sometimes they closed their eyes and murmured on, because they had no strength to move from the arc of the tree that crashed down on them. The two worked through such a day, when crystals of ice shot on the wind to sting the cuts that streaked their cheeks. And when it was already dark, they trudged back to camp to find a place where Cornelius might stay alive.

'The comrade seemed dead last night,' Eynarr told him. 'Then this morning when they came to take him from his bed, he refused to go. He made one last effort to remain in the world. The guard let him lie; he crossed himself and said a prayer. But this was his last day, I know.'

Cornelius followed between rows of windowless cabins until they arrived at a doorway hung with thick oilcloth. Eynarr raised the folds, and Cornelius pushed through an inner curtain to a room lit with the amber light of tallow candles. It was half filled with the smoke of a stove constructed from two jerricans and a length of pipe that stopped short of the roof. Eynarr inclined his head to show their direction, and they passed slowly between rows of wooden bunks, three layers high, the brothers of the beds he had seen on the day of his capture by the liberating army. As in that other place, he was met with stillness, and when he crossed the alley, listless eyes followed him, while from time to time he heard a feeble cough or moan.

'Well, brother,' said Eynarr, resting his hand on the grey blanket that covered the shoulder of a man who lay on one side, with his cheek resting on his palm. 'One day closer to freedom.'

The man remained motionless, but his eyes opened: the bright, expectant eyes that Cornelius had seen before in the sockets of the nearly-dead. The face was covered by taut parchment, marked with feverish blotches and drawn tight at the lips to expose clenched teeth. The giant Eynarr touched the thin shoulder with the utmost tenderness, and the dying creature constricted his lips to smile.

'Consumption,' Eynarr murmured. 'He has a fierce spirit, but his struggle is almost over. I will stay with him tonight, and you may use my bed. Tomorrow, when he has gone, this will be yours.'

They left the hut and walked to another one nearby, where Eynarr took van Baerle to his own sleeping place.

'Can you be sure he will go tonight?' Cornelius asked.

'Yes,' Eynarr answered. 'He has suffered long enough.'

Comradeship

SOMETIMES when he lay on the boards of his inside, above-ground bed, wearing all of the clothes he possessed, and with his warming tin clasped in the folds of his hunched body, van Baerle yearned for the smell of smouldering branches, and their warmth in the ground beneath him. But when morning came, and he still felt life below his knees, and in his back and shoulders, he knew he had arrived at a better place, a place where he could survive a little longer.

For forest workers it was a blessing of winter that the days were short. Van Baerle arrived back at his wooden home an hour after dark, and had two hours to wait before the others in his hut returned from work in their illuminated factories. He sat by the light of a single candle, made from the fat of a sheep, and fed the stove with wood he had brought the previous day, while laying out to dry the branches he had just retrieved. During this interval of recovery, Eynarr would come to visit the memory of his dead comrade. The two foresters placed their tin bowls on the stove to boil their water. They sprinkled it with roasted root of dandelion, and let it boil some more. Then they sat to drink, with their elbows on their knees and their bowls cupped in their hands, burning their faces in the glow that escaped from cracks in the stove. Eynarr was a veteran of the Finnish campaign, whose crime was to have seen foreign ways. He had warred across the northern snows and back again, but all his memories were of childhood, as if a curtain fell to keep that precious time from all that followed. Their conversations consisted of monologues, episodes suggested by the other's stories, and insights from the depths to which their lives had led.

'My mission was to bear witness to the other camps,' Cornelius recalled. 'I was to accomplish that by walking the landscape, and standing in the trees to watch from a distance.'

He paused, and the two regarded each other's firelit face until they both gave way to quiet, shuddering laughter.

'Quite a plan,' Eynarr allowed. 'Do you think perhaps some gentleman comes to stand in the woods and observe our situation? Perhaps we should clean ourselves up a little, to give a better impression.'

They laughed again, without bitterness, at the absurd expedition which had brought van Baerle to his present pass.

'We both look like trolls,' Eynarr admitted. 'But you should have seen me when I was nine, and I came home after a day of wading in the bog to collect cranberries. My face was torn by thorns, and both hands dripped scarlet juice. My mother fell to her knees and thanked God for visiting her with the Christ child.'

'And then?'

'And then she beat me, of course – not so much for destroying good shoes as for failing to be divine.'

Van Baerle resumed his own narrative.

'The troubling thing was that although my task was futile, and

I could see nothing of those people's lives, I knew what they consisted of. I understood by instinct the depravities to which they would be subjected. And when I went inside the camp, it was just so. I had been capable in my imagination of devising appropriate torture for creatures at my disposal. So: am I no better than the worst of those unfortunates' keepers, no better than ours?'

They fell silent a while, then Eynarr said:

'When I was a boy I kept rabbits. I stroked and spoiled them every day. Then one year the winter was hard, and we had little food. So I went out and killed my rabbits. They were the same rabbits I had loved and petted, but I killed them without regret, and we ate them and lived.'

Cornelius wondered if this memory bore connection with his questions.

'They were my family,' the big man explained. 'I loved them. The worst that man can be lies in us all. You have enjoyed the good fortune of never having to avail yourself of those resources. But sometimes the opportunity of behaving decently is denied us, and we have no choice but to behave like beasts.'

'Surely,' van Baerle suggested, 'we always have that choice: to yield or not yield to our baser natures is not a matter of circumstance.'

'You answer your own questions, tovarich. But place yourself in the position of a man who has the choice of behaving like a brute or being shot. Do you imagine the distinction between moral choice and circumstance would be so clear? Do you think these creatures who drive us every day are expressing their choice? Don't you believe in other circumstances they would be happy to share a cigarette with us?'

Van Baerle broke off his speculations about mankind's nature, and both men sipped their decoction of dandelion, and stared at the heat in silence, until Eynarr volunteered a coda.

'Some of my rabbits had escaped and become wild. They were the lucky ones.'

They each considered the mawkish conclusion of their philosophising, and gave way once more to quiet laughter.

The toll

NEW SUBJECTS for correction arrived, new enemies of the state. Some took abandoned pits in the heather ground, some slept on bare earth that was too hard to dig. Some, who understood that they would die if they lay exposed to weather, crept at night into the log huts, and huddled together like litters of ragged dogs. Every morning when van Baerle was trotted to the trees, he saw the corpse collectors' cart, piled high.

New men came to work in the forest, men with arms and chests roped with muscle, and fat on their cheeks. Van Baerle was separated from Eynarr and given an apprentice of his own. While he chopped and sawed without thought, he saw his helper agonise as he had done, and quake before the day was half-way through. The novice swung his axe arrhythmically, and buried it in the wood; he snatched the saw and held it back.

'Work slow and steady,' Cornelius called. 'And if you are unable to pull, just hold; don't hang on the saw.'

He saw the rounded face grow haggard in a day or two, the eyes seek desperately some sign of hope, and find none. He read the calculations in the new man's brain that multiplied his pain by ten years, twenty, twenty-five. There was no use in telling him he would forget those sums, those unjust numbers meant for someone else, and think instead of evening's rest, the stove, and sleeping through one night. He must arrive at that knowledge by his own route, or die of despair.

The dank days of late winter turning into spring brought new hazards to the amphitheatre of chopping and sawing. Sometimes when a cry went up from the tree fellers, the trimmers and the haulers were still searching for the hazard when the trunk of a tree materialised out of fog, and they were crushed. At day's end their bodies were stripped and returned to the camp for registration. If there was uncertainty about their state, if someone stirred or murmured, registration removed all doubt. If some naked victim raised his head while jolted on the ox-cart ride, a guard returned him to unconsciousness. There was no infirmary in the camp; its citizens were well or dead.

Eynarr still came to drink and muse before van Baerle's stove. When he was absent for three days, Cornelius went to look for him. The veteran lay on the rough wood of his cot, his eyes gleaming like splits in the skin of a yellow apple, the hollows deep below his cheekbones where his teeth once filled the space. Both men were sinewy shadows of the two who worked like clockwork blades before the winter came.

'Eynarr,' Cornelius murmured. 'Are you sick?'

The bundled figure stirred, and seemed to puzzle for an answer.

'I have no strength,' he rasped. 'Last week I had it. Then in one day it deserted me.'

He spoke of his strength as if it were an ungrateful animal.

Prisoners who came to the end of their resources did so gradually. Van Baerle had seen them wither day by day on every side. They grew thin, their teeth fell out, their hair, their fingers fell off, and their toes. They moved ever more sluggishly until their last reserves were gone. But Eynarr, though his skin shone tightly on his skull, and his hands had become large claws, had shown no sign of his decline. He had held himself firm, resisting small hesitations, denying that he faltered. He would not admit he was defeated. But he was, as were they all.

Cornelius raised his friend, and brought him warm water to drink, and fed him a fist of bread which he had stolen two days before, when the man who served their gruel had looked away.

'The worst of the winter is over,' he said. 'Work will be easier as the days grow less cold. You must work as slowly as you can, and I will try to find some food.'

Eynarr's tongue came out of his head and ran along his tight, dry lips.

'I feel that I must lie and sleep a whole week,' he whispered.

'Sleep now, and then tomorrow let your partner take the lead,' said Cornelius. 'If we still worked together . . .'

He interrupted his futile speculation, and covered Eynarr with his coat. Then he reached into a pocket for his warming tin, set the charcoal glowing from the stove, and pressed it into Eynarr's hands.

'This will help you to stay warm. Perhaps tomorrow you will have some of your strength again. Don't despair, friend: everyone here must expect to feel weak. But don't despair.'

It was a pointless message. When a man who has been strong all his life finds one day that he is weak, despair is required.

The next day, as van Baerle pulled his great saw like a boat oar, and braced his feet against the bole, a gang of haulers leaned to start a trunk from its inertia. Their harnesses crossed their shoulders and their chests, and from behind their backs a strap of wide leather was fixed that fell forward in a loop across the haulers' foreheads, so they pulled their load with their heads as well as their bodies. As they strained to get their tree in motion, their rag-wrapped feet churned the yellow clay for purchase. Among them, clasping at the harness on his chest, his eyes desperate as an animal's, was Eynarr.

Paint

AFTER A YEAR and a half in the forest, van Baerle too was finished for heavy work. He would never learn the technique of smelting magnesium from the dolomitic rock that every day was pushed in iron wagons to the furnaces. Men who had served in the forest had insufficient strength to quarry rock or to transport it. And they could not stand twelve hours before the ovens, half stripped, turning and re-turning briquettes of ore and flux which gave off blue-white flares on contact with the air, as if a photographer had called to capture their endeavours by flashlight. Van Baerle was good for nothing more than paint.

The settlement was built around the manufacture of pigments: a paint works had existed ninety years before, and ate the lives of men who were reduced to breathing lead and cadmium and chromium and zinc, in order to survive. Since few but derelicts volunteered for such careers, the ancient manufactory was annexed by the state as a punishment facility. Forestry and magnesium were introduced when too many prisoners were transported to be occupied in the corrosive traditional activity of the establishment. Radium was added to its inventory of materials.

The central structure of the factory to which van Baerle was allocated resembled that fortress of crusaders in Tripolitania: the Krak des Chevaliers. Its stone walls formed a high, circular keep, a grey cliff with no openings but one gate at ground level, and higher up, slit windows, such as archers might have used. Like a castle's, the building's single gate functioned not by opening inward or outward, but by being raised and lowered on a clanking chain hauled by the cogs of a star-wheel that took two men to turn. Cornelius walked in and saw a disc of ground fifty yards across, with scarcely a standing space free of human activity. The inside of the perimeter wall was supplied with a shed roof fifteen feet from the ground, which extended the same distance into the arena, and provided a ring of work space for processes that must be sheltered from weather. The open ground was segmented by rails, which converged on a central turntable. Material requiring transportation from one work station to another must be loaded into an iron wagon, pushed to the hub, turned to point in the direction of its destination, and delivered along the chosen track. If a consignment of ore required removal from one work station to an adjoining site three strides away, it must still be trundled via the spokes and omphalos, where a marshal stood to regulate the traffic. In the ground between the rails, men raised sledge-hammers to reduce a variety of ores to amenable sizes.

The special mission of the facility was to produce industrial coverings: paints to protect the hulls of battleships from brine, paints to coat the walls of dams below the waterline, zinc-white paint to write on roads, lead-white paint for submarines, paints that ate a surface layer of metal, paints that glowed in the dark. No artists' watercolours were attempted.

Van Baerle looked at men who were orange: orange in every

pore of their bodies and every hair of their heads, men who dreamed in orange. He looked at men who were ultramarine: nigger minstrels of ultramarine, whose pink-rimmed eyes and pink lips gleamed from their light-absorbing faces like illuminated fruit peel, who when they blinked looked like the dark side of the moon. He saw viridian men, and chrome-yellow men, and apparitions of such whiteness that their teeth, by contrast, seemed chestnut-coloured.

His allocation was to an array of flying hammers designed to reduce to powdered form the heavy cakes of precipitated metal salts, in every hue, delivered from ovens where the last moisture had been baked out of them. A transport worker braced himself in front of his wagon to stop its motion with his back, then spun a wheel to spill its contents on van Baerle's floor. Cornelius must shovel the dense heap, still radiating heat, into the hopper of an apparatus like an iron wardrobe. Inside, rotating shafts equipped with hammers smashed the crusts, which tumbled through to closer shafts, and down to pulverising blows from hammers small enough for elves. The shocked and shattered substance fell onto a sieve, which van Baerle must kick to let the powder fall down through a chute into a double paper bag, one hundredweight of pigment to a bag, which must be stitched across its top and carried to his railhead. This he must do from seven o'clock in the morning for twelve hours, every day.

One-third of the space beneath their circular awning was occupied by similar implements, which thrashed to charge the air with dusts of ethereal hue, drifting mists of pink and lemon, of emerald-green and blue, drawn out of cinnabar, galena, cyanite and malachite, and ores of chromium and cadmium and zinc.

The forms of prisoners clarified and dissolved endlessly in the poisonous clouds, while from the drying pans and ovens, coloured flames sprang up and died. The other third of covered space belonged to those who organised precipitation, who poured out acids on the raw crushed rocks and compounds, and harvested their magically vivid sludge.

At intervals around the stone circle, hanging like vines from the lip of the shed, rubber hoses connected the Saturnian atmosphere of the work floor with that of the outer world. Prisoners whose choking delayed their progress were permitted to place the hoses in their mouths to suck, at intervals, restoratory lungfuls of the natural air. Prisoners whose métier was the pushing and tipping of products, since they crossed and recrossed open ground, were not granted hose time, although at certain hours the entire enterprise, their space included, disappeared into a fog whose chromatic components were subsumed in an enveloping fuscous blanket.

The prisoners who worked in paint were men whose brute strength had been drawn out of them in the forest or the quarry, or in the laying of roads and railway track. They had delivered the best their bodies could offer, and arrived at a point of precarious equilibrium. More heavy work would destroy them. Colder weather would destroy them. A reduction in rations would destroy them. But if everything held steady, they might linger on for years, precipitating, baking and shovelling the valued product of the ancient plant.

The worst that could happen to a worker in paint was that his lungs filled with insolubles, he choked, and no amount of pounding by his comrades could free the plug that stopped his chest. He was destined to die of ruined lungs, no doubt, but the sudden drama of such exits seemed a larger insult. Sometimes, ill-baked cakes of colour clogged the iron wardrobes' hammers, prompting the inexperienced to intervene and prod. The shaft resumed its rotation unannounced, and in a thumbsnap pulverised a hand, an arm, a shoulder – it mattered little which, since each ensured that death was soon to follow. While feet and hands were routinely mangled during the transit of iron wagons from one point to another on its circumference, a fall into acid occurred only three times during the eight years that van Baerle laboured in that colourful amphitheatre. Explosions in the ovens might be expected at any time: their doors flung suddenly open, an envelope of accumulated gas ignited like dragons' breath, and fragments of shattered pigment cake, luminous with heat, zipped through the air like tracer bullets.

When he was still new there, Cornelius ran the tips of his fingers with a paper bag through the stitching machine, and saw them flattened, pierced and joined by twine to make one flap, which he cut free and wrapped in rag to carry on. He was entranced to see the orange powder that he worked, blown up with air to twice its settled bulk, spill from the bag he dropped and run across the work floor like a wave dying on the shore. It reached the outer wall, rose up it like foam, then fell and returned in diminishing ripples to his feet.

On summer evenings, when prisoners lounged in the alleys between their windowless shacks, it was possible to say precisely where a worker in paint was employed. While foresters and workers in magnesium spat blood from diseased lungs, the worker in paint delivered a specific phlegm of cadmium-red, or chrome-yellow, or malachite-green, a badge of his assignment. One moonless night, when van Baerle stooped to drink water from a barrel, a pale fish rushed to its surface. He drew back, and saw his own face in the water do the same. He glowed in the dark, from luminous powders in his pores.

In the stone-girt arena devoted to the manufacture of pigments, Eynarr was a pusher of wagons. When he came to van Baerle's station, the two men paused for breath and exchanged an almost imperceptible nod of the head. It was the merest inclination, but contained so much. Their eyes met, too, and in that nod and glance they said: Remember what we were that now are come to this. The days ahead cannot be worse than those behind. We have survived.

One twilight when day's work was nearly done, the two men stood beneath the canopy and saw a sky filled with speeding, mud-brown clouds, with yellow streaks between, which flew like ugly geese, then grew, conjoined, and wrought a gale of coloured dusts, that whirled and eddied in their stadium, until a deluge came and damped it down. In falling dark, torsos of rain-soaked slaves, heaving garish burdens on the rainbowed earth, were illuminated intermittently by lightning, and belches of blue flame from the ovens.

'This is our life,' said Eynarr.

Athletics

EVERYBODY knows that D. van Baerle, Dolboy, represented his country only once in the international athletics arena before his career ended abruptly and mysteriously during the first Soviet Spartakiad of the post-war era.

The nonpareil of his junior school, Dolboy progressed with plaudits to be senior *victor ludorum* in two consecutive years, National Schoolboy Cross-Country Champion (Open), and winner, in record time, of the one-mile event in the National Schools Athletics Championships. His triumphs were complete when, while still at school, he secured the National Senior Cross-Country title, an occurrence unprecedented and unrepeated in the history of the event. He was never beaten. But although he had been prevailed upon to perform his tricks for the glory of his house and school, after returning to his homeland he became increasingly reluctant to appear in races requiring him to run laps of a track.

To run a mile was hard enough: to run a lap and see the end post come and go, then come and go again, and then once more appear and disappear, until it finally fulfilled its function. The same faces came and went, then came and went, then did the same again, and then gave vent to spasms and to screaming. But slender Dolboy's glory, it was agreed, would be found in longer hauls: three thousand metres, five thousand, and eventually ten. The prospect of so many revolutions appalled him. His special talent, which seemed to him to be his self, his essence, was no commodity, to be apportioned and doled out by committees and selection boards of the athletics council.

'Given your mile and cross-country times, you would be untouchable on this continent at three thousand and five thousand metres too,' the chairman of selectors told him. 'Take your pick or run them both. We're happy to accommodate your wishes.'

Dolboy envisioned the laps, and asked himself the question: eight revolutions or thirteen? Neither was inviting.

'I'd rather continue with cross-country runs,' he offered.

Until that time, running in the landscape was the only kind that Dolboy had enjoyed: each stride was over different ground, the weather changed a course, and for long stretches he ran with nothing but the trees and fields for company, between the features hemmed by crowds. (Why was a bank or bend of interest, while ground which gave a runner chance to show his pace attracted few?) And, with exceptions, he had been able to run this event without concern for other athletes. He could hold a sprint start now for four hundred yards, which put him clear and let him continue to the end as if he ran alone. If sometimes another runner came abreast, he was happy with the company awhile, but found without employing tactics that his visitor soon flagged.

'Yes, continue with cross-country,' the official answered. 'But the season for those runs is limited, while on the track you have the summer long, more choice of runs, and greater glory. Don't think this premature, but you might soon be running for the greatest prize. A medal in the footsteps of Kuts.'

At the name of that suicidal devourer of distance, Dolboy was transported for some moments to cruise beside the great Kuts, to pound the earth relentlessly with him, and relieve the rhythm with exhilarating sprints, not because somebody threatened, or the finish came in sight, but for the joy of flying. Like Vladimir Kuts, he ran against himself, against the ground, against the air.

'The truth is: I don't care for track events,' Dolboy said.

'Don't care? Good God, you're a champion! You have a gift that is given to one man in a million, once in every two generations. You have a duty to care.'

'A duty?'

'Yes, a duty, not just to your country, but to your children and your grandchildren. Do you imagine you'll sit with them around a fire and recount that you could have been a great champion, if only you had cared for running on a track? No, my boy, of course not. Instead you will recall to your regretful self what honours you might have enjoyed. If you don't want to risk too much – your record or whatever – just let your name go through for one event: three thousand metres, if you will. You have years to move to longer runs. But make a start.'

'My record?' Dolboy asked.

'Everybody must be beaten some time,' the chairman told him. 'There's no shame in it. As you mature and grow in strength, you'll hold your own at any distance. Nobody minds if you have lost along the way – not that it's likely here in any case. What do you say? Name your distance in these games and we'll go along.'

'The marathon,' Dolboy answered.

'Yes, one day the marathon. One day. But for the moment choose something attainable, some distance you have already run across the country. You can't jump so soon from six miles to a marathon. What do you say?'

'The marathon.' Dolboy did not know from where this decision had arrived, but he felt certain it was a good answer. The chairman grew exasperated, but promised to discuss the notion with selectors.

'What was your event?' Dolboy asked him.

'My event?'

'You were an athlete, weren't you?'

'I threw the javelin,' the other answered, with irritation.

'And how many times must you circle the stadium to do that?' the stubborn runner enquired.

It did not occur to Dolboy that a marathon was more than he could run. Sometimes when he cruised victorious to the finish of a landscape race, he knew he could go on, and wondered why that arbitrary point was chosen for an end. Once, he trotted round a course three days ahead to reconnoitre, and then again to be sure, and finally he ran the route as if it were a race. The compounded circuits made the maximum an athlete runs, and though he stopped to drink between his laps, he knew the aggregate might easily be run continuously. Once, before he went away to school, when he was just a boy, he ran to Zutphen with a message and back home again, a distance of twelve miles.

'You should have ridden,' his aunt scolded gently. 'What will people think?'

But everyone who visited was told about his exploit, and amazed.

The chairman of the selection board of the national athletics council, however, required more tangible evidence before Dolboy was allowed to turn his back on the possibilities offered by the repeated circling of a track. He would only be considered to represent his country in the race that left the stadium when he had accrued a record of success in the event at the regional level. In the meantime, Dolboy was named to run for his country over three thousand metres in the continental games.

'How is it that I may premiere this distance internationally, but not the other?' Dolboy asked.

'You've run twice this distance with distinction in cross-country,' he was told. 'You have no record in a longer run. Perhaps you would cover half the course, then fade. Who knows? A year ago you were a miler. You can't win everything.'

It was true. Dolboy knew that he had reached the fastest he could run to win the schoolboy mile, and stronger sprinters would prevail if he repeated that event. His future lay in undertaking longer tasks, in which he could maintain his steady pace. But he had no interest in protracted circling. Three thousand metres through the woods or on a beach would be an ideal test. His thought was troubled by the chairman's doubt: that he might run half a course, then fade.

'I don't give up,' he answered. 'If I am entered for a distance, I don't fade. I run the distance.'

'I'm not saying it would happen.' The retired javelin thrower attempted to recover ground. 'Just that it's possible. It wouldn't be the first time somebody ran out of baskets with only half the eggs collected. Better it happens in our provinces than in Strasbourg, that's all.'

Dolboy remained perturbed.

'You think I can't stay a course?' he answered quietly. 'Show me a course, any course, and I'll complete it.'

'That's what we're doing, Dolboy. It's three thousand metres long. To some people that would be an obstacle, but we're confident you will complete it, and complete it before anybody else making the attempt that day. You are a great hope in our national team. You will go on to famous achievements. But please do so one step at a time.'

Dolboy was not dedicated to victory. If the chairman of selectors had said he believed Dolboy could not win an event, he would have considered it possible, a matter to be tested. But the opinion that he might not sustain his effort troubled him. How could anyone who knew his history hold such a view? He may sometimes have started too fast, or too slow; he may have burst into sprints too often, or not often enough; but when the finish came in sight, whatever distance he had run, over grass or mud or snow, Dolboy ran without error. He ran fast and he ran without faltering, however hard his heart beat. He never faded.

Dolboy prepared diligently for his international debut on the track. He remembered his first teacher's words: 'If you have trained for something longer, you will go on,' and repeatedly ran nine laps at a speed that would have brought him victory in eight. And when he had done his work, and gentlemen with stopwatches and crested blazers agreed he was a glowing hope, he threw aside his weapon shoes, the grass impalers, and went home to run his old courses. He set out by his uncle's mills, along the dyke, and breathed, as he ran, the odour of bean flowers and corn, and cows in the fields. He ran a route selected three strides before he reached it, sometimes veering without thought into woodland when the path turned another way, sometimes leaping over water when the track continued on the other side. This was his world and this was his joy. In all of his cross-country expeditions he attempted to recall this beloved anarchy, the blind plunging of his younger self through plantations and thickets, and though he saw the alders and the willows and the brambles of his home rush past in other lands, they were no substitute. Though he might have leaped an obstacle spectacularly, or inserted sprints for the fun of them, he must still hold to the prescribed route, the route that brought him to the corridor of back-slappers and cheering, the route that returned him like a performing animal to his trainers and his keepers. But in the *Graafshap* there was no route but that before his face. If he glanced left, that was his route; if he turned to the right, he ran to the right, through obstacles or open ground.

'If this is what you want to do, then it is worth doing,' said his aunt, narrowing her eyes to read his feeling.

'This?'

'Running for an audience.'

She had cleverly picked out that aspect of Dolboy's course that seemed most antithetical to its enjoyment.

'Thank you,' her nephew answered.

Six weeks later, as the continental games drew toward their close, D. van Baerle satisfied the expectations of the selection board of the national athletics council by capturing the three thousand metres title in a manner which suggested the other finalists were not worthy to compete. Coming into the home straight well clear, he slowed briefly to watch the progress across his track of a butterfly, occasioning a collective gasp before he redirected his attention to a concluding burst of speed.

'That could have been a record,' the chairman of the body complained.

The marathon race on the last day of the championships was described by *L'Équipe* in the following terms:

AFTER *a gruelling duel through the suburbs and parks of Strasbourg, in record heat, Emil Hasek of Czechoslovakia took the marathon title ahead of Gordon Peters of Great Britain and Eduard Dignon of France.*

An otherwise unsurprising contest was enlivened when, with the race in its last quarter, a runner broke from a group trailing the leaders by a hundred metres, caught them, and sprinted ahead. Officials were unable to identify the improperly numbered athlete, who wore sun glasses and a cap, but hesitated to challenge his contention of the event for fear of error.

With the stadium in view, the new leader ran strongly two hundred metres clear of his nearest followers, and seemed sure of victory. Then he appeared to lose his orientation, leaving the marked course to run into a side street. Spectators scattered from the barrier to call after him that he ran astray, but the mysterious athlete continued, and disappeared!

Hasek's winning time of 2hrs 24min was 20 seconds faster than that of Peters, while in third place the Frenchman clocked 2hrs 24min 45sec.

Two weeks after the event, the chairman of the selection committee of the national athletics council was puzzled to receive a clipping of this report, in the margin of which was written, in an apparently disguised hand:

'A case of fading?'

Return to the castle

AMONG THE MANY letters of congratulation which Dolboy received on his return home from Strasbourg was one from Mirjam van Doesburg, who studied art in Utrecht, and begged him to visit her during her summer holiday at the castle of Weisse. This note, which concluded with a cartoon figure breasting the finishing tape with both arms aloft, he read and reread, examined closely, interpreted, smelled, and held up to the light. Could he detect in the form of words she employed a motive for her communication after a silence of several years? Were her words of praise and encouragement politeness, or a message from her heart? Was that triumphant manikin a mockery or celebration? And had she forgiven his startling behaviour on the occasion of their last meeting?

Since that traumatic parting, Dolboy's despair had undergone an evolution designed by Nature, like evolution in general, to secure his survival and continuance. A period of shame and desperation, in which his ridiculousness and his unloved state were joined together in the forefront of his waking mind, was succeeded by one of melancholy, in which he failed to see how anything in this world could be pleasing. The distractions of schooling took his pain to a subsidiary place in his consciousness, but although it no longer occupied the greater part of his thoughts, it persisted like the numbness which remains, long after a nettle sting has ceased to throb. In dreams and reveries she swam up from where her memory was interred, and made his stomach leap, until he remembered that his foolish love had come to nothing, and returned her image to the vault of lost hopes.

Her letter occupied his speculation at every spare moment, and although he feared he might suffer further hurt if he responded, he knew he would be tormented by uncertainty if he declined her invitation. He replied, and they agreed a day for their reunion. When the time came round, all of his doubts were replaced by an enveloping calm, and instead of troubling his head over a winning combination of jacket and tie, or contesting with his hair an arrangement judged fashionable, he read all morning about Gregor Samsa's life as an insect, and at the last moment strolled in an open-necked shirt and tennis shoes to drive the old Opel saloon to his appointment. The iron gateway of the castle drive returned to him his boyhood thrill at entering there, and as the air from the open window made the points of his collar flap like two trapped butterflies, he smiled at the lost fantasy he dreamed: of driving with his bride along that avenue of towering trees in a gleaming landau.

Mirjam appeared at the castle door as he stepped from the car, and waited while he crossed the bridge, not with her twinkling, dimpled smile, but with an expression of serene pleasure that suited the graceful beauty she had attained. They kissed three times on the cheek, as was the custom, and her silvery hair gave up its perfume to his indrawn breath. A long dress with a smocked bodice replaced the dark, traditional costume that she used to wear.

'Dolboy, you look just as I knew you would look – like an athlete.' She smiled up at him. 'We're all so proud of you, our champion.'

While she hung deliciously on his arm, they promenaded down the hallway to a room he had not visited before, where diamond window panes of a greenish tint, in a frame that occupied the greater part of one wall, cast spangles from the sun and from the surface of the green moat too. The lozenges lay bright and rainbow-edged on the chequered floor, while on the plastered panels overhead they danced and spun with changes in the water, fading and strengthening as tree shadows made them jade, or apple-green, or mossy shades. It was a room that seemed a puzzle.

A silhouetted gentleman rose from a chair and approached them.

'Dolboy, my dear boy,' he proclaimed, 'you have completely spoiled my pleasure.'

'I hope not,' Dolboy answered, uncertain of Ivo's meaning.

'Well, yes, you have. How can I find anyone to run against you now? Who will lay out good money to take his chance against such a star?'

They held each other and patted backs, while Mirjam laughed and held them both, and Dolboy saw at last the dimples in her peach-complexioned cheeks. Ivo did not look precisely old, but he moved with the solidity of an important land-owner, an impression he reinforced by offering Dolboy a cigar.

'You smoke cigars now?'

'One must present an illusion of being serious.' Ivo spoke ironically.

All three rushed to speak at once, to ask and tell what had been accomplished in five years. Ivo had abandoned attempts to become educated, and given himself to following his father's examples in business. He had little idea of the principles involved, but offered himself at various offices locally and in the capital, as an empty vessel, eager to be filled with expertise. Dolboy recalled for them his school days on the offshore island, but resisted pleas for a detailed diary of his accomplishments in running.

'I just do what I always did,' he protested. 'But now it's measured and directed. If I had not gone away to school, I would still be running undetected, except by people in the fields.'

'Not so, Dolboy,' said Ivo. 'Do you think I would have let such a prodigy go to waste? The pity is: there's no money to be made from being a champion. You have to settle for the fame and a cabinet of medals.'

While they sat, a girl came in with and tea and cakes, and they suspended conversation while she distributed their requirements on a side table. Mirjam watched the china and the creamy food set out, while Ivo and Dolboy both looked furtively at the yellow-haired servant with ribboned plaits and upturned nose. She performed her task, then held her head up, looking down on them, and allowing the ghost of a scornful smile to cross her features. Ivo thanked her, uneasily, and Dolboy saw unreeled at once the hundred graduations of permissiveness through which their relations had evolved since he peeped in on them.

'She's Ivo's mistress,' Mirjam announced without embarrassment, when the girl had left.

'Please, Mirjam . . .' her brother began to protest.

'It's true,' she persisted. 'I only mention it so Dolboy doesn't
feel awkward when you two are play-acting.'

They contemplated their cups and plates in silence, until Ivo
shrugged and confessed:

'She has the most divine arse two hands ever held.'

Mirjam and Dolboy laughed out loud, while Ivo spread the
fingers of both hands and mimed the act of cupping something
substantial.

The sunshine on their teacups added flickering discs to the
angled shapes that dappled the ceiling, creating a constant distraction of movements overhead. And since the brightest light
bounced from the tiled floor, the illumination of their faces was
inverted, so that shadows of their cheeks fell upward on their
eyes, and their noses cast dark triangles on the green skin of
their brows. They appeared to be three tinted elves, observed by
firelight. This verdant tableau was supplemented when the door
opened to admit a fragile figure dressed in black, with translucent skin, which floated like a disembodied skull until she found
the pool of sun. Trixie's visitation promised to remain silent,
before Mirjam goaded her to speech.

'Trixie has followed all your triumph,' she said. 'She has become
tragic because she believes you never think of her.'

'Stop it, Mirjam,' the delicate girl ordered in a deep voice. 'The
fact that I don't dress like Bo Peep doesn't mean I'm in mourning,
for lost love or anything else. Congratulations, Dolboy, by the
way, on running.'

Dolboy was amused by Trixie's drollery. She had grown into a creature whose features were so fine and intricate they might be in danger of destruction if she turned over in her sleep. At their last meeting he had considered her a bizarre hop-o'-my-thumb. But he was overwrought that night. He saw now that she was striking.

'Thank you, Trixie,' he answered. 'It's true I have a collection of cups now. But I really don't know what to do with them.'

'No, not that running,' she continued, drily. 'I meant congratulations on running off from Ivo's party. It was the highlight of the evening. I can't have been much fun to dance with.'

Ivo groaned, and Mirjam shook her head. But Dolboy was not embarrassed.

'No, Trixie, it was not your fault,' he told her. 'I was confused, and not used to the excitements of a party with dancing. I was so ashamed that I could not even bring myself to apologise, but now I do, to all of you.'

Trixie's bluntness had exposed a topic which the others had in mind through all their conversation, but dared not mention.

'Well, that's cleared up then,' their grave visitor observed, and after stooping to kiss Dolboy passionately on his lips, she added:

'And so is that. It's true I've always adored you. But you knew that. If ever you want to make love to somebody with feelings, you know where to come.'

She flicked Dolboy's hair so that it fell in his eyes, and he looked at her in amazement, before she marched from the room.

'Kids!' Ivo declared.

'She has become so dramatic,' Mirjam added. 'But I can't help admiring her strangeness. It makes me feel so devious and false.'

Dolboy threw his head back and gave himself to a bout of laughter that made his chest shake, and through the tears that filled his eyes he saw the movement of green spangles on the ceiling, and was drawn into their scintillations, floated and swam with them. He felt the joy of being reunited with his family of friends within their puzzle room.

There remained one memory to be reactivated. Mirjam said:

'You'd better see my studio, Dolboy. In Utrecht, of course, I share with other students, but here I have my own. Can you guess where it is?'

'I think so.'

While Ivo sat and lit another cigar, Dolboy and Mirjam crossed the green water and walked together to the summer-house. The leaf-green fretwork on its verandah had been refreshed, and with the sun high overhead, the structure dazzled like a decoration made of sugar on a wedding cake. The foxgloves stood half changed to seed, half flowers, in rippling shadows cast below the birch, and rhododendron blooms flecked the perimeter of spruce.

Mirjam held up her key, and they exchanged in imagination their first words. I was just looking. Let me show you. She had resembled a figure from a children's story: Alice, holding up the key that offered entry to a charmed world.

'No longer my lepidopterium, you see.'

She opened the door, and he looked into deeply shadowed space.

'A strange studio,' he suggested. 'How do you see to work? By lamplight?'

Mirjam laughed, and guided him to a chair. She closed the

door, and they were enclosed in darkness, as if all the light of the building had been sucked out to fuel its sparkling shell. He heard her feet on the wooden floor, and wondered what her key would open now. Would she swoop like a moth and tease him with amorous courtship? Or would she be revealed like Ivo's domestic love, half bare, and standing on a table? Entombment in absolute night with the object of his desire allowed him whatever fantasy he dared.

He elaborated until the gloom was intersected by a cone of light, whose apex arose brightly from one wall, as its base performed a disc on that opposite. While it was less luminous, it was the disc that held his fascination. He peered at it and saw clouds in a blue sky, and as his eyes grew more perceptive, a world upside-down, of birch trees on their heads, with trunks ascending to a sea of flowers.

'It's my camera obscura,' Mirjam called from the apex. 'My dark chamber.'

'I thought you were a painter,' he mouthed into the blackness.

'That's true. But this is my summer fantasy. Come and see how it's done.'

He walked through the shaft that conveyed the outside world until he saw her face, dimly lit from the glow of the image on the wall. The window where she stood was covered with black card, and at its centre she held a lens in which the sunlight blazed.

'I tried a pinhole, but the light was too faint to carry,' she explained. 'I've covered every window just the same, and made a centre flap which can be dark, or hold the lens. Across from these five apertures I have white drawing paper where the image falls.'

Dolboy crossed to the inverted scene, and saw that it fell on large sheets of paper, held with pins.

'It's a camera, but one you can't take anywhere, or point. You must wait until a vision comes to visit. I have two viewpoints at the front and three behind, and when the clouds and leaves decide to please me, I mark their boundaries and make a photographic print. I'll show you.'

She opened the door and took a portfolio from the table to the verandah. Inside it, Dolboy saw large photographs of purplish-brown, with bright, clear birch stems under soft blurs of moving leaves, and foxgloves captured twice in one image, stirred by wind.

'These are prints from negatives I exposed on the wall,' she told him. 'But what I want, Dolboy, is you.'

He looked at her, and raised his eyebrows.

'Will you pose for me? I want you stepping from the woods into the clearing, as if you've run from home. This is my favourite place, and when it comes into my head, I always see you in it.'

So, while Mirjam stood in the doorway and called across the glade, Dolboy found a position she thought suitable, and remained immobile when she went in and closed the door. He had promised to hold his station till released – a period of five minutes – and though it seemed a torment after three, he kept his word. At last she called him over.

'Do you want to see where you were?' she asked. She closed the door behind them and stood in the cone of light that threw an image across the room. 'Here,' she said. 'That's where you stood. Of course, you must picture yourself head over heels.'

She pointed where the scene had fallen, and Dolboy saw clouds on her skirt, and flowers moving gently on her face, he saw the outside world reflected on her hair and arms, and as he too entered the zone of aerial imagery, the pair were incorporated with the universe of leaves and grass and trees in one brief masterpiece. He paused before her landscape-dappled beauty, then stooped to raise her chin and kiss her mouth. She touched his cheek, then held him in her arms.

Bread

HAVING SERVED his sentence of ten years in a corrective labour colony in the administration of GULAG, a thousand miles east of civilised society, Cornelius van Baerle had no energy to plan a journey westward. His only wish, while he was a worker in paint, was to cease. To wake one morning in his shack of logs, and stay to feed the home-made stove, instead of turning solid lumps to powder through the day: that was his dream. He wanted nothing more. The camp was his home, its slaves his family. When he looked out after a night of snow and saw fir trees bent double with its weight, and flashes of magnesium through the mist, he felt the comfort of familiar things. After he received the papers that confirmed his obligation to the state discharged, he moved to a settlement on the distant outskirts of the camp, where retired convicts eked out their lives. They had survived, and more: they had found their place in the world. Like men who have passed through war together, they were a brotherhood.

Van Baerle's days were occupied with the gathering of fuel, the exchange of his food coupons and the drinking of black tea. Their uniformity was punctuated weekly by a day on which he was called to assist in the collection and distribution of bread.

On those days, like a man who has been woken before dawn for ten years, Cornelius rolled from his bunk and dressed in darkness while he still dreamed. Three candles were lit, and a fire was started in the stove, to boil water for the first tea. He and five companions ate a little bread and cheese to remind themselves of their freedom, then, muffled against the cold, left their log shack while the sky took on a pearly greyness, suggestive of approaching dawn. Cornelius wore two coats, two pairs of trousers, boots swaddled in strips of sackcloth, and a hat made from the hide of a fox that had frozen by its mouth to the surface of a pond.

The party trudged in silence over slush that had solidified to make a rippled sea of ice, until they met a band of bundled women near a railhead. Exchanging few words, the augmented party walked along the line, some stepping from black sleeper to black sleeper, others crunching on the stones between, while all the rest formed lines outside the rails. The greatest number that could walk abreast was three: one between the rails and one on either side, for one step further to each side the snow stood untouched, chest-high. Outside the shelf of snow, after they had walked a mile, fir trees pressed in a palisade of glaucous blue, tall and close, so the trajectory of steel seemed in the distance like a dull knife lost in dark grass.

The line was dull because no other traffic used it. It had lost its shine. It ran straight, to a vanishing point where the corridor of trees was grey, like the ground, and the sky. The bread party walked at one pace, dictated by the ones who trod the sleepers and the gaps. The ones in front stared at the unchanging geometry ahead, while those behind watched footsteps, the swaying of coat-tails, or dreamed. The sky changed to sapphire-blue, with yellow streaks of cloud. Dawn had arrived somewhere, but the low sun would strike this canyon momentarily at some time later in the day, like the hurried beam of a lighthouse, and leave its gloomy shadows seeming deeper.

Two hours after they set out, the leaders sighted their objective: a speck. They trod on, and the distance to the speck seemed unchanged. It remained a speck for half an hour, and when they were a hundred yards away it still seemed little more. But when they arrived, and gazed up like climbers contemplating an unconquered peak, they wondered how they could forget the thing's immensity. It was a wooden box wagon, tarred against the elements, with iron wheels and a sliding door, held locked by a bar which swung across: the same enclosure in which they made their journey to the outpost, with space for fifty standing men. It lay on a spur, twenty paces from a line which ran through small settlements thirty miles in either direction. In each there was a bakery. Once every week loaves were transferred from a train to the waiting wagon.

Without looking in, the bread collectors circled their heavy transport to assess the chance of moving it. After agreeing that chance to be slight, they ignored their own conclusion, slackened the bar of the hand brake, and applied their weight to the inert container, some pushing with outstretched arms against its rear wall, others applying a shoulder to iron projections on its sides. Having confirmed what they already knew, and tested the futility of hoping for a miracle, they grew practical. Where icicles had thawed the previous day, and set like glass yokes on the axles, the retired convicts applied kicks and blows with rocks selected from the track. They tried again, and still the wheels held fast. More work was needed. They hacked the crazed globs once more, and when it seemed they might succeed, took turns to penetrate the frozen wheels with urine.

The wagon moved, and every helper called instructions to the others. Their messages were similar: Continue! More effort! Don't pause! Now that inertia had been overcome, they wished to keep their vehicle in motion. But since they could not hope for every soul to work without rest until they reached the camp, they took turns to drop their arms and recover strength, while others pushed at walking pace. After they had gone a mile or so by alternating their efforts in this fashion, an uphill incline made their work heavier. All hands pushed until the wagon slowed, hesitated, almost stopped, and then began to roll unaided down the other side. Now the first hump was passed, a halt was called, the brake applied, and the bundled labourers walked to and fro behind their load, pressing the small of their backs to unbend their spines. Cornelius stooped with his hands on his knees, and sucked the cold air.

When it was agreed they had recuperated, the brake was released and three men helped the truck along, until its tiny headlong rush diminished, and more hands were called to propel it to its next crisis, when everyone must strain again to overcome another crest. If they had to stop, which was inevitable, they did so where an incline helped the resumption of motion. Twice more they halted and observed the wall of trees which enclosed them, seeking nothing, and finding nothing. Somewhere outside the snowbound chasm the sun achieved its zenith. The shadows grew green. Twice more they began again, small within their big clothes, sinewy and half fed, until the stubbornness that made them live brought them to the end of the rails, their starting point, heaving their behemoth, black against the bright sky.

The pushers of the bread wagon stamped the dirty snow and exchanged the banter that workers employ at the successful conclusion of an onerous task. Then the bar of the capacious container was raised, and Cornelius saw on its floor three wooden trays, each holding twenty-four loaves of bread. When first he saw their load and counted heads, his sum told him they might have carried six loaves each, and left the wagon where it stood. He raised the question and received a variety of rebuttals to his argument. There might sometimes be more bread (there never was). Why worry about saving time when there was no further task demanding their attention? And that was the way it had always been done, therefore there must be a reason for it to be so done (a perennial argument in that nation).

When he had enlisted with the bread collectors a dozen times more, he understood that the mathematics of the enterprise was unimportant. He was enrolled in an expedition whose accomplishment was an exercise of will, a ritual, a defiant act. All week the souls of the perimeter colony dragged out their lives in dull acts of survival, but on one day they gathered themselves and said: You took our lives, and still we persist! On one day they shook their fists.

The ritual was not concluded. The bread collectors carried their trays between them to the shop, a hut of planks, with a window and two benches: one along its wall to sit on, the other, higher, held the trays of bread. Customers waiting on the bench had discussed for two hours the quality of the previous week's bread, its price, the bread their mothers made, and the omens for an early or a late delivery. If the weather turned, or more ice than usual gripped the wheels, or too few pushers volunteered to keep good time, the customers would sit for hours more to see their bread. Once, when a blizzard blew from nowhere for two days, the bread detail huddled in its wagon with the loaves, and met half-way the men who came to dig them out. The loaves came three days late, and one voice rose from the blank faces on the bench:

'A problem? Oy, you came. Who's complaining?'

Most citizens bought their bread and left, but one man remained to debate the price and quality of the product. He was a wiry, grey-skinned survivor, with a shaven head which his fur hat ate as if it were the egg of a small bird. On every other day he lived a silent, solitary life.

'I'm telling you: there's acorns in that bread. I've eaten acorn bread, and that's the way it tastes. Why should we pay for bread that only claims to arise from flour. That's bread of a different colour. This bread is of a cheaper grade. Nobody minds eating acorn bread – the holy virgin knows it's better than sawdust bread – but anybody in his good mind will choke to eat acorn bread which he has bought for the price of bread that's made from flour.'

The customer was addressing nobody in particular, and nobody in particular listened to him. But since the bread had arrived, and the purpose of his being there was to buy bread, he would have no reason to remain if he did so. Thus he must delay by whatever means his purchase. He embellished his complaint, sometimes on the topic of the bread's constituents, sometimes on its age and condition, sometimes on its price, and in between he carried on a civil conversation with whoever served the product to the customers, and with any other buyers who cared to join it. If demand for bread was strong, and the supply on the bench dwindled, he asked for a loaf to be put to one side for him, before rejoining his protestation that he would never buy such bread, at half the price.

Some buyers came and sat to drink tea. Some bought their loaf and left. Others came simply to look at bread, to wonder that it had materialised again, to dream about the world from which it emanated and imagine (mistakenly) the carnival of consumption which was enjoyed there. But the grey recluse came to socialise, and when Cornelius extinguished the lamp, and pressed his wetted fingertips to mop up the last morsels of crust and crumb in the tray, the garrulous customer remained to bid him good night, and promised to return.

Such was one day in the life of Cornelius van Baerle.

Dolboy in Moscow

IN THE TWO YEARS leading to the next Spartakiad, during
which he was enrolled as a student of law at the university
of Groningen, Dolboy secured marathon victories in six of
his country's twelve provinces. The outcome of his studies
remained uncertain, but the credentials entitling him to run the
great street race were established beyond a doubt: he was the
most prodigious athlete in his nation's recent history, expected
next to dazzle on the worldwide stage. Six hundred foreign
athletes competed in the first Spartakiad, prompting the chairman
of the Supreme Council of Physical Culture to declare:

'Competitive sport not only strengthens the various organs;
it helps a person's mental development, teaches him attentive-
ness, punctuality, precision and grace of movement. It develops
the sort of willpower, strength and skill that should distinguish
Soviet people.'

Those qualities distinguished Dolboy, too, and his talent
reached its peak in the year he travelled to the city where the
Jack Band played its last, and his father had communed with a
spider. The letter arrived, announcing his selection for the games,
and he was called to meetings on the topics of uniforms and
etiquette, transport and accommodation, documentation, famil-

iarity with the words of the national anthem, and restrictions to be expected in the capital city of a nation prepared for nuclear war and world domination. When they were judged ready, Dolboy and his team companions were supplied blazers and haircuts, and assembled for a group photograph. His aunt and uncle were among the proud supporters who waved his plane eastward.

The athletes' village at these jamborees seethed with intrigue, rumour, and schemes to secure, without recourse to a common language, copulation with the finest specimens humanity could offer. At this tournament in the city of onion domes, this hymn to socialism, the sportsmen's world was also closed and fortified. But though their every move must receive the sanction of the state, the athletes contrived to evade the vigilance of watchers at the gate.

So on his third day in the city, while contemplating the three weeks remaining till the marathon, Dolboy joined a group intent on investigating attractions of the night without official guidance. They proved to be few. Food, where it was available, was not the best, and strong alcohol was found in three brands, each one the product of the state monopoly. Recreation for Muscovites appeared to consist in getting drunk to a degree which precluded realisation that nothing further was supplied. The apparatchiks, however, the aristocrats of the socialist order and their hangers-on, had everything at their disposal: the best of ballet, of symphonies, of caviar and salmon, of good wine, and after the great leader's death, once more, of jazz.

Dolboy liked jazz. When he and his companions heard strains of trumpet and saxophone coming from the ballroom of a great hotel, they tried to enter, and were repelled. They tried again with the same result, and aimed their third attempt through a rear entrance used by kitchen staff. This time they were successful. They blundered through the department of bird evisceration, hurried in file past outbursts of flambé and emerged through vapour clouds tasting of celeriac and beet into a plush-carpeted hallway, highlighted with gilt. They tuned their ears to decide where next to go, and bore down on a double door which, before they reached it, swung wide to admit a posse of militia and a chef. The chef indicated them, with a spoon.

In his last year at school, Dolboy and his fellows had been visited by officers of the army, seeking recruits. Some boys enrolled, while Dolboy joined more cautious souls, agreeing once a week to learn the adversary's tongue, to better fight the war of threats. Now, as soldiers seized the party of intruders, he showed off his linguistic skill, but for answer, they laughed and made jokes among themselves. The athletes were dragged through the door and down a passage where the music sounded louder, until they stood close to another entrance. Here they were held, while one man went inside. Dolboy attempted the difficult language again, and again was answered with laughter.

At last the door reopened, and the messenger returned with a sturdy person whose head and neck had been shaved as an undifferentiated stump of muscled bone. Dolboy supposed everyone had muscles on his forehead, but he had never seen them so defined before, so superfluously gross. The moloch's eyes glistened tinily, and it occurred to Dolboy that he was a facsimile, in uniform, of the nation's president, a snowman of flesh. The newcomer's tunic was of fine cloth, and decorated with sufficient ribbon to commemorate battles going back a century. Dolboy joined his fellows in flaunting the crested badges on their chest pockets, while repeating:

'Atletika. Spartakiad atletika.'

The monolith examined them, and turned over in his mind the consequences of their crime. Good, bad, good, bad . . . Then he smiled like the man in the moon, the sportsmen smiled in return, and after comparing the demeanour of both parties, the militia nodded and shook hands. The officer waved them forward until they were inside a ballroom where the band played. He raised an arm in the air and shouted for the attendance of waiters, who scuttled from all corners with champagne and canapés. The guests were welcomed and congratulated from all sides, the honoured guests, the heroes of the running track.

The metamorphosis into something brightly spangled, of an evening which began as a dull glove, was completed when painted ladies attached themselves to the visitors in batches of three or four per man. They were ladies whom Dolboy suspected of being uninterested in sport, and slightly drunk, but whose curiosity was pricked by the presence of males selected for endurance and strength. Though they had long passed an age when they might have been attractive to the young, they fluttered in helpless obedience to a primal instinct, like old moths battering themselves against the glass of a streetlamp. Wherever the athletes moved, the perfumed tide flowed with them.

After the gate-crashers had spent an hour smiling and nodding agreement to compliments and proposals, and general assertions of which they understood not a word, the band set aside its instruments to salvage remaining fragments of food and dip into the free flow of alcohol. Recognising the

Spartakiadniks as strangers, like themselves, to the cadre of uniformed and suited comrades for whom the event was presented, the musicians gravitated to their party, and were soon gathering information about the world outside, in languages other than their hosts'.

Had the great enemy also put a man in space? Did everyone have television? And must you still pay for education in the West? These formalities observed, the outsiders moved on to gossip about chinks in the façade of the socialist ideal, places where a better choice of food was found, and drink, and women interested in dollars. Dolboy was learning from a trumpeter about the revival of decadent music in the union of republics, when the leader of the band joined in.

'Don't count your chickens too soon,' he told his colleague. 'Right now we're riding high, but believe me: things can change while you blink. I've seen it happen.'

He reached to shake Dolboy's hand, and when Dolboy gave his name and country, the jazzman smiled and shook his head.

'Do all you people have the same name? I had a countryman of yours in my band once, and he was called van Baerle too. Corny van Baerle.'

'Corny?'

'That's right: Cornelius.'

'Then you're right,' Dolboy answered. 'We don't have much imagination when choosing names. That was my father's name.'

'It seemed quite strange to me, but maybe it's like Dmitri Valevich, or Abraham Goldsmidt,' Rozner continued. 'They're ten a penny till you drop them elsewhere on the globe.'

'It's not a rare name, but not common either,' Dolboy said.

'What happened to your man? Did he play with you here, in this country?'

'That's right,' said Eddie. 'Right here in the capital. We played for the emperor himself, and he liked it, until he decided maybe he didn't. Van – I called him Van as well – was on piano, and he could play. Sometimes, if he'd drunk a couple more than usual, the rest of us could put down our instruments for ten minutes and wait till he came back to earth.'

He laughed at the memory of his pianist's flights.

'So why isn't he still with you?' Dolboy asked.

'Like I say: the emperor had a change of mind. The thumb that once was up, turned down. They threw us all in jail.'

'For playing jazz?'

'For playing jazz, for being foreign, for reminding the great panjandrum that he was human. Who knows?'

'But you were released. You reassembled.'

'The almighty one died, but we still had to serve our time. Most of my boys disappeared: van Baerle included. I came back and started up again with new faces, and now we're all the rage. They can't get enough of us. But you know what: I won't believe it till I'm dead.'

Eddie Rozner was not the svelte showman he had been twice before in his career. His lank hair straggled untidily over each ear from the gale of trumpet playing he had unleashed, and a two-day stubble reinforced the slack skin of his cheeks. He no longer pencilled a right-angled moustache on his upper lip. He was successful, but he was weary. He touched Dolboy on the shoulder, wished him luck, and moved on to a pole vaulter from Bavaria.

Dolboy explained to a clarinettist the demands of marathon running, and the joys, until the revellers grew restless with the hiatus, and the musicians began filing back onto the podium. Then a mouth close to his ear said:

'Zutphen.'

'Zutphen?' Dolboy repeated to the maestro.

'My van Baerle came from a place called Zutphen,' said Eddie. 'I think that's what it was. I've been trying to remember. Is there such a place? It sounds rum to me.'

Then he turned to climb onto the stage, stood before his troupe with a trumpet dangling from one hand, and with the other outlined rhythmically a tiny crucifix.

'A one, two, one-two, one-two.'

Dolboy's request

IN THE REALM of literature, Alexandre Dumas contrived to have a figment of his creativity, Cornelius van Baerle, perfect a black tulip bulb. And in the parliamentary sphere, a member of the Second Chamber named Cornelius van Baerle was disgraced for 'rescuing' from her tropic hut a long-limbed Indonesian girl, aged twelve, and conveying her to his country home for education. But in Zutphen there was a limited supply of van Baerles, and only one was named Cornelius in that century. Dolboy mused on Eddie Rozner's recollection before retiring to bed. By his family's account, Dolboy's father had been given to erratic decisions: sudden journeys, infatuations with unsuitable women, a passion for geneva after years of drinking curaçao. But nobody reported that he had attached himself to a jazz band. He had been musical, it's true, but performance outside the family circle was not among the memories his aunt had marshalled of the dear, dead parent. And yet there was no other Cornelius van Baerle of Zutphen. One word unearthed from Eddie Rozner's store had made a puzzle. Had Dolboy's father performed during one of his circulatory tours of eastern suppliers on behalf of the van Baerle enterprise? Was that before the war? Before Dolboy's birth? He was curious to know the extent of his late father's talents, and decided to return the next day to the hotel where Eddie Rozner played big-band jazz to people tired of folk dance.

The Hotel Moskva was not rigorous about security in broad daylight. Its foyer was being tidied like the ring of a prize fight between bouts. There was a sense of breaths being caught before the next onslaught, and the hotel staff was too preoccupied to concern itself with the deflection of drifting souls. Dolboy asked at reception if the whereabouts of the band leader was known, and it transpired he was resident. A note was sent upstairs. Dolboy sat and watched a parade of functionary uniforms pass by while waiting for the jazzman's response, and at length he was invited to ride up to a room on the fourth floor. It was more than a room: it was a suite. And it was more than a suite: it was a luxury suite.

Eddie answered the door in a silk dressing gown patterned with birds of prey. He wore leather Turkish slippers, turned up extravagantly at the toes, and his bony chest was bare between the faced lapels of his gown. Dolboy knew that under there was a tired body wearing underpants. At this time in the day the trumpeter was an exotic derelict. Several veins in his naked legs had given up, and lay dead and blue.

'I had an idea we'd meet again,' said Rozner.

'When you mentioned Zutphen I was sure you were talking about my father,' Dolboy explained. 'There are no other van Baerles there but us. And no one called Cornelius but him.'

The two regarded each other like instruments of destiny.

'It's a small world,' said the jazzman. 'You know, you look a lot like him. So, what can I tell you?'

'When did he play in a band here? None of us knew about that.'

'We came here from Minsk two years after the war.' Eddie looked at the ceiling of his large, deeply upholstered suite and saw his dog-eared dressing room at the Luxor Theatre, where plaster hung like white bats, in precarious triangles. He smiled. 'We had some good times there, before we were called to the capital.'

'After the war?' Dolboy was bemused.

'That's right, a couple of years after.'

'My father died in the last year of the war. He disappeared and died.'

'Well, he certainly played like an angel,' said Rozner. 'But he was flesh and blood when I saw him last. How do you know he died?'

That was a natural question, which Dolboy asked himself in childhood, until he grew to hold the view of older, wiser folk.

'Since he never reappeared, or wrote, it was assumed he was no longer able to do so. We were not alone in mourning someone who simply vanished.'

'You're not wrong about that,' Rozner shrugged. 'And you were correct to think he couldn't write. His hosts did not encourage contact with the world outside. But to be entirely sure we're talking about the same party, tell me how your father disappeared.'

Dolboy began to repeat what his grandfather had related of van Baerle's improbable mission to the camps of the east, and the band leader broke in:

'That's Cornelius. He told me about that crazy project. He

might have lost his life on such an errand, but instead he became a captive of the citizen army, and wound up playing Duke Ellington and Harry James.'

He recapitulated van Baerle's history, up to the day they both fell victim to a change in the Father of the Nation's feelings about jazz.

'I received a ten-year sentence in the camps. I never knew what happened to the others. I got a band together there and played at weekends for the officers. Can you imagine? Jazz in a punishment colony? I was lucky. But other camps were not like that. If you went to the worst of them, you might not live two years. They were a good crowd, the Jack Band, but I couldn't say if any have survived.'

Dolboy should have completed training laps that day, but thoughts of running had left his head entirely. It was full of fantasies.

'How could I find out what became of him?'

'There would be records of a trial and sentence,' Rozner mused. 'And of his destination, if he was imprisoned.'

'But that was years ago. How could I discover where he might be now?'

'Look,' said the old man, seriously. 'Don't hope for anything. Not everybody got a trial. Those who refused to sign a confession never made it to the courtroom. And most who went to the camps didn't survive, they didn't work out their sentences. If Cornelius was an exception, and his time compared to mine, he will have been discharged some years ago. He could be anywhere, or nowhere.'

'But who would know?'

'GULAG, our landlord, maintained excellent records. Who they were for is anybody's guess. When a prisoner died, his family received no news. The death was entered, for the record. Full stop. If he never showed up again, you could assume he was dead. But a death would be recorded, and a discharge.'

'So I could find out?'

Rozner shook his head and smiled as he placed a hand on Dolboy's shoulder.

'No, of course not. Do you imagine we're talking about a public library? You walk in and ask to consult the books? But I tell you what: as you can see, I'm comfortable here. I have acquaintances – I wouldn't call them friends – in every government bureau you could imagine. They love jazz. They will do anything for jazz. And here I am the living prophet of jazz. I'll ask somebody to consult the records. If your father was sentenced and discharged, it will be written somewhere. If he died, GULAG will have that information.'

'How long would that take? I only have three weeks here.'

'If a comrade made such a query, legally, as he is entitled, it could take three years. It could take for ever. But if I ask a bureau chief outside the system, with a sum of money mentioned, as I am not entitled, I might have an answer in hours. That's how things work. They shuffle paper till it's worth their time.'

'Hours?'

'Come back the day after tomorrow. At least I will be able to tell you where your father went after sentencing, assuming he remained alive. Anything more will take longer, but first come back to see if I can discover his punishment, and where he served his time – if he was given that option.'

Since Dolboy's event wound up the running games, he might have stayed at home for two weeks before joining his team. But irrationally, he had flown to kick his heels in an ersatz village. He had not known what impulse drove him there. But now he sensed some purpose.

Two days after his first visit to Eddie Rozner's suite at the Hotel Moskva, Dolboy returned. Eddie had shaved, and wore trousers and a shirt under a dressing gown of kingfisher-blue, with dragons. His hair lay black and streamlined on his skull, and he brandished a cigarette holder in the local fashion, with his fingers along its length, the little finger nearest his lips.

'The news is mixed,' he reported, frankly. 'Like me, your father received a ten-year sentence for spying.'

'He was a spy?' Dolboy felt a frisson of admiration for his parent.

'No, of course not. That was a common formula to deal with foreigners. It's not important. He had the ill luck to be assigned a camp a thousand miles from here, with a name for heavy work and high mortality. Not everybody died there, but it could be expected. Your father survived, however, and according to records of the Main Administration of Corrective Labour Camps, was released to live in a settlement attached to the colony.'

'A settlement? What kind of place?'

'There's work to be done at the camps beside that designed for punishment. Sometimes old convicts stay on, and pass their days engaged in menial tasks and foraging. Not everybody wants to start a band. Not everybody wants to return, to discover if his mother died, or his wife had six children while he was gone. Why Corny stayed I can't guess. But there you have it.'

Dolboy remembered his father's face. He remembered the

moustache and the clear brow in their wooden frame, to which he whispered every night: 'Good night and God bless you, father, until we meet in heaven.' And he recalled, before that prayer, his other, hopeful supplication: 'Good night and God bless you, father, and soon come safely home.' It was this prayer that now rose up in his heart.

'I must go and see him,' he blurted when Rozner concluded his report.

'Wait a minute. The record says where he went on discharge. That's some years ago. It doesn't say where he is today. He could be anywhere.'

'He might still be there. And if he's gone, then someone there might know where to.' Having received information he would not have dreamed about, Dolboy did not propose simply to note it. His impulse suggested a wilder course. 'No. I must go there. I must see what has become of him.'

Why he felt the impulse, he could not say. But he felt it, and it would not be resisted.

'Your papers, presumably, allow you to stay in the city, and nothing more?'

'Yes. That's true.'

'And you understand that in this country you must have documents to authorise a journey? That you must have a reason to travel a thousand miles?'

Dolboy was not deflected. He puzzled a moment, then informed Rozner:

'They will do anything for jazz, your acquaintances. Get them to write something for me: something that will give me safe conduct.'

The refurbished jazzman paused for some moments. While stroking the newly-shaved skin of his cheeks and chin, he strolled the length of the room, surveyed the great vista of the city's roofs, and then strolled back.

'Why not?' he answered. 'You're right: they can't say "no" to me. Just now.'

The journey east

A TRAVELLER on a train moving at forty-two miles an hour will cover a thousand miles in twenty-four hours. That is, if it doesn't stop en route to pick up passengers. And that is, also, if only one engine is required to pull the train, without having to be changed because of connecting rods worn to breaking point. That calculation also assumes the traveller proceeds from his point of departure to his end point in one stage, without transfers in the middle of the night to subsidiary trains travelling to the general area of his destination. It assumes no stops for coal and water, which might in a better-regulated undertaking have been supplied in advance. It assumes that timetables have been revised within living memory.

Dolboy's father had made his journey of a thousand miles in ten days. In that case there was no urgency. His transport was left to stand on spurs for two days at a time, while more vital cargoes, like horses for the army, and twenty thousand shovels packed in grease, received priority. Dolboy's travel lasted less than half that time.

Eddie Rozner drove him to the station in a black and chromium Volga (he had not yet seen the armour-plated Packard with thick glass) and outlined Dolboy's itinerary. He gave him appropriate travel documents, a map, and a letter of authorisation from an elevated apparatchik who (it said) insisted the bearer be given access to whatever folkloric occurrences he chose to photograph for *Soviet Weekly*.

'In fact, a foreign traveller could not take two steps without a chaperone,' Rozner warned. 'So don't speak to anybody official. Just flash your papers and the letter. This man amounts to quite a threatening name.'

He indicated the title of Dolboy's sponsor. Then he handed over a camera and film, for credibility, and waited an hour with Dolboy before the functionaries responsible for departure coordinated their approvals.

'If you find him, tell him I'm still looking for a good pianist,' the generous man called. 'Preferably somebody who knows "Little Brown Bear".' Then he waved Dolboy out of his life, and returned to a career which was to make him rich and famous, before he slipped into obscurity for ever.

Dolboy turned from the grey monoliths of public buildings and apartment blocks that streamed past the windows to study his intended journey on a map. His instructions were that he must leave the train, which travelled comfortably from west to east, after eight hundred miles. Then he must wait six hours at an important crossroad of railways, without entering the attendant town or speaking to its citizens, before taking a minor line to one of two settlements nearest to the penal colony. Here the expertise of people in the capital expired. From this point he was alone in the hinterland, with his determination and an incompletely commanded language.

The train was crowded, but Dolboy did not dread the prospect of two days in close proximity with fourteen citizens occupying a space designed for ten. He had a purpose, a hope, and neither the gaze of many idle eyes nor the odour of many bodies could make it dimmer. In the event, his transport stopped three times within an hour, and disburdened of three-quarters of its occupants, assumed a steadier pace, intended to persist. Only four other people remained in his compartment, and since they had examined each other to the exclusion of further curiosity, they turned to an observance of the landscape, and then to reverie.

Dolboy did the same. The geography of his own country had seemed uniform, but that of the land through which he now glided possessed only two features: horizontality and an unvaryingly drab greenness. Sometimes a river reflected the silver sky, but that too, by the transit of the train, was transformed to the engulfing hue. The verdant ambience of the land seeped into the compartment like a fog which dulled his receptivity to stimuli, so that his eyelids closed, and the gentle rocking of the carriage persuaded him he travelled in an earlier time, when his father gathered him against his chest and covered his eyes against the truth, as their wagon moved beneath them. After he had woken three times, he gave way to his dream and lay on the dusty fabric of the seat, with his pack for a pillow.

When he woke, it was another day, but the land outside was the same, and he dreamed on, upright, into a future as nebulous as any other, but containing a parent. When night fell again, the train was within sight of the important railway junction which was its destination, but its early arrival required it to be banished to a siding until an appropriate delay had passed. At some time between nine and ten o'clock the next morning, when it was allowed to inch under a great canopy containing several platforms, bundled travellers lying against baggage congratulated each other on their good fortune, while Dolboy looked for a bench on which to wait. Six hours later he entrained again, and moved again into an unchanging landscape.

There was no civilian rail approach to van Baerle's camp. Rozner had advised that Dolboy seek a means of road transport from one of the two settlements nearest to van Baerle's colony. But when he arrived in the region, he found they were connected by a further train, which if he took it would set him down halfway, where a defunct line gave access to the camp, for travellers unperturbed to walk six miles. He took it, and sat for the ultimate portion of his journey hemmed on a wooden bench by silent women, and workers with crossed arms and tight mouths, who studied the trees when he met their eyes, and when he turned away examined him.

After an hour, the train connecting Talvertni to Chashnovo slowed and stopped. An official of the railway, with a receipt book and a pencil in one hand, walked along the track until he reached the carriage he'd noted. He called Dolboy to climb down, and people leaned out to see who had interrupted their smooth passage. Those who knew better assumed the train had stopped to pass on bread, and they were right. The official pointed out Dolboy's direction, then wiped him from his memory. Inside the curve of an abandoned branch line a black wagon stood. The official lifted the bar of its door, slid the door open and lifted out a shallow wooden tray. He carried the tray back to the train, climbed up, and after a pause of two minutes reappeared, balancing the tray, which he had filled with loaves. He walked briskly to the open wagon, deposited the tray and took another. He repeated his duty three times, counted every loaf present to assure himself the number agreed with that which he had tallied in Talvertni, then took his pencil and entered a mark of approval in his receipt book. Dolboy watched the entire procedure, but might have been a tree for all the busy man cared. After he had barred the wagon door afresh and returned to his post, the engine gave vent to a veil of soot, and stuttered once more into motion. The train continued north, and vanished into woods, a line of faces still staring back at something different.

Dolboy shouldered his pack and walked past the black wagon along the dull track, down an alley of pine. The sun pursued a shallow course in the West, and there was no sound beyond the hooting of owls, and his footfalls on the ground. Sometimes he walked on the stones between the sleepers, sometimes on the wood. Soon it seemed more troublesome to maintain a stride dictated by the spacing of the timbers than to pace the sandy path between the pine trees and the rails. The path was over-grown with heather fronds, but it was soft, and roots below the fibrous surface worked like springs beneath his feet. He jumped the fronds, and spongy ground returned him to the air. The space between the jumps he filled with lighter steps, and still the ground assisted. It was an ideal surface. His pack was light, and soon he trotted in the dusk, and interspersed his progress with leaps, as if he crossed the surface of the moon. The silence was broken, still, only by his celebratory tread, and calls of owls.

The rosy sun slipped below the forest's rim, leaving the sky subdued, but not dark. Beyond the trees he saw drifting clouds lit with unnatural blue flashes, and in an hour the glow of work lights made a yellow dome. Emerging abruptly from the corridor of fir, he saw the camp spread out ahead, its working parts festooned with smoke and steam. It resembled an ugly, abandoned toy, clanking and hissing where it lay thrown on its back in the dark wilderness.

He knew it would be unwise to approach the colony at night. There was a broad fringe of heather where the railway line met the clearing, and at its outer edge, below pine trees, it formed a thick bed. There he pressed a resilient nest, then laid his head on his pack, covered himself with his jacket, and slept. It was his first night in the open air since he journeyed westward as an infant, and although his memory of that time was faint, he felt at home on the ground, he felt comforted. The odour of bruised heather, and the prickling of his bed, were familiar. To sleep beneath a roof of branches was not a bad thing, in summer.

The sick man

HE WAS WOKEN by shouts, words he did not understand, but recognised as orders. He raised his head and watched where prisoners emerged from huts, while others rose from open ground. Guards did their jobs, and those they guarded performed their movements too, accepted that dreaming had given way to reality, and trotted in lines at double speed, to lives in timber, and magnesium, and paint. Dolboy watched the sky grow luminous. He had no plan except to wait. He would see where people came and went. He would see who was approachable.

He sat in the heather and followed the exploration of its purple flowers by ants. He watched the sun glide from a black horizon through the merest sliver of clear air, into the covering cloud, so everything grew silver. He watched a party of men and women, their jackets tied with string, come near, then walk along the line that brought him there, talking and laughing together. They were not prisoners, he felt certain. They had no guard, and walked at their own speed. But he was not sure enough to approach. From where he lay in shadow he would keep watch a little longer.

The space between the heather and the pine boughs was two

feet. No one could see him. He was safely installed. But as the morning advanced, he learned nothing. No one else came near, and he was too far away to see what happened in the area of factories. He ate the last bread and chocolate he had brought, and found himself in need of drink. He had seen men dip their heads at a barrel by the nearest huts, and when the clouded sun moved overhead, he could wait no longer. It was quiet, and no one had passed for an hour, so he left his place and approached.

When he reached inside the barrel and brought his cupped hands to his mouth, he found the water had a bitter taste, but he was glad to drink it. He took his fill and turned to go back to his lookout. But as he did he heard a rumbling noise, the sound of iron wheels, and saw a dark thing on the rails. It was the wagon from the day before, which stood where he began to walk the line. On either side of it were men and women bent to push: the ones he saw set out at break of day. It was too late to hide, and since he had seen no other folk he dared approach, he felt glad to be discovered.

The bread collectors let their burden roll until it stopped. As he approached, they regarded Dolboy without interest. They were people who had learned to concern themselves only with what they knew beyond a doubt to concern them. The men wiped sweat off their brows, and the women wiped it from folds below their eyes. They stretched themselves and loosened buttons, glad their effort was behind them. When Dolboy uttered a polite greeting it was returned, and when he said his father's name, they repeated something like it.

'Van Baerle? You know van Baerle? Cornelius van Baerle?'

'Biyerle. *Da.* Biyerle.'

They nodded, conferred, shrugged, made gestures with their hands, crossed themselves, and created a confusion of impressions. They were neither helpful nor unhelpful. The nodding and discussion continued while trays of bread were removed from the wagon they had hauled, and when they moved off they beckoned Dolboy to go with them. He followed until a woman who had taken the responsibility on herself led him in one direction, while the main party steered its cargo of bread another way. He and she walked together to log cabins that had windows, near the trees, and seemed spaced randomly, as if avoiding order. Some had sod roofs, some had thatch, and Dolboy's helper stopped at one with thatch and rusted tin on top. Although the weather was warm, wood smoke drifted from a pipe.

'Biyerle,' she nodded, and he confirmed:

'*Da*. Van Baerle. I'm looking for van Baerle.'

Behind hanging sacks there was a door of wood. The air inside was hot. A headscarfed woman with an Asiatic face looked up from the stove. The one who led him spoke to her, and they were encouraged into the building. The women consulted between themselves, then each addressed Dolboy to no effect. He made no sense of their speech. The resident beckoned him to a corner opposite, and he saw they were more than three in the cabin. A wooden bunk, covered with a blanket and a coat, concealed a man, but for his head. He slept, with sunken mouth and sunken eyes, and on each cheek red patches glowed, like two geranium petals.

'Biyerle,' his guide enunciated. And again, indicating the unconscious head: 'Biyerle.'

This was nothing that Dolboy had pictured. The creature

lying there might answer to Biyerle, but that did not mean he was van Baerle, Cornelius van Baerle. Dolboy drew his father's face from memory, and laying it on the one below, discovered no resemblance. And yet, if that mustachioed, clear-browed man had lost his hair, and missing teeth had sunk his cheeks . . .

He tried again to question the women, but his words only prompted them to resume a dialogue with each other. He saw for one instant that his errand was ridiculous, and like his father before him, he had placed himself in a situation, far from help and home, for no other excuse than a whim. If he had not wandered out and heard the sound of jazz, if he had not met Eddie Rozner, if Rozner had not uttered: 'Zutphen'. But these thoughts occurred only for an instant. Dolboy was there, and so it was his fate.

While he still looked at the sick creature who devoted his strength to the effort of drawing breath, his guide approached and delivered a further narrative he could not understand, gesturing at the same time that he should remain, should sit, while she went elsewhere. That much he understood, and having no better prospect in mind, he sat. His hostess offered him a glass of tea, baring teeth like interlocking beech nuts, and nodding in a satisfied way when he drank.

Quite soon the first woman returned, accompanied by a tall, broad-boned man with the face of a Roman gladiator. The big man examined Dolboy and decided he was satisfactory. He nodded and extended his hand, a gnarled and knobbled thing, decorated with scars. Then he bent tenderly and brought his face close to that of the one beneath the covers. He looked at him awhile, then spoke to Dolboy, to no effect. One year of the tongue for spies was not enough. The two tested each other's languages further, and found understanding in German.

'*Gott sei dank*,' said Dolboy. 'I was lost with these women, in spite of their helpfulness.' He smiled aside at both and they smiled back. 'I am looking for a countryman of mine: Cornelius van Baerle. He was a prisoner in the camp, and I have been told he lives here still. Is this the settlement for convicts who are freed?'

'It is.'

'And is he here?'

'Why do you come for him? And who are you?' Although his days of servitude were past, Eynarr remained a cautious man.

'I am his son. I believed him to be dead. I learned only a week ago that he survived.'

'How did you arrive here?'

'I have travelled by train for more than three days.'

'From where did your father come here?' Eynarr could think of no reason why this young foreign man should arrive like the first swallow of summer, and he was reticent by nature. He did not believe in relatives conjured from across a continent.

'He came here from the capital, where he played in a band. He went there from Minsk, and the home he had left was in Zutphen.'

At last Dolboy had proffered information which Eynarr recognised.

'It seems a miracle, but you have come almost too late,' he murmured. 'This is your father. This is Cornelius.'

Dolboy drew again from memory the framed face of his bedtime prayers, and tried to match it to the ruined head. He bent to kiss the brow, and felt its furious heat.

'He has pneumonia,' Eynarr said. 'His lungs were ruined by work. His strength was taken, and his health. We survive here by a slender thread. Pneumonia is common. It takes people every year. Cornelius has endured well. But in winter he caught a chill, and this is where it ended. It's God's grace that you have come now. In three days or so he will be at peace.'

Dolboy remembered a boy at school who caught pneumonia, and was well in six weeks.

'Pneumonia? He doesn't have to die because he has pneumonia. Can you be certain?'

'People here die of many things. Pneumonia is one of them. I've seen it many times. I've seen this' – he looked down – 'many times.'

Dolboy did not believe his destiny had brought him randomly to his father at that moment. If he had come a year ago this crisis would not have been foreshadowed. If he had come next month he would have received an account of his father's passing. But to arrive precisely when his life was poised to cease, to be with a dreaming man, with him but not known, seemed a fate he was unable to decipher.

'What does the doctor say?' he asked. 'What treatment does he have? Can nothing more be done?'

Eynarr enclosed Dolboy's shoulder in his palm.

'I am his doctor, my boy. Everyone here is each other's doctor. I make a tea of rosehips and juniper. That is his medicine. But mostly our medicine is hope and prayer. For Cornelius, now, just prayer.'

'But you are no longer prisoners. Is there no doctor here who can supply something more?'

'No, we are no longer prisoners, and yet we choose to stay here, where there are no doctors. That is our choice, and we know its consequences.'

But Dolboy felt his stubbornness dissent. It said: This is not my destiny. This will not be. Whatever choice he may have made, my choice is other.

'Where is the nearest doctor?'

'He won't come,' said Eynarr.

'Where? How far away?'

'In Talvertni or Chashnovo.' The two towns connected by train.

'If I walk to the train line, I can ride to either place in an hour. I'll bring a doctor, and medicine too.' Dolboy was resolute.

'A train passed yesterday,' said Eynarr. 'The next one is in two days. Then you must travel back the same way. I don't think Cornelius will wait for you.'

'Is there no other approach to either place?'

'To both. A dirt road for farm carts and the like.'

'How long is that route?'

The released convict was silent for a moment. He had not been far along the road, but knew its course.

'To Talvertni thirty miles, a little less to Chashnovo.'

'What sort of country does it pass?'

'Up and down. More up to Talvertni. The road to Chashnovo traverses lower woods and then finds fields.'

'That sounds the better way,' Dolboy decided. 'Is it plain to follow? Will you show me where it starts?'

'There is no traffic on the road. A farmer moves a mile or so, a woman takes a cart to visit her mother. Sometimes a truck may travel there from our camp. But there is nothing for you to ride today.'

Dolboy took from his pack a pair of shoes: his running shoes. 'I'll go on foot.'

Eynarr admired the resolution of the young man who had appeared like a wood wraith to dance at the death bed. It was a long time since he had seen a face that glowed with health, an unlined face, and soft, shining hair. It seemed as if the spirit of van Baerle's youth had come to protest at his departure from the world. He saw that you could not dissuade a creature of that mark.

'It will be dark before you arrive,' he advised. 'Better wait till morning for such a walk.'

But Dolboy laced his shoes.

Dolboy's purpose

IT WAS NOT YET the end of the afternoon. Men in the forest licked their dry lips and calculated how many trunks they must saw before they stopped to drink. In the stone amphitheatre of the paint works, men pigmented like ancient warriors pushed wagons to and from the turntable, and dripped chromatic sweat. The great doors of the magnesium shed were open at both ends to admit air to those who worked by lightning flash. And where a dirt road passed the rim of the industrial clearing, a large-boned man with weathered features watched a slim figure run into the blue-green shadow of encircling trees.

Dolboy carried little in his pack. He tied its bottom straps around his waist, so that it moved with his body, instead of jolting counter to his rhythm, and set off with his familiar, energetic tread. The fir woods on either side were like the woods of home, the heather and the earth the same. But instead of lying flat for miles, the landscape rose and fell beneath his feet, like his cross-country course at school. Sometimes he flew down the rolling road, and at its trough increased his speed to meet the rising ground, and kept his pace until his heartbeat rose, and he must moderate his stride to match it. He liked the uphill climb, the earth that came to meet his feet before his leg was stretched, and each time he reached a brow, he felt glad that he had triumphed over something sent to try him.

Sometimes when the road ahead was clear to see, he marked its course and veered into the woods, trampling ancient needle beds and stumps before emerging where he knew the track went on. This was his delight: to run on unfamiliar ground; to plunge, not knowing what lay two strides ahead, and let his body think what it must do to carry on. He loved the woods, their air, their shade, their silent floor, propelling him aloft, receiving him, and launching him to fly again.

The exultation that flooded his body when it worked at speed was joined by something more: an intuition that the clockwork of his life had ticked inexorably to this. A vision that the logic of his running was complete. This was his purpose. This day was why he ran: the end and reason for his impatience with a slower pace. His trotting on dirt roads and dykes, his headlong flight through trees, his victories over landscape and track: all led to this.

'Dolboy runs as a bird flies. It is his nature to speed through life.' His aunt remarked the fact, but not its explanation.

It was more than Dolboy's nature to run through life; it was his destiny. He understood. His coming to this country and this place, prepared to run for thirty miles, prepared for up and down, for rough and smooth: this was why his father brought him from the war. He kept no thoughts in his head, but gave himself to speed, and knew he was unbeatable.

No one consulted a watch and no one cheered. But people gazed along his course. A herdsman paused, speechless to see the slim figure flit by the spot he worked. A farmer travelling in a cart held up his whip and crossed himself when a pale shape appeared and grew, then passed him like a ghost in shaded woods. People returned home with the story of an apparition, or of some solitary athlete they had seen, or someone running to escape, or something like a deer on the road. An hour passed, and he ran strongly; two hours and still his pace kept steady. He had trained for more.

While the sun still shone he saw the town: a scattered place with homes of silvered wood, and roofs fringed with filigree of pine. The church tower leaned, where wood had shrunk, and at its top there was a gilded dome of wood. The station where the engine stood was wood. It was a town of wood.

He stopped at an apothecary, with earthen jars and dried roots in its window. Inside he asked where he might find a doctor. That, at least, his knowledge of the language allowed, and he was directed to a house no bigger and no better than its neighbours, with no brass plate or other indication of its function. Inside, three ancient female comrades exchanged news, sitting under framed photographs of pinewoods in snow. They paused to examine Dolboy as he walked past them and entered a door meant strictly to be opened only from its other side.

The doctor made no attempt to be polite. He told Dolboy plainly that he regretted his indifference to the fate of creatures outside his jurisdiction, but it was a fact. The province was divided clearly, and the domain of his responsibility did not contain the punishment colony, or its satellite of unfortunates unwilling to return to responsibilities in the wider world.

'I am happy to pay whatever is needed,' Dolboy offered, and displayed a considerable sheaf of roubles.

'You must know that medical care is free here,' the doctor answered. 'Your need may be pressing, but there are channels through which it must be expressed. Money is no part of that process.'

'What process? What channels must I use?' Dolboy imagined he saw a means of making progress.

'The situation of the colony is anomalous. In terms of regional responsibilities, its administration lies not with a local authority but with GULAG. Any request for help must be directed to that body.'

'It is an urgent case,' Dolboy insisted. 'There is no time for telephone calls to centres of administration.'

'Letters,' the medical man corrected. 'Such an approach must be in writing.'

He had a comfortable life. The three ladies waiting to apply for his assistance that evening were happy to continue their conference indefinitely. When he was ready to admit them, they would complain of pains and aches and gynaecological imaginings, and be happy with the iron tonic he supplied in such cases. There was no reason why he should concern himself with the health of a retired convict thirty miles away.

'Where is there another doctor?' Dolboy asked.

'In Talvertni. But I believe you will receive the same answer,' the doctor told him. 'Look at the case from my perspective. If I were to concern myself every time someone fell sick out there, I should be constantly in motion. I should have no time for matters here. What is that, incidentally? What do you have there in your bag?'

Having drunk water from a bottle in his pack, Dolboy had left it agape.

'What?'

'The camera. May I see it?'

He still carried the leather-cased apparatus which Eddie Rozner had supplied to support his subterfuge of recording Soviet folk life. He handed it to the doctor, who opened the case and examined its contents reverently.

'German engineering,' he murmured. 'Even the case is perfect.'

He held the flat, black instrument in one hand, and pulled out its silver lens barrel with the other.

'Does it contain film? I don't want to waste any.'

'No, it's empty.'

'Do you mind if I try it?'

Dolboy assented, and after viewing every aspect of his room through the viewfinder, the enthusiast cocked the shutter once for every speed on the dial, and pressed the camera's body to his ear while firing. He closed his eyes and smiled as he listened.

'Smooth at every speed. It's perfect. Why trouble to dominate Europe when you can make cameras like this? This is supremacy in the palm of your hand. May I open it?'

He took off its base and looked inside. He unscrewed the lens and watched the shutter blinds process like curtains. He turned and operated the machine like a child with a clockwork toy.

Dolboy and the doctor looked at each other, and concluded an agreement without resort to words. Only its details required confirmation.

'The camera is yours if we leave at once,' Dolboy said.

'The morning would be more convenient.'

Dolboy held out his hand to repossess the treasure.

'We must go now, and take whatever medication is needed.'

The doctor had no arguments. If Dolboy had suggested they ran back together, he would have made the attempt. A Leica came that way once in a lifetime, and he would agree to any condition for its transfer.

The waiting patients were informed of the changed plan, and the doctor waved at the pictures on the wall.

'My work.'

He looked again at the camera with which chance had made his life complete. Then they took a sturdy car equipped with three forward gears, and proceeded at a pace only slightly faster than the one that brought Dolboy there, back along a track which seemed completely strange to him, and fit perhaps for sheep.

Since it was as dark as a northern summer can be, that is twilit, when they arrived at the satellite colony, the Chashnovo doctor was obliged to include in the price he was willing to pay for a rare camera a period of duty as a night nurse. He examined Cornelius in a detailed way, injected him, bathed his head, regulated the temperature of the cabin, and administered the first doses of the medication known to be effective in combating *Diplococcus pneumoniae*. The next morning, a crowd gathered outside and stood in silence, waiting to demonstrate arthritis, blindness, goitre, symptoms of malnutrition and a range of coughs to the medical man who had been conjured magically from his distant station by a young man light on his feet. The doctor refused to emerge until it was dispersed.

'What he most needs is new lungs,' he told Dolboy before leaving. 'But penicillin is all I can offer. I've seen it save a hundred lives that would have been lost thirty years ago, but there's no guarantee. His treatment should have started earlier, but there, what can I say? His temperature is steady now, but if it rises, bathe him. Make sure to continue with the medication. And if he survives, he must rest and take light, nutritious food.' He realised where he was, and corrected his advice: 'Ideally speaking, that is. You must find the best you can here. But rest is essential. If he survives.'

In his mind he was already winding-on film, and listening to the silky click of the instrument through which he would henceforth scan the landscape. He left without looking back.

Dolboy sat by his father's cot. He refreshed the sick man's mouth with water when it grew dry, and sponged his head when it burned. Cornelius lay like a flushed corpse, radiating warmth. At first he seemed bent on death. Like Eynarr, he had seen its progress many times, and knew its signs. He conformed to the formalities of his extinction, and was prepared to slide by numbers to a proper end. But then he seemed to hesitate, as if his attention to a fatal course had been distracted by signs from a world whose existence he had disproved. His illness progressed to a stage of babbling and restless tossing, as though he debated with himself a matter of importance. His words arrived in several languages, sometimes in sentences, sometimes in phalanxes of verbs and troops of nouns, sometimes in a curse repeated till he slept. He made no sense to anyone who listened. Then, after three days, he opened his eyes and gave indication that they were still connected to a brain. Eynarr crossed himself, the high-cheeked woman brewed more tea, and Dolboy welcomed him, in his native tongue, to his second birth.

'Is it possible he might live?' asked Eynarr, who had never seen that conclusion to pneumonia before.

'Why do you think I came?' Dolboy replied.

The next day, Cornelius was raised from the horizontal to recline against a pillow containing hay and chicken feathers. His sharp shoulders jutted beneath his shirt, and his face had assumed that angularity of suffering seen crucified in oak from Aachen to Dresden. His neck lacked the resolve to support his head, which leaned forward so his chin wedged on his chest. His eyes glistened like the eyes of a bird that has struck an unseen pane of glass, before they fade and grow dull.

Dolboy administered the medication grown from mould, and van Baerle's woman added to a barley gruel meatballs of rabbit and eggwhite, which she fed him from a spoon. After two more days, the Lazarus had strength enough to understand who sat by his bed, though the mechanism of Dolboy's arrival remained mysterious to him. Eventually, he conversed coherently with his son in a language he had not spoken for sixteen years, and which assembled itself on his tongue after his brain had moved forward to another thought. The two van Baerles looked at each other and saw themselves in other times: Cornelius when he dazzled every girl in Zutphen, Dolboy in his ruined ancientness to come.

'Do you remember anything of our journey?' asked the father.

The son answered without reflection.

'Everything, though not in words.'

Cornelius slept for his required rest, then asked:

'Tell me about my father.'

His father had not yet died. He persisted. He lingered.

'Tell me about my sister.'

Then it was Dolboy's turn.

'Tell me about my mother,' he asked. But Cornelius fell asleep.

Together

A T NIGHT in van Baerle's hut, the runner lay on a bed of boards and listened to the infinitely varied orchestrations of rain on the tin roof. He heard its music where it splashed in puddles on the ground, he heard its trickling continuum in a pipe, a tinkling in a barrel. He heard a pattering irregularity which returned him to his mother's loft, the chilly cell that was his first world. He watched the roof above him rise and fall with the wind, as if it breathed, and the yellow flame of a candle turn at its point to a wisp of smoke that rose like a black thread, then wavered jaggedly and vanished. His mother's fingers flew again among the bobbins. Dolboy remembered these things in his bones. He felt them as the dawning of his history.

His more complete mythology had been provided by his aunt, who told and retold the story of his coming to the *Graafschap*. When he was still the small and perfect toy she groomed until it shone, he often begged for that strange tale, to which he listened with undimmed interest, mouthing silently the words she spoke out loud, en route to 'nesselrode'. She also told him of his father's fate, his bravery and sacrifice. But of his absent mother she told him one invented thing: that duty held her fast while she permitted his release.

The distant pair who hovered in his memory had taken on the quality of wraiths. Now that he lay under a roof with one of them, he searched for questions which had brought him there, and found a dearth. It was enough that he and a parent breathed the same air. It was enough that they were together. At the end of night, when diaphanous light outlined the profile of the invalid, Dolboy's gaze ranged the cragged and hollowed features of his father, and felt the peace of his proximity. When Cornelius woke, they sat for long intervals in silence. The prayer Dolboy had held in his heart from childish habit, that Cornelius should come safely home, would not be answered. But he was familiar, now, with the logic of his father's vanishing. That puzzle was resolved. One thing remained.

'Tell me about my mother,' he asked again, and when Cornelius answered, his eyes narrowed as if to discern some particular of a distant horizon, while an expression of disbelief possessed his features.

'Your mother? Yes, I remember your mother.'

And he recounted his remembrance.

Sitting half upright to drink one day when the low sun patterned an opaque window with the dappled play of tree leaves, van Baerle expelled a slow sigh, and told his son:

'My life was something that I chose. And though it led me where I never dreamed to go, it is my life: this hut, this woman, these comrades. This is my life. I chose it.'

Like his father, Dolboy followed an impetuous course. He too could say: this is my choice.

Now that he had fulfilled his purpose as a runner, now his father had been pulled back a little while from death, Dolboy knew he must soon leave, or be a captive in the country, without papers authorising his presence or his departure. A week after he arrived there, he left his father's bed. Father and son memorised each other's face, and embraced in the knowledge that they would not do so again. Neither knew what drew them twice together, and having drawn them, bound them: the man to an ugly child, the young man to one considering death. Each had followed his path with no thought for the other, but at their parting, neither could distinguish an emotion beside one consisting of great joy and great sadness. It was the emotion of love.

As Dolboy hitched his pack between his shoulders, Cornelius asked him a favour. He mentioned the foreman in his father's concern, the man who had enlisted him, and said:

'Tell him, if he's still there, that I saw everything.'

Dolboy nodded. Having reached the cloth-covered door of the hut, he looked back to see three faces: that of the Asiatic woman, who lifted a hand, the impassive Eynarr's, and that of his father, its eyes glinting in the shadowed, smoke-washed tableau where he lay raised on one elbow. Then he turned and ran from the cabin to the track which had led him there, not slackening his speed until he was three miles along it, and the sounds of industrial punishment had been swallowed by the forest.

Soon he stood again where the dull rails stopped, and brighter steel traversed the miles from Chashnovo to Talvertni. Once more, when the train connecting the two settlements nearest to the penal colony slowed to stop, a line of peasant faces peered out. The railway official who had entered bread in his receipt book now entered Dolboy's embarkation, before allowing the

End of the race

THE GAMES which occasioned his visit had delivered four-fifths of its entertainments, but the marathon performer's absence had gone unreported to anyone outside his delegation. The men who broke bounds to explore the city's nightlife with him were questioned daily, but offered no insight to his disappearance. The authorities who ran the games would have to be informed if nothing changed, but for the moment his countrymen persisted in the belief that Dolboy would overcome the depredations of alcohol, or women, or both, to end his truancy in time for his event. They were not aware that he had given up athletics.

A radiant morning, perfumed with maple leaves and cooking oil, attended his return to the city. As he strode toward the athletes' village, he noticed that more people than before stood in the streets, and soon he saw officials of the games, and bigger crowds, and coloured tape demarcating pavements from a road devoid of traffic. Although he had ignored the passage of time since starting on his journey east, he knew today to be the day of his event. He recognised a section of the route he had inspected weeks before. Now he looked along the course and could not suppress the tensing of his muscles, the dryness of his mouth.

He could not suppress his accustomed excitement as he craned to see a distant bend of the road. And then he heard the shout, faint and far away, then rippling near, that said the runners approached.

He saw the bobbing throng head-on, joined like a dragon in a Chinese street parade, until it grew close and stretched into a thread. He looked along the course and saw himself, sprinting, then keeping to his steady pace, then sprinting once again when everybody thought him spent. The leaders moved like automatons, their impassive faces betraying no sign of their intentions; the followers strained and rolled; and those behind grimaced while displaying every degree of suffering from breathlessness to crippledom.

When he ran a marathon, he heard the constant hubbub of spectators along his route. But when he stood in one place to view, the contest had a different sound: the cheering grew, then trailed, became polite, and then ironic as the runners passed. He watched until the last labouring soul, a famous athlete in his own land, drove himself on, when all the crowd had gone. He watched until the runners were a distant, diminished thing, and then he watched the empty road.

The inquisition at the athletes' village was perfunctory. The officials of his party were relieved to see him back, before exchanges were engaged between their governments. The question of his non-participation in the games would be examined at a later date, they said, and in a fitter place. His team companions were curious, but soon content to greet his silence with allusions to liaisons, protracted revelry, or spying. Dolboy met their speculations with a shrug, a smile, a simulation of inscrutability.

He had no intention of offering an account of his journey, of Eddie Rozner's influence, of a country doctor's passion for photography, of his father's life. That was a private, convoluted tale.

As promised, Dolboy was called after his return home to a special sitting of the selection board of the national athletics council, to answer for his abstention from the race he had been expected to win. He was polite, but apologised without shame, without any display of real regret, and most vexingly, without an explanation of his absence. In answer to repeated requests for enlightenment, he replied simply:

'I'm sorry: it was a private matter.'

'On the contrary,' the chairman of selectors informed him. 'It was a very public matter. Everybody in this country was aware of it. It could not have been less private.'

'If people were disappointed by my absence, I'm sorry for that. But it was occasioned by a matter of private concern.'

'You weren't there in a private capacity,' the official persisted. 'You had no business attending to matters of private concern. You were there as a representative of your country, instead of a dozen other athletes who would have been delighted to make the journey, and turn out to compete in the bargain. What do we tell them?'

Dolboy gave a shrug and nodded.

'It's true. They have the right to be aggrieved.'

'Damn true! And why? Because you met some woman? They lay them on to trap folks from the West. We warned you in advance.'

'No, there was no woman. I was not trapped.'

'What then? Give us a clue. You disappear for two weeks and tell us to forget it happened?'

'It was an honourable affair, but private.'

'What help do you imagine this is for your career?'

'My career?'

'Your athletics career. You begged us to let you run the marathon. It was your ambition. And now what? How can we put your name forward again? How do we know if you will run, or find some private business to attend to?'

'I didn't beg,' Dolboy corrected the agitated man. 'I said that was the distance I chose, and I beat all contenders in the country when I ran it. But please don't bother your head over my career. I don't propose to run again.'

The chairman and the members of the selection board of the national athletics council had every intention of reprimanding Dolboy, of awarding him some punishment, of shaming him in some degree. But they had not intended that such a shining name should be wiped from their entry list for ever.

'Just tell us something: anything. Something we can enter in the record. Something that will round things off,' the chairman pleaded. But Dolboy was adamant. He would not end their curiosity. He would not invent an Olga for their satisfaction.

Works of art

CONTRARY TO practice on such occasions, all of the paintings at the exhibition opening which Dolboy attended in Amsterdam, to mark the debut of Mirjam van Doesburg, were covered. He stepped from cobbles on the *Herengracht* into a vaulted chamber, painted white, which warehoused wine a hundred years, and now was hung with pictures, draped in cloth. Mirjam saw him enter, and left her group to welcome him.

'Dolboy. Thank you for coming.' They kissed, and pressed each other more firmly than onlookers knew. 'This whole thing would not have been complete without you. You are in fact my guest of honour.'

Dolboy signalled his incredulity with raised eyebrows.

'Honour? Well, thank you, Mirjam. That's something I've not heard much lately. But I'm honoured to be here, to see your career begin. I hope one day to look back and say: "Yes, of course, she is our most eminent artist. I was present at the start of her dazzling career."'

Ivo, still almond-eyed, his hair brilliantined in a fashionable quiff, strolled over with his elbows tucked into his waist, and each forearm raised at an angle of forty-five degrees to his body,

301

a cigarette in one hand, a wine glass in the other. He placed the glass on a table and shook Dolboy's hand.

'Excessively good to see you, Dolboy. I admired that disappearing tactic, by the way. Now nobody knows what to think. Should they not bet on you because you are odds-on favourite, or should they not bet on you because you might evaporate on the day? You have created confusion, for which you are to be congratulated.'

The two men laughed, while Mirjam scolded her brother for touching a topic which nobody mentioned, though everybody burned to raise in Dolboy's presence.

'Well, my little dabbler, when do we see the masterworks?' Ivo went on. 'If we wait much longer I shall be too far gone.'

'Now Dolboy's here,' she answered. 'Now we can continue.'

Consistent with practice on such occasions, a self-appointed authority on art delivered a preamble lasting fifteen minutes, which touched on Mirjam's ancestry and predilections, and promised that she would go gloriously forward, despite her disavowal of the abstraction to which her contemporaries (along with all other servants of the nation's fine arts) clung. Ivo examined his empty glass, then looked at Dolboy and rolled his eyes upward. Another guest consulted his wristwatch.

Applause greeted the peroration, but before it faded, it was spurred to a louder, more excited plateau by the snatching away of the cloth masks which had concealed the art. People exclaimed in surprise, and laughed and clapped their encouragement to the artist, who smiled back and waved like the queen. Dolboy also was surprised, first when he saw three walls of gleaming, varnished images, and then when people turned and clapped for him. They clapped, then led by Ivo, uttered cheers. Mirjam too began to clap, and could not prevent herself from launching forward and throwing both arms around his neck. The two embraced each other, laughing, while the celebration reigned.

The object of the gathering, her art, hung large and blue, with skies and clouds and distant hills, and blue shadows under trees. Each image was a scene: a landscape, or a picture in the air, or on the sea. In one the world itself was seen, a wreathed blue orb against a universe of indigo. A vista of polders receded to a mist, fields of barley bent in silvered waves, the leafy *Graafschap* flourished, a paradise of streams and rivers, birch and oak and pine. And in every dreamlike scene a figure ran, white across the blue-green fields and woods. He trod the crests of waves, he strode on clouds, he flew through trees. On every face of Nature that she drew he ran. It was himself.

'It's called *De Renner*,' Mirjam said. 'The runner. No longer the little runner. Do you mind? Was it wrong?'

Dolboy looked up and saw his likeness touch distant points on the spinning world.

'No, Mirjam. You were not wrong. You see exactly what I do.'

He felt his arm clutched, and looked through cigarette smoke into the expressionless face of the third van Doesburg child.

'Hero worship,' Trixie judged. 'Naked hero worship. But I suppose she's got a likeness. Have you a spare kiss for me?'

Another quest

A T THE END of his law studies in Groningen, Dolboy joined the van Baerle enterprise in Zutphen. There he sought out the individual his father had named, and found him seated in an oversized leather chair, at a desk on which that day's newspaper lay open. The manager invited the newly-invested lawyer to join him for coffee by a deep window, which looked out over the market place. Here Dolboy delivered van Baerle's report.

'Saw everything?' the executive enquired. 'What does that mean?'

'He witnessed what you asked him to.'

'Are you sure your message is meant for me? Are you sure it comes from your father?'

Since Dolboy's vanishing from the first Spartakiad of the post-war era, some people were reminded he had always been a soul apart, inhabiting a private universe. Now he delivered messages from the dead. But he was the company heir, the young master. Dolboy saw that the promoted foreman had changed priorities from those he held in other times, and did not question his refusal to recall van Baerle's mission.

'I'd like to see the records of my father's journeys,' he suggested.

'Yes, we kept account of his comings and goings.' The manager left his window seat and crossed to a tall cupboard inlaid with patterned veneers of walnut and cherry. Without expressing disrespect, he implied that van Baerle's travelling had been aimless.

'I wish particularly to know his itinerary before this date.' Dolboy wrote down the day on which he first tasted nesselrode, the day on which he took his name.

'Yes,' the manager muttered, holding something like a marbled ledger open in one hand, while running down its entries with a finger. 'We have a record. See here: he listed visits to a dozen towns. There's Ceske Budejovice, Plzen, Jelenia Gora, Zielona Gora, Gorzau Wielkopolski, Dessau, Rostock, and so forth. Does that help?'

'It could do. Tell me: do any of these companies still trade? Can we still buy from them?'

'Not all. Some vanished in the war. But others are extant, though now there's such red tape. They all lie in the zone beyond the curtain. They want to trade, but need official sanction. But yes, we buy from some.'

'I'd like to visit those we know.'

'We never go there now, of course.' The book was closed.

'But all the same, I'd like to go.' Dolboy appreciated that his status as his father's son gave him some power in the enterprise.

'There's no need now. Our supply lines are set up. We get what we need; the prices are agreed.'

'All the same. I'll go.' Dolboy closed the discussion, and enjoyed the pleasure of behaving wilfully, without fear of consequences, which was his nature. The manager thought of the useless heir he had despatched, and now disowned. He looked at the son who came to take his place, and wished him too in some remote repository. He raised no further obstacle to Dolboy's whim.

After two months, when visas had been obtained, and permissions from bureaucracies concerned with commerce, Dolboy travelled by aeroplane, and then by train, to tour his father's footsteps. Cornelius had told him that his mother was a woman of great beauty, who made lace. He mentioned too the village where she lived: a place called Lom. There was a Lom near Teplice, another near Görlitz. There were Loms to take a pick of. But Dolboy looked for those between the towns recorded in his father's book.

According to his permits he must visit only places listed in his documents, to meet distillers of liqueurs, suppliers of toys made by machines to look like the products of human hands, embroiderers of tablecloths. In some regions he was accompanied by representatives of the state security apparatus, in others by a trade official, and in one by a committee of bureaucrats with identical haircuts and identical suits, who insisted on providing him a tour of a plant manufacturing motor cars which changed gear by means of a rubber belt. But in whatever company he found himself, he slipped away whenever Lom appeared in reach. Once, to free himself of an adhesive guide, he simply ran. The overweight official gaped about him on the street, as if searching for a billboard on which instructions might be found for dealing with such an eventuality.

A yearning for his concealed history beckoned Dolboy, as it had beckoned him to wander from the games. He wished to find his mother and explain his being to himself. His father clarified a part of what he was, his mother would complete the quest. Those who grow with parents from their origin are curious to know what lies beyond their town, beyond their country's borders even. But those who swim in myths about their parentage hold one enquiry paramount: they long to see their parents' faces, know their truths. And so it was with Dolboy.

In Lom that was closer to Leszno than to Görlitz, and closer to Legnica than to Teplice, he asked again to see a craftswoman with his mother's skill, and was directed to an unexpected place. While menfolk worked in fields and factories, their women came from miles to see the lace invented there. Dolboy joined the crowd who fingered doilies, runners, valances, and saw it was no ordinary lace. The woman who spread the work on tables was calm and beautiful, as if she had some purpose no one present knew, some higher role which occupied her thoughts, and caused a smile which never left her lips. She raised the knotted folds of lace to show its worth, and smiled. She bantered with her customers, and smiled. She smiled much as Dolboy smiled, and like his, her hair fell in fine waves, her brow was clear. She too thought they were alike, and paused when her gaze fell on him. She saw herself.

How perplexing that he had crossed the continent to find his facsimile, but not his mother. For the lace seller was younger than Dolboy by two years. He offered to buy everything she had, but she denied him, for fear of leaving her regulars unsatisfied. He bought examples of all she offered, and when he left, sensed his own presence in strange doorways, and on the road enclosed by shivering trees.

Epilogue

SOMETIMES in the satellite settlement attached to the penal colony a thousand miles east of the city in which Dolboy's athletics career came to an abrupt and mysterious end, a pusher of the bread wagon approached Cornelius van Baerle's hut with a parcel from the world outside, sent for delivery to the railway in Talvertni. Sometimes van Baerle received a letter from his sister or his son, and once he replied. He wanted nothing further. One day when Dolboy walked with his aunt in the garden of her *Graafschap* home, a silence fell on their talk, and they looked up to where a stork flew arrow-straight. When it was overhead it made an arc, a circle on another, then higher still it soared, until it faded into clouds. In place of their habitual greeting of the bird, his aunt admired it silently, and Dolboy murmured:

'Goodbye and God bless you, father, until we meet in heaven.'

In Berlin an old man died without a penny to call his own, while crooning the wordless melody of 'Nuages', by Django Reinhardt. After achieving a fame that made him richer than everybody but three others in his adopted country, Eddie Rozner had yearned to see his former haunts again. He was granted permission to leave the union of socialist republics only after giving up everything he owned: his wealth, his property, his trumpet. His name was expunged from accounts of the nation's cultural life, and his recordings in official hands were de-magnetised.

People in the *Graafschap* still spoke about the boy who ran the woods and dykes and roads around, and sometimes a farmer told his wife he'd seen him just that day, striding in the distance, as he used to stride. Sometimes it was the truth.

In a room where a purplish-brown photograph hung, of a boy in a white shirt, pausing as if in interrupted flight at the edge of woodland, a lawyer sat down to write. He listened, to hear his own voice; he closed his eyes to make time run backwards; then he began:

'I looked in the mirror and saw a room lit with tasselled lamps in pastel shades. I saw striped walls of leaf-green and pink, blotted with cherubim prints. I looked in the mirrors of my mirrored eyes and enjoyed the ignorant bliss of wanting nothing. And then it was gone.'

In the beam of light cast by his lamp, two autumn moths fluttered against the window glass.